SON OF THE THUNDER PEOPLE AND TUMBLEWEED TRIGGER

ALSO BY GORDON D. SHIRREFFS

SON OF THE THUNDER PEOPLE AND TUMBLEWEED TRIGGER

Two Full Length Western Novels

GORDON D. SHIRREFFS

WOLFPACK
PUBLISHING
— EST 2013 —

Son of the Thunder People and Tumbleweed Trigger
Paperback Edition
Copyright © 2023 (As Revised) Gordon D. Shirreffs

Wolfpack Publishing
9850 S. Maryland Parkway, Suite A-5 #323
Las Vegas, Nevada 89183

wolfpackpublishing.com

Paperback ISBN 978-1-63977-992-5
eBook ISBN 978-1-63977-592-7

SON OF THE THUNDER PEOPLE AND TUMBLEWEED TRIGGER

SON OF THE THUNDER PEOPLE

Grateful recognition is given to
Dr. Morris E. Opler
Professor of Anthropology, Cornell University
for reading and criticizing the manuscript

To Carole and Brian

CHAPTER ONE

Alan Warden shifted in his saddle and looked at the country about him. If this was typical of Arizona Territory, he wondered why his father and the other settlers in the small wagon train had ever left the green rolling fields of Illinois.

The country was harsh, naked, and dead to the eye, and the mountains seemingly half buried in the sand. The yellow dust dripped from the groaning wagon wheels and then wreathed up behind them to shroud everything in the area. The dust caked beneath soggy collars and chafed sunburned necks. It masked the faces of the people who rode on the wagons or plodded alongside them in stolid discomfort. Here and there across the parched land, stippled with prickly pear, mesquite, and ocotillo, a wind-devil would rise as though conjured from the desert floor, whirling about rapidly in its aimless dance, rising higher and higher only to vanish as mysteriously as it had come to life.

The first defile of brooding Apache Pass was just ahead, and there was no sign yet of the cavalry escort from Fort Bowie. Now and then, Gila Simmons, the civilian scout, stood up in his stirrups and eyed the pass. Jim Warden, Alan's brother, and at seventeen already as

good a man as any who was with the wagon train, was
beside Gila, as he had been ever since Lordsburg,
learning the ways of the Apaches and of the new country
to which the Warden family had committed its future.
The sun glinted dully on the brass trim of the Henry rifle
that Jim had been allowed to buy at Independence. It was
a sore spot with Alan, that rifle, for he had as his sole arm
a battered old double-barreled shotgun. Jim was Alan's
senior by three years, but Alan could shoot almost as well
as Jim could.

Gila thrust up an arm and circled his roan on the
forehand, waiting for the first wagon to reach him. The
wagons came to a halt, sending a billow of dust sweeping
along the twisting trail. Big Bill Warden, Alan's father,
wound the reins about the brake handle and looked at
Gila. "Well, Gila, where are the troopers?" he asked.

"Ain't here, it appears," Gila said laconically.

"What do we do now?"

Gila eyed the darkening northern sky. "Storm
acomin'. 'Bout two more hours of daylight. We'd best
form the wagons into a corral and wait for the horse
soldiers to get here."

Alan swung down from his little sorrel and led it up to
the lead wagon. His mother was beside his father, her
worried face shaded by a sunbonnet. Bill Warden's jaw
was set. Alan knew the signs. His father wanted to go on
through. "We've got twenty good men here, Simmons,"
he said quietly, "with repeating rifles they know how to
use. You mean to tell me you're scared of some half-
naked Apaches?"

Gila shifted in his ornate Mexican saddle and rested
an elbow on the pie-plate pommel. "Now, Bill," he said
slowly, "don't yuh go to sayin' Gila Simmons is scairt. I
ain't. But I know no white man ever got away with under-
estimatin' an Apache in his own country. If we go into
the pass without troops, we ain't likely to get through.
The pass is lined with the graves of people who was

foolish enough to try it. Mail riders and coach drivers get double wages to travel through it. Yuh got wimmen and children with yuh. Yuh want to get them massacreed?"

Bill Warden slapped a big hand on his thigh, sending up a little cloud of dust. "No one is going to get massacreed, Gila."

"So?" asked Gila quietly. "Look!"

A lone horseman had materialized on a low ridge west of the wagons. His thick mane of hair was bound with a red cloth. A line of white paint was across his nose. Even as the settlers watched, he vanished as though manipulated by strings held by a puppeteer.

Alan shivered a little in the cold wind. The warrior hadn't seemed real.

"So?" asked Bill Warden. "One warrior? He's just looking for a stray most likely."

Gila waved an arm angrily. "Where there's one, there are others. I'm warnin' yuh!"

Bill Warden looked at the silent homesteaders who had gathered about his wagon. "We can take care of ourselves," he said stubbornly.

"Out here in the open yuh kin. Sure!" said Gila. He pointed at the brooding pass. "In there yuh'll be penned at the bottom of a canyon and wiped out, and yuh won't see a blessed thing except for gun flashes and wisps of smoke. I tell yuh, Mister Warden, *yuh won't have a chance!*"

The wind was rising steadily, sweeping across the wastes, driving tumbleweeds ahead of it, piling some of them against the wagons or rolling them with incredible speed across the rutted road into the sandy desert beyond. Alan felt chilled as his sweaty shirt began to cool. The brush thrashed wildly, and the drab wagon tilts flapped.

Bill Warden unwrapped the reins from the brake handle. "We go on!" he said loudly. He slapped the reins against the dusty flanks of the mules and drove on without so much as a sideways glance at the others.

Slowly at first, and then with quicker strides, the others went back to their wagons. They followed the Warden wagon up the slope. Gila Simmons shrugged and rode on. He might have known there was no use in arguing with Bill Warden once he made up his mind. Gila looked at Alan. "Yore dad will make a spoon or spile a horn," he said gloomily.

The darkening mountains were stark and bald except for sparse timber stippling the lower slopes. Here and there in the canyon were great crevices and eroded faults. Scrub pines, spruces, oaks, manzanitas, and aspens sheathed the banks of a water course. Alan placed a hand on the cantle of his saddle and looked back down the long slope. The desert was already dark from the approaching storm. A brooding uneasiness was in the air.

There was a sharp crack as though an axle had snapped. Alan turned to see Milo Hankins, a man from his hometown, stand up on his wagon and grip his left shoulder. He drew his hand away and stared stupidly at the blood on it. His huck shirt was already darkening with blood. A puff of smoke wreathed up from a brittle bush. Then came a sound as though someone had run the length of a picket fence, dragging a stick along the pales.

Something hummed softly past Alan's head. A bullet!

The little sorrel reared. There was the sound of a stick being whipped into thick mud, and the sorrel bucked, throwing Alan sideways. He gripped at the saddle horn, but it was too late. He hit the ground hard as the sorrel raced off through the mesquite. Blood stained its withers.

Gila Simmons was yelling in a hoarse voice that almost outdid the noise of the rushing wind. He fired, dropped from his roan, and hit the dirt in a gully. Jim Warden also fired and dropped beside the scout. The homesteaders opened fire blindly, searching the brush with wild slugs. A mule screamed like a frightened woman and then went down, kicking and thrashing in its traces. The homesteaders crawled beneath their wagons and into gullies as they churned out fire from their repeating rifles.

Alan snatched up his shotgun and rolled into the brush, wincing as catclaw ripped through his clothing and raked his skin with dozens of tiny hooks. The sorrel was standing in a clearing, whinnying plaintively. Alan ran toward the horse. The guns were crackling like the flames of a forest fire. Alan hadn't seen any of the ambushers. He cocked both hammers of his shotgun and hastened toward the wounded sorrel. Suddenly hooves beat a tattoo on the hard earth. Alan leaped into a gully and dropped flat.

Half a dozen horsemen thudded past the gully. They had glossy hair, bound by strips of dingy cloth. Thigh-length, button-toed moccasins covered their legs. A horse raced past Alan, scattering gravel into his face. The mounted Apaches opened fire, yelling and screaming as they drove off the sorrel and two other strays. Then they were gone as quickly as they had come.

Alan scuttled down the gully. Sweat greased the stock of his shotgun. His throat went dry, and his heart thudded against his ribs. He poked his head up over the edge of the gully and felt as though his blood had suddenly congealed. Apaches were between him and the besieged wagons. The firing was still going on. Guns rattled from behind rocks and wagons.

He worked his way along the gully. There was a chance that he might circle back down the trail and reach the wagons. The sky was much darker now, shot with streaks of forked lightning, which lanced into the distant peaks. The wind roared through the pass. Alan reached an area of land that Gila would have called malpais, or cut-up land, and thick brush. He glanced back at the wagons. Then he tripped and fell hard. His head smashed against a rock, and he seemed to drop swiftly into a pit of blackness. He knew no more.

IT WAS the cold that aroused Alan. He opened his eyes and winced as he touched his head. There was a big knot on it caked with sticky blood. The sound of firing was gone. A terrible sickness came over him. Had they been wiped out? Alan tried to get up and grunted in pain as his weight rested on his left ankle. He felt it gingerly. It was swollen from a sprain. How long had he been lying there? He felt about for his shotgun. It was nowhere to be found. He lay back against a rock and drew out his sheath knife with a shaking hand.

Long minutes drifted past. A faint sound came to him —the beating of shod hoofs. The Apaches rode unshod horses. Some of the men from the wagon train were looking for him! Then the noise seemed to move away. He yelled with all his might. The beating noise came again, closer this time. Alan smiled.

Lightning flashed eerily across the sky. Alan yelled loudly, with a strong feeling of panic in his soul. Something was moving around at the top of the cleft into which he had fallen. Gravel and pebbles cascaded over the edge and fell on his legs. Alan braced an arm to help himself up. Then he froze, staring at the figure that stood at the edge of the cleft. He wore no flop-brimmed hat. Thick mane-like hair was etched against the lightning flashes. Alan felt a flood of green fear pour over him. He was trapped!

Two more Apaches joined the first one and stood there, looking down silently at the boy beneath them. One of them held a lance. His face was a mask of hatred as he poised the long weapon, pointing down, aimed at Alan. He was ready for the hard, killing thrust.

Alan tensed himself, and a prayer formed in his mind. The lightning crackled viciously, blinding him a little before he saw the Apache with the lance cast the weapon from him and shriek with fear. There was a strong electrical odor in the charged air. The bolt had struck very near the cleft.

Alan pulled himself to his feet and blinked to regain full vision. He held his knife ready. The Apache who had poised the lance was staring up at the sky. He looked down at Alan. A thick-bodied warrior spoke in a strange tongue, pointing first up at the weird sky and then down at Alan. "*Ittindi!*" he said. He thrust his right hand into a buckskin bag that was slung from his waist. He cast a powdery substance toward the sky. "*Gun-ju-le, Ittindi!*" he called out.

The big warrior dropped into the cleft before Alan could move. The odor of sweat and greasy buckskin clung about the Apache. Alan thrust out with his knife. The Apache's left arm flicked out, lashing a quirt about Alan's wrist and pulling it high. His right hand smashed against Alan's head. Alan's weakened ankle gave way, and he staggered back. The knife clattered against rock. Alan went face downward on the floor of the cleft. He waited for the killing thrust in his back. It never came. Instead, his wrists were tied tightly together. Strong arms raised him to meet the outstretched hands of the other two braves.

Alan was carried to a pony and thrust up on it. His legs were bound beneath the pony's barrel. In a moment, the three braves had mounted, and they were off toward the gloomy mountains, alternately illuminated by flashing lightning or plunged into darkness.

The roaring wind brought a spit of rain, which was soon followed by sheets of water that swept across the parched earth. The naked brown shoulders of the Apaches gleamed with wetness when the lightning flashed. Thunder pealed in the canyons. Then they were in a narrow gorge, riding swiftly with a sureness borne of long familiarity. Alan looked back. Somewhere in the windy darkness were his family and friends, lying in the downpour, staring up at the sky with eyes that did not see.

The hours drifted past as the rain kept sluicing down. They climbed higher and higher into the mountains. Alan thought they were traveling in a southerly direction, but he wasn't sure. In fact, he wasn't sure of anything at all. The sudden attack; the separation from the wagons; being cut off by the Apaches; falling into the cleft and being captured—it all seemed like a wild nightmare from which he would surely awaken. But the throbbing of his head and the pain of his twisted ankle were real enough.

Water roared in the gullies and arroyos, curling swiftly along, carrying brush, drowned animals, and small rocks. The streams frothed and danced as they raced down to the lower levels.

The bitter journey went on after the cold rain stopped. The Apaches seemed oblivious to the cold.

At dawn, they rode through a canyon hung with ghostly tatters of mist. The warriors ate as they rode, gnawing at dried meat and quenching their thirst with water carried slung across the withers of their horses in the long greasy intestine of some animal. Alan was given a chunk of sweetish-tasting meat, hard and stringy, which he could not identify. He was allowed a drink from a gut canteen. He almost regurgitated the meat after tasting the greasy water. His throat felt as though it had been thoroughly sanded.

Alan wondered what would happen to him. The Apaches were said to be as cruel as devils. No escape was possible now. A rawhide noose had been placed about his neck, and the end of the *reata* was held by one of the Apaches behind him. If he made a break for liberty, either he would be strangled or would be choked into insensibility. It was a journey into fear, from which there was no escape.

CHAPTER TWO

The watery sun rose above the mountains. Alan tried to drive away his fear by studying the silent warriors. All three of them were rather short compared to white men, averaging about five feet five or six inches in height. Their shoulders were broad, and their chests were deep. They had high cheekbones, broad faces, and Roman noses. They were deeply bronzed from the suns of the Southwest. Their heads were well-shaped and appeared to be enormous because of their thick hair. Their eyes were liquid brown and seemed to have smoldering fires in them.

They wore thigh-length moccasins folded down just above their knees. The soles were thick, and the toes rose into big buttons. They wore dingy loincloths which hung to a point above the knees in front and hung down almost to their heels when they stood erect. Buckskin belts held the loincloths in position. From the belts depended ornamental bags for the powdery material Alan had seen one of them cast toward the lightning the day before. Knives in wide sheaths were thrust through their belts. The men were naked from the waist up. They carried carbines across their muscular thighs. The stocks had been studded with brass tacks in ornamental fashion.

One of them had a huge old-fashioned Navy cap-and-ball Colt in a battered black holster.

They must be Chiricahuas, guessed Alan, from what Gila had told him about the country. The Big Mountain People. There was another reason for him to be worried; Gila had said the Chiricahuas were the fiercest of the tribal divisions of the Apaches.

It was close to noon when they reached a narrow trail that wound upward against a naked shoulder of granite. A turkey suddenly gobbled from somewhere up the trail and was instantly answered by the leading brave in a perfect imitation of the big game bird.

A head appeared from behind a rock. Alan looked into the eyes of a young Indian, not much older than himself. The guard waved them on without a word, but his eyes never left Alan until he was out of sight.

Higher and higher they went until Alan was afraid to look to his left, down into the rock-studded canyon far below. Then they reached the top of the trail. Another warrior passed them on from his guard post.

The pungent odor of burning wood drifted about Alan. He looked across a thickly wooded mesa to see curious humped shapes scattered about among the trees. They were lodges, formed by tying together thick brush branches and covering them with blankets and skins. Smoke rose from cooking pits and drifted up to mingle with the light mist that overhung the mesa. Warriors, women, and children came toward the new arrivals. Young boys seemed to sprout up out of the grass or drop from the trees like ripe fruit. *It wouldn't be long now*, thought Alan.

The women looked impassively at Alan. Their strong brown hands were held flat against their thighs. Several of them fingered their knives and glanced at their cooking fires. The leader of Alan's little party raised an arm and spoke to the people. There was awe in his eyes as he spoke and pantomimed what had happened. Alan didn't understand one word, but it wasn't necessary, for the Chiricahua's simulation of what had happened was well-nigh perfect. Eyes widened as the people stared at Alan. Some of them drew back from him.

A stout squaw with a badly scarred face waddled toward Alan holding a long-bladed knife in her right hand. Alan was tense, but he didn't want to show fear. It took all the control he could muster, but his fears were groundless, for she merely severed his bonds. He was helped to the ground. His legs felt as though they had needles in them as the stout squaw helped him through the crowd. There was no hate on the dark faces, just polite curiosity.

He was guided to a big wickiup. She eased him down on a woven mat and then rolled up his trouser leg to study his swollen ankle. She cut loose the shoelace and pulled off the heavy brogan. She touched the swollen flesh and then shook her head. After busying herself preparing some kind of mess in a pot, she smeared it on his ankle and bound a soft cloth around it.

Alan looked out through the doorway. Some of the warriors were seated in a circle, solemnly passing a bowl from hand to hand and sipping fluid from it. Blankets had been spread on the ground, and on them had been placed weapons, saddles, horse blankets, several hats, and a pair of boots. Six horses were hobbled not far from the warriors. Alan recognized some of the horses with a sinking heart. They were from the wagon train.

The squaw clucked about Alan like an old hen. She waddled to a fire and roasted strips of dark meat. Then she served him on a flat piece of wood. Alan ate quickly, thoroughly enjoying a dark-red food, which looked like strawberry jam. The squaw smiled broadly as she watched him eat it. "*Hoosh,*" she said.

Alan nodded. He guessed *hoosh* was preserved fruit. That was one Apache word he had learned.

There seemed to be a prevailing good humor about

the woman. She pointed out at the sky and made swift darting motions with her plump hands. Then she looked at him and nodded her head.

Alan shook his head. She was trying to pantomime lightning. She spoke swiftly and smiled, pointing at the sky again.

Suddenly it came to him. She wanted to get something across to him about his capture. She took an arrow from a quiver and darted it downward.

Alan smiled and nodded.

The squaw pushed him back on some blankets and then closed her eyes, simulating sleep. She touched him on the head and left the lodge, lowering a piece of canvas before the doorway to close it. Alan shut his eyes. The lodge smelled faintly of skins, wildflowers, and food. It was quiet and peaceful. He dropped off to sleep.

When Alan opened his eyes, a boy was squatting at the door, watching him curiously. He wore a sketchy breechclout and low-cut moccasins. The afternoon sun was warm on the roof of the lodge, and the light came down through the trees forming dappled patterns on the ground. Alan had slept for several hours. His head still throbbed a little, but his ankle felt better.

Alan looked at the boy. He touched his own chest. "Alan," he said.

The boy showed no interest. He drank from the water olla and left. The haft of a knife showed at his waist as he walked away.

Alan looked about him. Blankets and skins were neatly rolled into bundles. Several short bows hung from pegs, and the arrows were held in a quiver of bobcat skin with the tail depending beneath it. There were brass and iron pots and various woven baskets filled with meal, seeds, acorns, dried fruit, and meat. A partially finished pair of moccasins lay in a big basket. A turkey-bone awl with a length of sinew threaded in it was thrust into a hole in the tanned leather.

Feet padded softly outside. A shadow darkened the doorway. Alan looked up to see the leader of the warriors who had captured him. He squatted beside Alan and looked at the bandage around the boy's ankle. He nodded as though pleased at what he saw and then he left the lodge.

They seemed in no hurry to dispose of him. He lay back and listened to the sounds of camp life. The thin notes of a flutelike instrument drifted to him. He crawled to the doorway and looked up at the cloud-dotted sky. The sky was intensely blue, and the air was fresh and clear with a winy odor to it.

The long afternoon drifted past. Evening came, casting shadows across the mesa. Alan ate a little dried meat and fruit and then drank from the water olla. He looked out of the lodge to see the same boy who had visited him earlier that day. The boy was whittling at a piece of wood. His eyes held Alan's. Alan went back into the lodge.

When night came, fires flared up throughout the camp. The people ate at their own lodges and then gathered about the central area as though expecting something. A wizened old man began to thump gently on a small drum. His hooped drumstick beat out an insistent rhythm. There was a movement among the trees. A woman came out of the darkness. It took Alan a little time to recognize the placid-looking squaw who had taken care of him. She had painted her face and hung her full body with amulets, feathers, and the claws of birds. She scattered a shining powder about her to the cardinal points of the compass. She called out in a low voice and then ended her words with a sharp exclamation. "Ek!"

Silence followed her chanting. She paused for dramatic effect. Then she began to speak again, pointing at the dark sky, imitating the jagged strokes of lightning and the swift downpour of rain. When she was done, the people gaped at the lodge where Alan stayed.

She circled the fire and came toward the lodge. Alan didn't know what to do. He could snatch up a weapon and put up a fight, but he wouldn't last long. She beckoned to him. He fought down his fear as he crawled outside and propped his back against a tree.

She began a low chant. She dipped her fingers into a buckskin bag hanging from her waist. She applied glittering powder to his forehead, marked a cross on his chest, and then walked about among the people, applying a little of the powder to their dark foreheads. They touched it with a finger and then put the finger into their mouths. She came slowly back to him and took something from a pouch. It was a charred twig hanging from a thong. She ceremoniously placed it about his neck and stepped back, vastly pleased with herself. The tribesmen began a slow stamping dance which they increased in tempo as he watched. They seemed to have forgotten he was there.

CHAPTER THREE

I n the days following Alan's acceptance, he learned that the people meant him no harm. Now the smaller children would come to the wickiup to stare at him and then scatter like flushed quail if he made a movement toward them. He stayed in the wickiup, as much a part of the family as the warrior who had captured him, the squaw who had cared for him, the boy who was their natural son. Yet they spoke very little to him, other than naming various articles for him so that he might learn their language.

He had been captured by Coyote, the leader of the particular band of Chiricahuas who had raided the wagon train. He was a renowned warrior among his people. The squaw was Looking Glass, and she was a well-known person in her own right, for she was a medicine woman held in respect and fear by her people. The boy was Never Still, a name that fitted him well, for he was always engaged in doing something. Alan learned their names, but it seemed as though the Apaches had no great concern over names, seldom using them among themselves.

In time Alan was able to hobble about the busy camp. If he went too far, no matter how careful he was, a warrior would suddenly appear in the vicinity and watch him until he went back to the camp.

The warriors hunted almost continuously. The women put in long, busy days. The older boys played their strenuous games. They would imitate warriors creeping up on an unsuspecting enemy. It was all very realistic: the careful approach; the study of the camp; the swift assault; the aggressive gestures. Then the miniature warriors would vanish as they had come. Alan liked best to watch them when they practiced with their small bows, shooting at marks so small that Alan wondered how they hit them so often.

The warriors were back from the hunt one lazy afternoon, sleeping in the shade, when Alan wandered over to watch the older boys at their wrestling. Never Still was matched against Yellow Snake, an older and heavier lad. Yellow Snake was strong and vicious, asking no quarter and giving none. They fought back and forth, straining against each other. Suddenly Yellow Snake shoved Never Still over a rock. He went down hard. Yellow Snake threw back his head in triumph.

A squat warrior was lying beside Coyote. He was the father of Yellow Snake. He smiled slyly and glanced at Coyote.

The victor paraded back and forth, shoving the smaller boys aside. He stopped in front of Alan and thrust out his chin. Alan looked about. They were all watching him. He stepped back, undecided what to do. The cocky boy followed him. Then the young Apache suddenly thrust out his hands and shoved Alan back over a log. Alan bruised his elbow as he hit the hard ground.

He got up slowly. He forgot he was on a mesa in Arizona facing an alien boy. He was back in his school-yard in Illinois, facing a bully. Alan held out his hands. They faced each other and then locked arms about each other's waists in the approved fashion. They strained against each other, and suddenly, the Apache threw his full weight against Alan and maneuvered him over a rock. Alan fell heavily. The squat warrior's face was a mask of pride as he looked at his victorious son.

Alan rubbed a scraped hand against his shirt. He got up and held out his hands again. They locked in struggle, swaying back and forth. Yellow Snake tried his same tactics, but this time Alan side-stepped, broke free from the other's grasp, thrust out a leg, and shoved hard with both hands. The boy went down with a thump, and his breath rushed out.

Yellow Snake got up quickly. The blood flooded into his broad face. He rushed Alan, reaching out to wrap his arms about Alan's waist. Alan shoved a hand up under Yellow Snake's chin, driving his head back. The Apache slashed at Alan's eyes with his right hand. The pain caused a flow of tears. Yellow Snake then slapped at Alan's face, yelling in victory.

Alan moved back. Yellow Snake came on. Alan thrust out his left fist. The boy smashed into it. He yelped in surprise. Alan crossed a hard right, which connected solidly. Yellow Snake went down and stared up at Alan with an open mouth. Blood trickled from his nose. The squat warrior spat and walked away. Coyote looked down at Yellow Snake and then up at Allen. It was the kindliest look Alan had ever been given by Coyote.

Yellow Snake got up. Alan held out his hand, but the boy ignored it and walked sullenly into the woods. The rest of the boys looked at Alan with admiration. Never Still placed an arm about his shoulders. They walked back to the camp. At the lodge, Never Still got his bow and arrows. He handed them to Alan and then led him to a cleared area where some of the boys were shooting at a mark. Alan studied the flat bow. It was made of mulberry wood and was about three and a half feet long. The outer surface, or back of the bow, was painted red, while the inner surface, or belly of the bow, was marked by a series of serrated lines. The bowstring was of sinew. The arrows were in a buckskin quiver. They had been made of hardwood and had been fletched with what looked like hawk feathers. The arrow points were roughly shaped from flint, inserted in a split in the shaft which had been tightly wrapped with sinew. The shafts were decorated with bands of blue paint.

Never Still took the bow and nocked an arrow to the string. With hardly an effort, he released the shaft. It flashed through the sunny glade and struck at the bottom of a mark painted on a piece of cloth that had been pinned to a bank of soft earth. He handed the bow and an arrow to Alan.

Alan had used a small bow back in Illinois. It had been made for him by Jonas Harper, who had once lived with the Crows. Everybody in town thought old Jonas was crazy, but he had been a good friend to Alan.

Alan nocked the arrow and raised the bow. Some of the boys were smiling broadly. Alan drew back the bowstring and pushed out on the bow as he had been taught. He sighted down string and arrow and raised the point a little. His release was smooth. The shaft flashed through the air and plunged into the mark so closely that it crossed Never Still's arrow and rested against it. The boys' eyes widened.

Never Still walked to the target and freed both arrows. He gave them to Alan. Alan turned to put them into the quiver. The Apache boy shook his head. He pushed the arrows into Alan's hands, pointed at them, and then at Alan. "*Cikis,*" he said with a smile.

Alan was now accepted by the other boys, and some of his loneliness left him. He wrestled with them and shot at marks with the bow and arrow. He was often beaten in the foot races, was never defeated in wrestling, and held his own with the bow. But always in the background, he saw the scowling face of Yellow Snake, the boy he had defeated so conclusively at wrestling. He had made a real enemy in a place where he had expected to find everyone an enemy instead of a friend.

Alan began to learn the language of the Chiricahuas by naming food items, clothing, weapons, and other articles common among them. As his knowledge of the language grew, he learned why he had been saved, miraculously it seemed, by the stroke of lightning that had lanced down an instant before he would have been pinned to the ground. Lightning was thought to be the arrows of the supernatural Thunder People. These strange beings were much like ordinary people. Some of them were good and others were bad. A good thunderstorm did no harm, while a bad one killed people and ruined their houses. The Thunder People lived in the clouds, and their arrows were the lightning. Power could be obtained from them. The Thunder People could cause anyone to be struck by lightning if they wished to punish him. The flash was the arrow's flight; the thundering noise in the heavens was the shouting of the particular member of the Thunder People who had loosed the shaft of lightning.

The most obvious evidence that the Thunder People were displeased with someone would occur when the individual was struck by one of the lightning arrows. Fright was also a powerful weapon of these strange beings. Coyote had known that Alan was to be spared and had saved him. A person who had so been saved would be likely to have derived power from the Thunder People. Thus, it was that Alan was known among the members of the band as Son of the Thunder People. He had been accepted as one of the band. There were many times when he lay awake at night, looking through the doorway at the clear stars, wondering what Alan Warden, the son of an Illinois farmer, was doing in the wild mountains living with primitives.

In time, Alan learned to speak a curious jargon of English, Chiricahua, and sign language. It carried him along as he increased his knowledge of the Apache language. The days were spent by the men in hunting or on scouting expeditions. The women did most of the work about the camp. The small children whiled away the summer days; the older boys and girls trained for the future.

Old Jack Rabbit was an honored member of Coyote's band. He was a wizened warrior whose body was scarred from battle and whose wrinkled face was pitted with smallpox scars. He was an old man wise in the ways of the war, the hunt, and the tangled mythology of the Chiricahuas. Coyote assigned the old veteran as mentor of Alan as well as of Never Still.

Alan had always envied what he had thought of as the carefree life of the Indian. To him, as a boy on his father's farm, helping with the never-ending chores, the life of an Indian boy had seemed ideal. Jonas Harper could tell tales that made an Indian's life seem perfect for man and boy. Jonas hadn't deluded him, but he had left out one important fact: an Indian's life was a rigorous one of hunting and warfare. To live, he had to be trained. Alan learned that it was indeed Spartan training.

Jack Rabbit was a patient but firm instructor. The boys learned to smoke bees from the honey trees and to bring back the sweet treasure without complaining of the stings and the eyes inflamed by smoke. They learned to make arrows of carrizo reed or hardwood. The reed shafts were fitted with a hardwood foreshaft, much like the footed arrows made by the famous English longbowmen Alan had once read about. The shafts were straightened with the teeth or by being pressed against a heated rock. Tail or wing feathers of the red-tailed hawk, the eagle, or the buzzard were used for fletching. Turkey feathers were considered a poor substitute. Three feathers were used, fletched to the shaft with pinon pitch and lashed with wet sinew. The heads were of flint, which could be found in many places, although chipping the flints into better shape was not practiced. They were considered as being already shaped by the Thunder People, who had cast them about while hunting. The shaft was split, the flint head inserted in the split, and the shaft bound tightly against the flint by means of moistened sinew. Sometimes the tip of the shaft was pointed and hardened in the fire. Arrows were sometimes fluted by being scraped with a sharp stone. Three channels were thus grooved into the shaft. Sometimes these grooves were spiraled, as were the feathers. Zigzag incisions were sometimes used because the arrows of Child of the Water, the great supernatural hero who had saved the Apaches and taught them how to live, had been so made.

The reed arrows were usually about thirty inches long while the hardwood shafts were a few inches shorter. The reed shafts were tipped with pointed wood, but flint was used on the hardwood arrows.

Bow-making fascinated Alan. The favorite bow wood was mulberry, although oak, locust, and maple were also used. The bow was usually the length of two arrows, sometimes less. The bow wood was greased, after being well seasoned, and worked until it was slick and shiny. The bow was bent over the knee or against a tree, then tied and placed in hot ashes until it took its permanent shape. Ten days were allowed for the drying after the heat treatment. A double-curved bow was shaped between two young trees growing close together.

The back of the bow was painted a solid color, while the belly was marked by the maker with his own personal design. Never Still marked his with a series of serrations. As a special privilege, Alan was allowed to mark his new bow with the zigzag markings of Ittindi, the Lightning. The dyes were made from various mineral or vegetable substances and were made permanent by mixing them with the juice of heated yucca leaves.

Sinew from the loin of a leg of deer was used for the string. The sinew was soaked in water and separated into strands, which were rolled together, three at a time, against the naked thigh to form the string. The boys were taught always to carry a spare string. The tough fiber from the mescal leaf could be used as an emergency string.

Alan was taught to release the arrow from the bow by holding the string between the thumb and first finger, assisting the draw with his second finger. He was also taught never to leave a bow strung when it was not to be used. It took the two boys almost a month of hard work to make up a sheaf of arrows. Never Still's ambition was to kill a mountain lion and make a quiver from the lion's skin, for such a quiver was considered to make a man lucky in warfare and hunting.

Wrist guards were made of rawhide and laced up the left wrist with a projecting piece to protect the hand against the snap of the bow string.

With their principal weapon made, the boys were taught how to hunt. They were warned never to think of the game they were hunting, for this was considered bad luck. They were allowed to go after small game and were punished by being sent to bed hungry when they failed. Jack Rabbit taught them to vanish swiftly at a signal from him. In time, they were allowed to hunt bigger game. It was a great thrill for both of them when Never Still drove a shaft into the side of a bobcat and was allowed to make a quiver from the pelt.

One day the two boys, while on a hunt for a bobcat from which to make a quiver for Alan, reached a high point overlooking a strange wonderland of rocks. Before them was a tremendous panorama of rugged mountains, decorated with the dark blues and greens of trees. Here and there were cascading streams and patches of wildflowers. Beyond them was a wilderness of yellow rock, cracked and eroded, forming countless needles, spires, turrets, pinnacles, and towers. The yellow and buff-colored rock was shaded here and there into glowing salmon and bright pink. The dark mouths of caves showed among the fantastic formations.

Magnificent evergreens formed a backdrop for the scene. Pines, firs, and spruces intermingled with groves of white-stemmed aspens. Flowers of every hue and type were scattered as though by a lavish hand—golden helenium, iris, verbena, larkspur, columbine, Indian paintbrush, silene, penstemon, and many other varieties.

The woods were full of game: bears, mountain lions, white-tailed deer, peccaries, porcupines, and raccoons. There were jays, occasional parrots, and plenty of wild turkeys. It was a vast land of beauty and plenty.

Never Still swung his arm, encompassing the landscape. "Big Mountain," he said proudly.

A strange feeling came over Alan. This was Never Still's home, not his. Alan would always be a stranger here, away from his family. He bowed his head.

Never Still placed a hand gently on Alan's shoulder. "Homesickness," he said quietly. There was strong sympathy in his voice and manner. It was not the first time the boy had seemed to know what was in Alan's innermost thoughts. In a way, they were much closer together than Alan had ever been with his real brother.

All at once, Never Still grew tense. He pointed down the slope. A big bobcat was poised on a boulder watching something below him. Alan forgot his homesickness as he followed Never Still silently down on their quarry. He wanted that pelt in the worst way.

The wind was blowing hard toward the two boys, rippling the tall grass. Closer and closer they went until the big cat was twenty yards away, unaware of their presence. Never Still looked at Alan and nodded.

Alan nocked his best arrow, the one he had won from Never Still the first day of their friendship. He drew back the string and anchored the shaft. He held the draw for a fraction of a second and then loosed the arrow. It flashed in the sunlight and plunged deep into the shoulder of the big cat. The bobcat rose into the air as though propelled by springs and vanished beyond the boulder. The two boys nocked arrows and cautiously approached the boulder. The cat lay on his side in the grass. He was dead.

Alan slid down the slope and looked proudly at his prize. Never Still smiled.

They climbed up the slope in the late afternoon sun, carrying the cat between them. It was a world so far removed from Alan's earlier life that he almost felt as though he had been transported to another planet. He could hardly believe that he had not seen his own family for well over a month and was living with the people who had killed them. Yet he found it hard to hate the Apaches. He had been as well treated as though he were one of them. Someday he would escape. Someday he would rejoin his own people and perhaps help them to exterminate the fierce Chiricahuas. Until then he had no choice but to live their way. He looked at his companion. It would be difficult to hate Never Still.

CHAPTER FOUR

Horses. Horses. Horses. They became as much a part of Alan's life as his bow and knife. For the horse was an important part of the Apache economy. It was used as transportation between campsites; for swift, slashing forays into the lowlands; even as food. A man's wealth was in his skill with weapons and his possession of horses. Mule meat was considered tastier than horse meat, but horse meat was a basic part of the Apache diet, and Alan came to like it.

Alan had always prided himself on his knowledge of horses back home in Illinois, but now he knew he had been through only the primary grades in that intricate and vital subject. There was rarely a time when the smell of horses wasn't in his nostrils or impregnating his clothing. Gradually he either wore out or lost the articles of clothing he had been wearing when he had been captured. His shoes fell apart and were replaced by low moccasins for camp use and the practical desert moccasins for rougher terrain. The thick soles of the desert moccasins turned aside thorny growths and sharp stones. They could be pulled up over the thighs to protect them or folded about the knees. The folds were handy for small articles such as sinew thread, an awl, bone needles, a hone for his knife, spare thongs, and even small quantities of food. He wore the breechclout of tanned buckskin and went with his upper body, bare even on the coolest days. His hair grew long and was cut in approved Chiricahua fashion.

Jack Rabbit taught them how to get the most out of a horse, using methods that sometimes sickened Alan. There was a way to get an extra burst of speed from a flagging horse after he should have fallen from exhaustion. They were taught which were the best cuts of horse meat and how to remove the long intestine for use as a canteen. The boys rode bareback, although some of the older warriors used captured Mexican or American saddles. Alan learned how to spring onto a horse's back and become part of it, like a brown centaur. The boys learned to distinguish the leaders of wild herds and to capture or kill them first so as to get the rest of the herd under control.

If a horse broke a leg or was permanently injured, he was killed at once for his hide and meat. It would have horrified Alan's father and brother to see what he had to do under the stern tutelage of Jack Rabbit and the inflexible Coyote, who had no peer in the handling of horses. The boys of the band were the horse herders, and woe to the one who lost a horse or permitted it to stray. He was not beaten, but he went without food and was in disgrace for a long time if he made a mistake.

There were times when the warriors would leave the camp and reappear days later with horses taken from the Mexicans or Americans. Mule had been named so because he had once captured eight mules from an unsuspecting camp of troopers near Dos Cabezas. Black Bear had once outrun a pursuing party of Mexicans, had circled around behind them, killing three of them, and had escaped into the hills with two captured horses. Jack Rabbit had earned his name by outrunning mounted Mexicans on the side of a hill, leaping from rock to rock like a jack rabbit, and then outrunning the tired horses on level ground. It had been a great deed.

There was a time when a tenseness settled over the camp. Two warriors had not returned from a raid into Mexico. Big Head and Eagle had been killed by the Mexicans. Coyote-Saw-Him, an honored medicine man, who specialized in forecasting the best time to go on the warpath, vanished from the camp, staying by himself in a small lodge near the rushing stream.

Late one afternoon when the long shadows were creeping down from the forested heights, Alan looked up from his work of fletching a cane shaft. A faint, eerie whistling noise came from the woods. The warriors gathered about a large fire in the center of the camp. The women faded into their lodges. The boys hid in the brush.

Coyote-Saw-Him appeared, dressed in his best robe, which was decorated with the symbols of the sun, moon, stars, lightning, hail, rainbow, fire, water beetle, butterfly, snake, centipede, and other mystic symbols, to pray to in time of need. His headdress was made from the skin of a strangled fawn, and his skinny neck was strung with various charms and amulets. The whistling noise emanated from a rhombos, or bull-roarer, which had been made from a piece of fir wood that had been struck by lightning. It was called the Sounding Wood. He twirled it about his head, rapidly and uniformly, and then from front to rear. It sounded like a rising, rain-laden wind. The shrill whistling noise rose above the soughing of the wind in the trees.

He walked through the camp and then through it again, north to south, east to west, making incantations at the four cardinal points of the compass. He stopped by the fire and threw powder upon it. Pungent smoke flared up. He lifted his face to look at the evening star. He chanted, with many arm gestures. Then he stopped, bathed with sweat. He tottered weakly as he announced that the time would soon be good for the warpath, that many enemies would be killed, and many horses taken.

A stiff hide was brought and beaten in time with a drum. The warriors made themselves up as though actually going to war, tying their long hair in place with a headband, and bringing the back flap of their long loincloth through between their legs and tucking it beneath the belt, then bringing the shorter front flap down beneath the crotch to tuck under the back of the belt. They slung on their bandoleers of cartridges and grasped their weapons.

Four warriors came from the east to the fire. They marched abreast. Four times they circled the fire. Two of them stopped on the north side, and two of them on the south side. Singers gathered about the drum beater and the man who beat on the hide. The four men began to dance. They danced toward each other, changed sides, turned about, and went back. Four times this was done. Everyone began to sing and shout.

The women had gathered silently beyond the light of the fire. The dancing warriors put cartridges between their fingers and in their mouths. They swayed violently, dropping on one knee and then springing high into the air, firing their guns or loosing arrows. They made a soft grunting cry: "Wah! Wah! Wah!"

The dancers saw imaginary enemies whom they charged, scattered, and killed. Now and then a warrior from the side lines would signify his intention of joining the war party by coming out during the singing and marching once around the fire.

At every new song a new set of four men would come out while the others went to the side lines to pray. A man looked at Mule. "You, Mule, many times you have talked bravely! Now brave people in Sonora are calling to you!"

Mule joined the dancers. Man after man who stood by was called by name and invited to go to war for revenge. Few of them held back.

Mule beckoned to Coyote. He began to sing:

> *"Coyote, they say to you,*
> *You! You!*
> *They call you again and again!"*

Coyote joined the dancers. Coyote-Saw-Him called out man after man. No one could refuse him. This was to be a big war party. "You are a man," he would sing. "Now you are being called. What are you going to do when we fight the enemy?"

Even the boys were affected. They swayed and grunted in time with the singing. Never Still seemed to have been transported into another world. Alan went to the lodge and watched the singing, posturing braves. It was like a carnival of demons. Even the women were taken in by the frenzy.

The dance went on and on. When the "fierce dancing" ended late that night, it was followed by social dancing. First was the "round dance" for everybody. Then came the "very partner" dancing in which the men were invited to dance by the women. A man *had* to dance and then give his partner a gift to pay for the privilege.

Alan fell asleep about midnight, listening to the drumbeating and singing. There was a vague uneasiness in him, and he rested fitfully.

A hand gripped Alan's shoulder. He looked up into the tense face of Never Still. The cold light of dawn filtered into the lodge. "We must run to the mountain this morning," said the young Chiricahua.

Alan shivered as he got up.

"We must be back before the sun rises," said Never Still.

Some of the older boys were waiting for them. They ran through the wet grass and up a long slope, slipping and sliding. Alan ran easily. He had done this before. It was supposed to give them strong bodies, minds, and hearts. It was hard going. Some of the weaker boys fell behind. Yellow Snake slogged along just ahead of Alan. Alan was determined that he would not return behind his enemy.

Alan was weary when they reached the top of the height. There was no time to rest. Down they went, passing the struggling, weaker boys. Never Still plunged into the cold stream first, without hesitation. Alan went in feet first just behind him. The frigid water drove his breath from him. He struggled across. Yellow Snake stopped at the edge of the stream and merely wet himself with the water.

Never Still waited for Alan on the bank, looking across at the cheater. He spat contemptuously and strode back to the camp. They wrapped themselves in blankets but stayed away from the fires. The sun just tipped the eastern mountains as they sat down.

"The fierce dancing will go on for three more days," said Never Still. "There will be hard training for us."

"Why?"

"They expect some of us to volunteer for the war party."

There was no letup from then on. Warriors who had been designated to train the boys, drove them through a series of trials. Mule sent his son out into the open space near camp. The boy stripped off his shirt and stood there waiting. The stern warrior began to shoot just past the boy with a heavy Sharps rifle. The boy did not flinch as the slugs chewed into the ground or screamed eerily from rock.

The boys would fill their mouths with water and run swiftly for several miles, returning to show their teachers that they had not swallowed the water. This was training to teach them not to breathe with the mouth.

The next night while the fierce dancing was going on, the boys were taken into the woods by Jack Rabbit. A course had been laid out, and the boys trotted through the moonlit woods, silently and grimly, determined not to come in among the stragglers. There were no halts, and at dawn, they staggered into camp after an icy plunge. They had had no sleep but were allowed to eat and then return to their training.

On the afternoon of the third day the boys were lined up in two parties facing each other across a wide clearing. They each had their slings made of a diamond-shaped piece of rawhide, pounded and softened, with four perforations through the median line of its width. A rawhide string was attached to each side, one of them being looped. The loop was placed about the middle finger of the right hand, and the free string was held between the thumb and first finger. The sling was drawn back and whirled just once; as it came forward, the unlooped string was released to cast the stone. There were piles of smooth stones on each side of the clearing. They were about two and a half inches long and about an inch thick.

Warriors stood in the neutral area. At a signal, the opposing teams began to cast the stones at each other. There were four boys on each side. Alan was beside Never Still. Yellow Snake was with the other team.

Alan was worried. He had never really mastered the sling. The other boys had learned when they were small, long before bow-and-arrow training. The stones whirled through the air. It was dodge and duck, cast your stone, snatch up another and avoid a missile as you put it into your sling. Wait your chance and then cast. You must try to hit a member of the other team. There was no protection other than your ability to dodge.

Never Still cast a stone that smashed against the arm of a slight boy. The boy dropped his sling and held his arm. There was no outcry from him, but Alan knew the arm was broken. He wondered how long he could keep it up. A stone skinned past his face. Yellow Snake had singled out Alan. Never Still fought silently and with great skill. Yellow Snake bounced a stone from Alan's left shoulder. Alan dropped his sling as the pain filled him. Yellow Snake moved closer. Alan snatched up a stone and threw it with all his might. It struck Yellow Snake's head. Blood streamed down his face.

Yellow Snake's father scowled. "Knife and awl!" he cried to Jack Rabbit, pointing to Alan. It was a common cry of frustration.

"It is mock war," said the old warrior. "Would you have Son of the Thunder People stand there defenseless?"

"*Ahagahe!*" yelled Yellow Snake's father.

Jack Rabbit stepped back. There was no literal meaning to the word, but it did mean one thing—the man was ready to go for his weapons and fight.

Coyote came forward. He held up his arm. "Enough," he said.

The boys lowered their slings. Never Still came close to Alan. "There will always be trouble for you from that one," he said quietly.

"Why are we doing this?" asked Alan.

Never Still looked up at the clouds. "When a boy is old enough, he is expected to go to war."

Alan pressed a hand against his bruised shoulder. "I don't want to go."

Never Still twirled his sling. "Some do not volunteer. They are looked down upon. If a boy does not go, it is thought that he is not strong enough."

Alan sat down on a rock. "You are going?"

"Yes. We must go on a horse raid or on a war party four times to be considered a warrior. I am eager to begin."

"I said I didn't want to go."

Never Still studied Alan. "You are a fast runner, the best of all the wrestlers. You are skilled with the bow. You know horses. What can you expect but to go?"

A hawk circled just above the trees. Never Still placed a stone in his sling and cast it upward. The hawk fell heavily. "A good omen," said Never Still as he went to the dead bird.

Alan walked to his friend. "You want me to go with you; is that it?"

"You are my brother," said Never Still simply. He walked toward the camp with his kill.

Alan followed him. He knew it was not customary to take untried boys on a war party, but the band was small, and they needed trained warriors. The boys would not be expected to fight and would be protected as much as possible. Their job would be to take care of the extra horses and do the camp chores. He didn't want to go, but he valued Never Still's confidence in him. "I'll go," he said quietly.

Never Still smiled. He drew Alan close with one arm. "I knew you would," he said.

They walked back to the camp together.

CHAPTER FIVE

C oyote was wearing his buffalo-hair headdress from which protruded two yellow painted buffalo horns. His war shield was covered. His Spencer carbine shone with the deer fat with which it had been greased. He was watching Coyote-Saw-Him passing out the head-scratching sticks and water-drinking tubes to the novitiates. The medicine man had already passed out the caps that would protect the boys in time of battle.

Alan looked at the head-scratching stick and the water-drinking tube. They had been tied together with a thong. The cap was like a skullcap, covered with conventional Apache designs, and it had a chin string. It had been used many times before, he guessed, from its worn appearance.

Never Still tied on his cap. "An untried brave must never scratch his head with his fingers nor allow water to touch his lips," he said.

Alan looked at the alien articles again. The stick was made from the branch of a fruit tree and the tube from a carrizo reed. "Why?" he asked.

"Why, if you scratch your head with the fingers, your

skin will get soft. If you do not use the tube, your whiskers will grow too fast."

Alan tried not to smile. Actually, he felt little like smiling. There was no way of avoiding the war trail now. Looking Glass waddled up to her two sons and silently handed them a sacred medicine cord. It was one of her duties to make the cords, and she had done well for Never Still and Alan. Their cords were powerful, for they were four-stranded, strung with turquoise, petrified wood, rock crystal, eagle down, hawk, and bear claws. There were also pieces of twigs that had been struck by lightning.

She sprinkled them with her sacred powder. It was not the pollen of the tule, such as most of the Chiricahuas used, but powdered galena, which was great medicine. It was difficult to obtain, but she was able to secure some because of her claim to having escaped from the claws of a mountain lion when she was a child. Her scarred face bore witness to that fact.

Those who were to stay behind, gathered at the edge of the camp to watch the warriors and novitiates leave. The quivers were full; the pouches were fat with cartridges; blades were honed to razor edges; food bags were plump, and gut canteens were swollen with water. The horses were fresh, and the warriors had rested a full day after four days of dancing.

Coyote led the way down the trail. The women gave a cry of applause as the long file of men and boys rode down the narrow, twisting trail. Alan's bobcat quiver bumped against his back. He had not poisoned his arrows as some of the other boys had.

There was so much to remember. He must not be unreliable or disobedient. He must not turn around quickly and look behind him without glancing over his shoulder first. To turn about, he must always turn toward the sun, or ill fortune would befall the war party. He must not eat warm food, for that would make the horses worthless. If he ate entrails, his luck would be bad with the horses. He must not gaze upward, or a heavy rain would fall. He must not laugh at anyone, no matter how humorous the situation might be. He must talk respectfully to the older men. He must stay awake until given permission to sleep. He must not eat too heartily or eat anything from the inside of an animal. There were about eighty form words that must be used instead of the ordinary forms of speech. The other boys had learned them long ago, but Alan had been allowed certain privileges in this respect because of his ignorance of the language. The one compensating factor about the whole thing was that the novitiates must be closely protected, for the loss of one of them would reflect on the leader of the war party. The untried boys were there for experience only.

They camped for the night in a cuplike canyon which overlooked the vast San Simon Valley. Alan spent a good part of the night, bow in hand, guarding the horses. He watched the stars winking icily in the dark-blue blanket of the sky, wondering where he would end up within the next week. It was bad enough that he should be part of a Chiricahua war party, without the sickening thought that someday he might be expected to fight against his own people.

They were on the trail before dawn, winding ever downward, riding silently, each of them alert for signs of enemies. They traveled in groups of two and three, with several warriors far ahead and some out on each flank. Apaches dreaded surprise and always camped high, even if there was no water available, to have the advantage of altitude. While traveling in the low country they were as alert as animals.

By mid-afternoon, they were in the foothills, which opened toward the great valley. Here, signs had been left for the main party by the scouts: a partially displaced stone, which was always carefully placed in its original position by the last warrior to pass; a bent branch; a disturbed clump of herbage. Never Still and Alan noted each sign, competing with each other to see who spotted them first.

The second night's camp was fireless, for they were within a few miles of the Mexican border. Three veteran warriors went on ahead, scouting into Sonora. That night Alan saw the somber, humped shapes of the mountains south of the border. What would happen to him there?

Hours before daylight the main party followed the scouts. The Chiricahuas seemed to be gifted with an uncanny sense of direction. Alan could distinguish no landmarks, but the leader went on as though the darkness were lighted by lanterns along the way. There was little sound except the muffled thud of the hoofs, now encased in rawhide boots. There was no talking, and a novitiate who made unnecessary noise was frowned on by the warriors.

By dawn, they were hidden in an arroyo. To Alan, who had expected to find Mexico quite different from the United States, the terrain was exactly the same.

The scouts returned shortly after sunrise. They were not riding the horses with which they had started out. The boys squatted outside the circle of warriors as Mule made his report. "There are many Mexicans," he said, "with ten soldiers. There are a few women and children. They are camped near the River of Little Stones. They are tired and careless. There are many fine horses and mules. The mules are heavily laden with goods. The Mexicans are traveling north, toward the great canyon not far from here. The one that crosses the border."

The veteran warriors had ridden at least fifty miles on their scout. No wonder they had returned with different horses! The original mounts must have been ridden to death on the trail.

Thirst thickened in Alan's throat as he watched the council, but he must not drink until he was told he could do so. It was part of his training.

Coyote began to sketch a map on the sand, using a pointed stick. They would angle southeasterly to reach the great canyon. The leader spoke quietly as he sketched. Coyote thought the Mexicans would travel in the canyon all day and would in all probability camp in it that night. The Chiricahuas would be in position to attack at dawn, their favorite time. The extra horses would be kept in a smaller branch of the canyon, guarded by the boys and a few of the older men. Coyote stabbed the stick down hard. "Here is the only water for many miles. They will camp there!" he prophesied.

Each warrior was allowed to speak his mind in the council. Broken Hand, a minor sort of medicine man, prayed for success. Later the boys guarded the horses while the warriors rested.

The sun beat down from a pitiless sky all that day. The mountains changed their coloring from dark to lighter gray, from dark brown to a tawny color, fading away in the late afternoon to purple and then to black as the sun went down. When it was dark the warriors began to check their weapons. They tested bowstrings, gun actions, knife-edges, and war clubs. The boys inspected the rawhide boots of the horses. Each warrior striped his face with a line or two of white bottom clay mixed with grease.

Never Still rested beside Alan after they came off guard. All the boys seemed nervous on the eve of their first battle. Alan's mind was filled with many thoughts. Never Still had but one thought over and over again in his mind: would he be brave when the time came to face the enemy? Four times he must go on the warpath before he could take another name and wear the paint of a warrior. He was the son of a chief, but that did not necessarily mean he would follow in his father's footsteps. He would have to become as great a warrior as his father to become a chief.

Alan looked up at the bright stars. He had no warrior

father to emulate, yet he dare not fail in his duties, or he would be struck down by the warriors as though he were a Mexican. He winced as he thought of it. He wondered why God had done this to him. Was there some obscure purpose in it? He prayed for the first time in many weeks.

Coyote led his warriors to the south long after darkness had fallen. It was a weird, ghostly land through which they rode, with the gaunt arms of saguaros pointing up at the sky. The mountains were humped and dim, brooding in the quietness. Now and then a coyote lifted his voice in a melancholy wail. This was good medicine, for were not the warriors led by Coyote himself?

Alan felt as though he had wandered from the face of the earth into some fantastic dreamland as he accompanied the warriors. There was never a word or a gesture as they rode through a silent land that had no visible trails or markers, yet through which they all moved with uncanny accuracy.

A cold wind sighed across the desert. There was a feeling of death in the brooding land. The men Alan rode with had been trained from childhood for war. The novitiates were already skilled in the fundamentals of war. War was as much a part of their lives as food, clothing, and shelter, and yet they could not see the inevitable ending of it all. They had no real conception of the power of the hated Americans. "A handful of naked warriors trying to stem the march of an empire in the making." The words had been his father's, not Alan's, and up until now, riding swiftly through the desert night to kill and loot, Alan had never fully realized what his father had meant.

They passed through a cut-up land, dropped lower to cross sand flats, then rose again until they were in rough-shouldered hills. At last, Coyote signaled for a halt. The chief went on with Mule. Time drifted past until the howl of a wolf was repeated four times out of the darkness to the south. The party rode on until Alan felt, rather than saw, that they were riding not far from the lip of a deep canyon. The warriors halted again. The horses were left with the boys while the warriors faded into the darkness. They were like phantoms retreating to the safety of limbo at the coming of the hated dawn.

Alan and Never Still were sent to the canyon's edge to stand guard. The eastern sky was faintly gray with the coming of the false dawn. The wind moaned softly through the great canyon. The sky turned lighter and then it was possible to distinguish things: the sharp edges of distant peaks; the mounded shapes of the higher mountain masses; the far edge of the great canyon. But the bottom of the canyon was still dark. Alan strained his eyes looking down into the mysterious blackness, but it was Never Still who first saw the Mexicans. He gripped Alan's arm and pointed them out.

They were camped near a shallow rock pan which was filled with water. They were scattered about on the rough earth, wrapped in serapes and blankets, shielding their faces with their great peaked sombreros. The pool turned a dull pewter color as it grew lighter in the canyon. Many horses and mules were tethered in a hollow. Heavy rawhide packs, shaped to fit the backs of the mules, lay in a line near the hollow. A sentry dozed against a rock with his rifle lying across his thighs.

Never Still moved close to Alan and whispered softly. "These people come this way often. It is the band of Don Luis, the trader. Mule knows him well."

"But they are peaceable people!"

The young Chiricahua's face was as hard as flint in the graying light. "No! It is they who killed Big Head and Eagle. They are fools, these Mexicans. Always they travel the same route at the same time of the month. That is how Mule knew they would be in here. That is how my father knew they would camp here. Do you not see it?"

Alan felt a coldness settle on him. Vengeance. An eye

for an eye. Big Head and Eagle must be paid for in blood. If there was much loot, so much the better.

Never Still hissed the scout warning. "*Tsst! Tsst! Tsst!*"

Shadowy figures moved among the rocks on the slope overlooking the camp. The warriors were closing in. There was a slight movement up the canyon where a few mounted warriors were getting into position. A warrior moved in among the picketed horses and mules, cutting the picket lines. The sentry stirred, raised his arms, and then yawned. He nodded again. A mule snorted. The sentry jumped up and raised his rifle. He walked toward the animals. It was too late.

The hidden warriors were close to the camp now. Rifles were leveled and bows raised. The shafts whirred through the air and plunged into the blanketed figures. The rifles crashed with a noise like the ripping of thick cloth. The sentry yelled hoarsely and turned to look up the canyon. The mounted warriors had launched their attack.

Powder smoke swirled about the Mexicans. Arrows plunged into those who ran about. The rifles kept up a steady, searching fire. The horsemen were almost at the hollow, trailing blankets behind them. The warrior who had cut loose the horses and mules now sank his knife into the sentry's back. The mounted warriors rode over the crumpled body.

Some of the Mexicans fought back, firing into the thick smoke, jerking their heads back and forth as they tried to see clearly. Now and then, one of them went down with an arrow or bullet in him.

The hard-riding Apaches closed in on the herd, screaming and waving their blankets. The herd stampeded right through the demoralized Mexicans, scattering them like tenpins. A few scattered shots rang out from the surviving Mexicans. Apache bullets sang as the brush blossomed with rifle fire. The herd was far beyond the camp now, driven by the shrieking horsemen.

The Chiricahuas closed in on the wounded. Warriors arose from their hiding places as though conjured up by a wizard. Knife and war club did deadly work among the helpless wounded. In a few minutes it was all over.

Never Still turned to look at Alan. There was fierce pride on his dusty face. "Are they not great warriors?"

Alan felt a sour taste in his throat. He looked away from the frightful scene of carnage below them, but he could still see it plainly in his mind's eye. It was the Apache way, the guerrilla way. Pick your ground and attack when your enemy least expects it.

Alan forced himself to look again. He saw a movement in the brush beyond the hollow where the mules and horses had been kept. A head bobbed up and quickly vanished. Alan looked at Never Still to see if the keen-eyed young Chiricahua had seen it. But Never Still was standing up, trying to count the number of horses and mules that had been taken. At least there was one survivor, provided he made good his escape.

CHAPTER SIX

The boys went to get the Chiricahua horses. They drove them down the canyon trail to water them. Alan kept looking away from the bloody scene. Coyote had taken but one scalp, for a ceremony. It was not Apache practice to scalp. Jack Rabbit had once told Alan that the Mexicans took scalps long before it was ever done by the Chiricahuas. Sometimes the Mexicans had taken scalps with the ears still attached, sometimes the whole head.

Some of the Mexicans lay tangled in their serapes and blankets, staring at the sky with eyes that did not see. The warriors were rifling the bodies and piling up other loot. Alan was glad when he was sent to help with the stampeded horses and mules.

There was a quietness about the camp when Alan returned. Despite the cheap victory and the many spoils, the warriors were not happy. Curly-haired, a young warrior, lay cold in death among the rocks. He was the only casualty among the Chiricahuas.

Broken Hand took care of the body. Belt, a close relative of the dead man, fired a good many cartridges into the morning air. The face of the dead man was washed, and his hair was combed. The face was painted red. The body was placed in a cleft and covered with rocks. Curly-haired's horse was brought close to the grave. Belt cut its throat. Those warriors who wore any red-colored clothing removed it and threw it away as a mark of respect for the dead.

Time was not wasted. The rawhide packs were placed on the mules. The dead Mexicans were stripped of their clothing. Scouts were sent out to ride ahead. Coyote led his men to the north, riding swiftly. Alan looked back at the silent canyon. There was a callousness about the whole thing which sickened him, but he knew the Chiricahuas would have received the same treatment from the Mexicans. Don Luis's men had killed Big Head and Eagle; Coyote's men had killed Don Luis and his men; someday, a band of Mexicans would seek out Coyote's band for revenge. There was no love lost on either side in the age-old warfare.

A mare strayed from the driven herd, and Alan was sent back for her. She stopped in a thicket. Alan dismounted to get her. Something moved in the brush. The mare suddenly shied and blew, stepping back nervously.

Alan swiftly nocked an arrow and studied the brush. He saw a thickness in the growth that should not have been there. Alan stepped behind a boulder. The peak of a sombrero showed above the brush. Alan knew it must be the lone survivor of the attack. The Mexican spoke softly to the mare. She looked beyond him and whinnied. The Mexican whirled. He was a young man. His eyes were wide in his fear-contorted face. Blood smeared his face. He whipped out a long-bladed knife.

Alan knew he could drive a shaft into the Mexican long before the other could throw the knife. "Wait!" he called in English. "I am a friend!"

The Mexican's jaw dropped. "You speak the Ingles? You are not one of them," he replied in English.

"I'm an American. A captive."

The frightened young man looked down the canyon. "Where are the others?"

"Down there. They will be expecting me."

The Mexican wiped cold sweat from his face. "Let me have the mare."

"No! I must bring her back."

The young man nodded. Then he spoke swiftly in Apache, but there was a slight dialectic difference obvious in his speech. "They are Chiricahua? The Cokanen?"

"Yes. The band of Coyote from the Big Mountain."

The Mexican held a hand to his forehead. "I too was once a captive of the devils. But I was with the Red Paint People, those who are known in New Mexico as Mimbrenos."

"The eastern band of the Chiricahuas." The same.

"Perhaps Coyote will let you go."

The frightened eyes held Alan's. "No. The Chiricahuas seldom take adult captives. I am a man."

"You are hardly more than eighteen."

"That *is* a man according to their standards."

Alan turned. "Some of them are coming."

The Mexican raised his knife. "I'll kill to get this mare!"

Alan drew back his bowstring. "I can drive an arrow up to the feathers in your belly. Besides, you cannot outride them on that mare. Come with me. I'll save you."

Never Still called from down the canyon. "My brother! Where are you?"

"Come," said Alan quietly.

The Mexican shrugged wearily. "I am Bartolome Amadeo. I was called Socorro among the Red Paint People. They captured me at Socorro when I was a small boy."

Alan drove the mare out into the open and then mounted his own horse. "There is a Mexican here, Never Still!" he called out.

Coyote appeared. He quirted his horse up the slope. There was anger on his face. "Is he wounded? Kill him!"

Bartolome looked about in fright. Coyote drew in his plunging horse. He swung up his Spencer repeater to cover the Mexican. Bartolome called out in Apache. Coyote's eyes widened.

"Throw down the knife!" called Alan.

Bartolome did as he was told. He closed his eyes. "I hope you know what you are doing," he said softly. "Before the Blessed Virgin, *I hope you know what you are doing.*"

Bartolome opened his eyes and looked at Coyote. "I knew He That Is Just Sitting There of the Red Paint People."

"Mangus Colorado? Red Sleeves?"

"Yes. I was once of the Red Paint People."

Coyote looked up the canyon. "You are a Mexican," he said harshly.

Alan kneed his horse beside that of the chief. "He spoke to me. He could have killed me from ambush. Instead, he asked to see you. He was tired of his life with the Mexicans. He wanted to be with The People again to live the old free life."

Coyote digested Alan's execrable Apache. He looked into Alan's eyes. The boy had never lied to him. Bartolome's life hung in the balance. "How are you called?" Coyote asked the Mexican.

"Socorro."

Coyote slid from his horse and searched the Mexican for weapons. Then he bound Bartolome's hands and boosted him up on his horse. He noosed his *reata* about the Mexican's neck and placed the end of the *reata* in Alan's hands. "He is your prisoner, Child of the Water," he said.

There was a feeling of pride in Alan, both for saving the Mexican, and for being called after the great hero of the Apaches. It was high honor coming from Coyote, who gave little praise at any time.

When they joined the rest of the war party, Coyote told them what Alan had done, how a boy on his first war party had captured a full-grown Mexican armed with a knife.

Never Still rode alongside Alan and glanced back at Bartolome. "Why was he not killed?" he asked.

"He was once of the Red Paint People."

"They are our allies. There are times when we graze our horses in their country and feast with them. They have a great war chief—Red Sleeves."

"So he told me."

Later, as Alan rode with his prisoner, Bartolome spoke to him. "What will they do with me?"

"They need warriors. The band is small."

"You have been with them long?"

"About three months."

"Where are your own people?"

Alan looked away. "They were massacred at Apache Pass."

"I am sorry to hear that, my friend."

"Where were you going, Bartolome?"

"That was the band of Don Luis the trader. We were on the way to Tucson to trade silver dollars for goods. Every month it was his custom to do so. Some time ago they killed some Apaches not far from here. I knew Don Luis would pay for it. The Chiricahuas never forget."

The lithe Andalusian mules trotted on beneath their great rawhide panniers. The silver bells on their collars jingled sweetly. "They are laden with much money, my friend," said Bartolome. "Do you know what that means?"

"The Chiricahuas do not use money."

"No. But *your* people do! There are white men who will come to sell fine rifles and much ammunition to the

Chiricahuas for those silver dollars. The border will flame. There will be no peace."

The yellow dust hung like a pall about the swiftly riding raiders. Alan looked to the northwest, toward the great San Simon Valley. There was no chance of escaping. "Do you know this country well?" he asked.

"Very well, although I have lived near Durango for some years. Why do you ask?"

"I want to escape."

Bartolome nodded. "Count me in, as you Americans say. But we must wait. Patience."

They rested at noon and then went on. Several weak horses and a mule fell by the wayside. They were killed at once, and the choice cuts of meat were hacked from them. The party went on with the red meat dangling over the backs of the horses to be cured in the hot sun. There was a terrible haste in the raiders to get back to their citadel—the Big Mountain.

Alan felt strange as they rode on. Never Still was like a brother to him. Looking Glass had been more than kind to him. Even the stern Coyote had treated him well. But the sights Alan had seen that dawn had turned him against the Chiricahuas. They intended to make a true Chiricahua out of him, and with their logic, they were sure they would. But Alan had matured a great deal in the past few days. In time they would expect him to raid and kill as they did. He would say nothing, but from now on, he would plan for escape and nothing else.

That night, camped in the hills, he spoke quietly to the Mexican. "I can't stand this much longer, Bartolome."

Bartolome shrugged. "It is not a bad life. There is good hunting, and the mountains are beautiful. Many white men have turned Indian and liked it. You may become a real Chiricahua in time."

"How can you say that?"

Bartolome's face saddened. "I told you I was captured. That is not true."

"What do you mean?"

"I was born in the camp of Red Sleeves."

"So?"

"My mother was a Mexican from Sonora. My father was Apache—Yellow Tail, a minor war chief."

Alan felt cold all over as he looked at the half-breed. Perhaps he was more Apache than Mexican. There were many strange stories about such men. Gila Simmons had told Alan of men of mixed parentage who at times were more wild and vicious than those of pure Indian blood.

Alan silently went to his hard bed. Fear came to him that night, an unseen bedfellow, who kept him awake most of the night. If Bartolome betrayed him to curry favor with the Chiricahuas, Alan would die slowly and horribly, and not even the fact that he was known as Son of the Thunder People would save him then.

CHAPTER SEVEN

The mountains seemed to have changed overnight as the victorious warriors returned to their natural stronghold. It was the time of Earth-Is-Reddish-Brown. The fall was upon the Chiricahuas, and in time, winter, or Ghost Face, would be upon them. Black Bear rode ahead of the returning party. His horse was splattered with foam and dust, but Black Bear's face was proud, for Coyote had picked him as the messenger of victory because he had been the most outstanding of the warriors in the battle.

Bartolome was afraid, for he knew that the death of a brave warrior like Curly-haired was sometimes revenged by turning over a captive to the women to be put to death.

It was late afternoon, with the bright sun sifting down its rays through the leaves, mottling the grass, when the warriors reached the mesa top. The women had gathered to give their cry of applause. They were dressed in their finest deerskin robes, wearing strings of seeds and shells about their necks. They had perfumed themselves with mint and dried flowers.

Guns flashed and roared, awakening echoes as the smoke drifted about the camp. The family of Curly-haired had been privately notified by Black Bear of the death of their man. They had removed their festive clothing and had cut their hair. They withdrew from the camp. The rest of the people in the camp had swiftly removed any articles that were red in color so as not to affront the grief-stricken family.

The victorious warriors gathered in the center of the camp to receive their share of the spoils. The horses and mules were distributed among them, and each of them was allowed to keep any of the enemy's possessions that he had obtained in the fight. A big fire was kindled. All the warriors had on the clothing they had worn in the battle. They were immensely proud of themselves as the dances began. They repeated the fierce dancing they had done on the four nights before the expedition. There was singing, feasting, and social dancing.

The singers told what each man had done. "Mule," they would sing, "you have done a great thing. Come out and show us what you did."

Mule came out, and in pantomime, showed what he had done, while the other members of the war party would sing of his brave deeds. Each warrior, in turn, took his place in the dancing area to follow suit.

The people danced the round dance, the couple dance, and later on, long after midnight, the men and women lined up in two rows facing each other and then moved back and forth in time to the music. The dead warrior was not mentioned in any of the songs. The Mexican scalp was displayed during the first dance and thereafter hung on a tree. Those who had handled it burned "ghost medicine" to purify themselves. It was a great night for the band of Coyote.

Bartolome was held in the lodge of Coyote, for he was considered Alan's prisoner. No one bothered him. Alan knew then that they intended to take him into the band.

Alan received the fine silver-chased knife he had

taken from Bartolome. It was part of his booty. The eyes of Coyote were fierce with pride as he told how his adopted son had captured a full-grown Mexican. All the novitiates had done well in this, their first test. It had been unusual to expose them to the rigors and dangers of a war party on their first trial, but there was a feeling of urgency in the band necessitating the initiation of the boys as soon as possible so that they might strengthen the band.

Alan and Never Still stayed close together. There was plenty to eat—horse and mule meat, mesquite bean cakes and prickly pear fruit, nuts, and seeds. Alan took food to Bartolome, who ate well. He looked up at Alan. "Coyote is very proud of you," he said.

"I didn't do much."

"You are destined to be a great warrior."

"You could have escaped from me, Bartolome."

Bartolome waved a hand. "To them, you did a great deed. They are proud of their strength and their way of war, no matter how they win."

"What can I do, Bartolome?"

"They consider you one of them now."

"I don't want to kill white men."

Bartolome shrugged. "In their conceit they think you cannot be any other way now that you have proved yourself on your first expedition."

Alan felt sick. "I've got to get away!"

Bartolome helped himself to some fruit. "Then you had better do it quickly, for the time of Ghost Face is coming."

"So?"

"These people winter far to the south. There is a stronghold of theirs down there. Five days' journey below Casas Grandes, somewhere in Chihuahua. It is called 'Pagotzin-kay.' If they go there, you will have to go with them."

Alan looked out at the dancers. They had been at it

for hours. It was not long before dawn. He was big for his age and had grown during his stay with them. Already he was as tall as Coyote, and there was no boy in the band with Alan's muscular structure, which he had inherited from his big father. He was five feet seven inches tall, and if he followed his father in build, he would reach six feet in height, heavy of bone and muscle. He could take care of himself in the mountains. He was sure of it. But he didn't trust Bartolome any longer. The Mexican, now that he knew he was not to be killed, had seemed to accept his fate casually.

This was as good a time as any to make the break. The warriors would dance and celebrate for three more days, dancing at night and sleeping all day.

Alan waited until the weary Mexican went to sleep. Then the boy took his weapons, some dried meat and bean cakes, a blanket, and spare moccasins. He crept through the rear of the lodge and sped into the shelter of the tall trees.

The moon was low in the sky, affording fair light as he picked his way to the west, avoiding the regular trail. An owl hooted from a tree. A bird of ill omen. An Apache would have turned back instantly, for the owl was considered to be the ghost of a person who had been evil during his lifetime and continued to be vicious after death. There was an eeriness about the soft call of the night bird.

Alan glanced back over his shoulder. He had a feeling he was not alone. One of the guards might have seen him slip from the camp. He sank down behind a boulder. Behind him there was a high outcropping of naked rock. There was no movement in the night. A bird rustled in the trees and flew off. Moonlight sifted down into a clearing. Never Still appeared, carrying his bow. He was looking at the soft earth at his feet.

Never Still had missed Alan. If it had been any of the others, Alan would not have hesitated to wound or kill so as to make good his escape. But Never Still was his adopted brother. Alan drew back. He dislodged a stone which clicked loudly.

Never Still looked up. "I see you, my brother," he said.

Alan stood up. "Go back," he said quietly.

"You plan to leave us?"

"Yes."

"Why?"

"I must go back to my own people."

"*We* are your people!"

"No. Ghost Face is coming soon. If your people go south, there will be no chance for me to go back to my own people."

"We are your people," insisted the boy. "You have eaten our food and slept in our camp. You have been trained with me to be a warrior. You have hunted with me, and we have traveled the path of war together. You have been honored for capturing the Mexican. We will be great warriors together."

"My skin is white and yours is red. You worship different gods. Your people fight mine and kill them. I can't go on with you. I will soon be a man. I must go back!"

The owl hooted. Never Still shivered. "This is an evil place. You heard the owl. He speaks the language of the Chiricahuas. Listen to him!"

The owl hooted again. Closer this time.

"There is a ghost in his body," said Never Still shakily. "The call is powerful. It can get inside of you and cause evil."

"Farewell, my brother!"

Never Still raised a hand. "If the warriors discover that you have left, they will track you down. You know our secret trails. You know how few we are. Perhaps you will bring the soldiers back with you."

"No. I just want to be with my own people."

Never Still shrugged and dropped his hand to his knife. He cast aside his bow." Then we will fight. If you win, you can go; if you lose, you must come back with me."

Alan looked incredulously at him. The thin veneer of friendship seemed to have dropped from the primitive boy facing him. The moon glittered on the long knife. It was held blade down, as in meeting a man. Alan dropped his bow and drew his Mexican knife. He didn't want to fight, but it had been forced on him. Suddenly he hated the boy facing him. This was not play. It might mean life itself.

They circled slowly. Never Still was thick through the chest like his father. His arms were long and muscular for his age. He moved like a cat. Alan was taller and heavier but not so light on his feet. They circled in their silent moccasins. Never Still closed in, sweeping with his blade. The knives clicked together. Alan threw him back.

The Chiricahua was skilled with the knife. He could have raked Alan easily. Alan knew Never Still meant only to disarm him. The Chiricahua moved in swiftly. Alan side-stepped and threw out a leg, gripping Never Still's left wrist with his left hand, dragging the boy toward him. Never Still sprawled across the outthrust leg. He hit the ground and rolled over, springing up on his feet like a cat. The blade flicked out, scratching Alan's thigh.

Never Still stamped his feet and moved back. Alan wanted to disarm him, but he wasn't fast enough. There was a movement atop the ledge of naked rock. Suddenly, as though materializing out of the rock itself, there appeared a long, tawny shape. The ears were set close to the rounded head, and the waving tail was thick like a club. A mountain lion! A big one!

"Look out!" said Alan. "Behind you!"

Never Still shook his head. "An old trick, my brother."

The mountain lion's tail stiffened out. He launched himself through the air. Alan closed in on Never Still, feeling the knife rake deeply across his left biceps, and then he bowled the older boy to one side, meeting the crashing descent of the great cat with a sharp upthrust of his knife. He went down under the heavy body, stabbing steadily with his blade. Blood ran down his left arm. The cat snarled at the odor.

The cat was like a bundle of springs and wires. Claws raked Alan's legs. The mountain lion drew up his hind legs to rake and disembowel. Never Still closed in, wincing as a claw scored his thigh. He drove his knife in hard behind the tawny shoulder.

The cat growled in savage fury. The knives drove in again and again, splattering the boys with hot blood. The cat rolled away, screaming like a frightened woman. Alan cut weakly at the exposed belly. The hind claws sank into Alan's chest just below his jugular vein and raked down hard and deep. Alan rose. He staggered over the thrashing cat and vomited thickly. The last thing he remembered was the sight of Never Still standing poised, a heavy shaft drawn back to his ear, aiming his arrow. The arrow drove in deep. Alan sank into a black void and knew no more.

CHAPTER EIGHT

The time of Ghost Face was almost upon the Chiricahuas. The squaws were finishing winter garments, new moccasins, woven baskets, and hide bags for food. The warriors furbished their weapons, made new bows and arrows, and hunted almost every day. The leaves were turning, and the winds were cold. It was time to travel south.

Alan lay in Coyote's lodge, thin and weak, with the terrible scars on his chest healing slowly. There had been days of delirium after his encounter with the mountain lion. The medicine men had worked all their powers to help him.

Never Still hovered constantly about Alan. He had never mentioned that Alan had planned to escape. The owl had been blamed for the whole mess. Alan found that he was regarded with deep awe by the people. Had he not been saved from death by the arrows of the Thunder People? Had he not captured a grown man on his first foray against the Mexicans? Had he not fought a mountain lion, armed only with his knife, to save the life of his brother? This was great medicine, indeed.

It was Bartolome Amadeo who one day gave the solution of the big problem to Alan. "You should have waited for me to help you to escape," he said. "However, the damage is done. In a way, it is a good thing, for now these simple people regard you as being especially favored by the gods. You have but one way to go when you recover. You must become a warrior and someday fight against your people and mine. Yet there might be another way." Bartolome leaned close to Alan. "Any young Apache man or woman can follow the life of a medicine man or woman if he can convince the others that he is able to dream medicine dreams. Then he can be apprenticed to a medicine man to learn his ways."

"I'm a Christian," said Alan stubbornly.

Bartolome waved his hands. "Yes, and I am too, but would you kill Americans and Mexicans rather than do as I suggest?"

"I just can't do it!"

"Look at it this way: perhaps their Supreme Being, the one they call 'Life-Giver,' is the same as our God. Perhaps their Child of the Water is the same as Jesus. Who knows?"

"What do you mean?"

Bartolome shrugged. "You will be like a priest or a minister."

Alan shook his head. Bartolome's strong fingers dug into Alan's arm. "Look! These are not games they play! You must be clever, much more than they are. Tell Looking Glass that you wish to study medicine under her tutelage."

"And if I don't?"

Bartolome spread out his hands, palms upward. "Who knows? You will be forced to go on three more raids or war parties. You will be expected to kill men. Is it not better to become a medicine man?"

Alan closed his eyes. Bartolome was right. It *was* the only way out. "All right," he said quietly.

"Good! I will tell her you are willing." Bartolome left the lodge.

Alan eased his left arm. He thought of the months he had been with the Chiricahuas. He had been captured on July 26. He had kept track of the days. With a start, he realized it was November 10, his fifteenth birthday.

Looking Glass came in and placed a cool hand on his forehead. "You are getting well, my son," she said. "Socorro has told me you wish to become a medicine man. Is this true?"

It was hard to look into her wise eyes and nod, but Alan managed to do so. Actually, he had always been interested in the mythology of the Chiricahuas. Learning it would be far better than being forced to kill his own people. It was a means to an end.

"You must convince us that you have the gift. It is said that you have power from the Thunder People. One can take or leave power. Sometimes it is too dangerous to accept it. There are times when the ceremony offered to you is not right, requiring that you do evil things. Perhaps you might think it is a good power when it is actually an evil one. You must be careful."

"How do you know when you have this power?"

She shrugged. "The power will come to you. You might hear a voice or see a sign. You must always be on guard so that the voice does not cheat you into becoming a witch."

"What would happen to me then?"

She looked out at the nearest campfire. "The fire. That is the only way to execute a witch."

"Will the power be for everything?"

Looking Glass shook her head. "There are powers for finding lost horses, to cure the sick, to bring rain, to find the enemy, to pick names for children, to have success in the hunt. There are many of them, my son."

Alan closed his eyes. He knew he faced a long and tedious training.

"You must rest now," she said. She left him alone.

At dusk, Alan was awakened by Never Still. He

squatted beside the pallet and handed Alan a bowl of food. "It is said that you will become a medicine man," he said.

"It is so, my brother."

"Good! Together we will work for our people—I as a great warrior; you as a great and wise medicine man. Are there medicine men among the Americans?"

"Yes."

Never Still digested the thought. "Do they find lost horses?"

"No, but they do find lost souls."

Never Still looked surprised. "Do they help them to the House of Spirits?"

"In a way. Perhaps one of them will come here someday and tell your people of Jesus Christ."

"Is he like Child of the Water?"

"In some ways."

Alan groped in his mind to remember the lessons he had learned in the little white church back in Illinois. He was ashamed to recall so little of them. "Jesus is the Son of God," he said. "Perhaps the mother of Jesus is the same as White Painted Lady in your religion."

"It is possible?"

"Who knows?" The mystery of it all closed about Alan as he ate. He was still sitting there, deep in his own thoughts, when Never Still left the lodge, glancing back uneasily.

Alan was able to get about quite well, but he did not associate much with the other boys as he had in the old days. Yellow Snake seemed to resent the fact that Alan had been chosen for medicine man training rather than himself, for he had swiftly completed his four raiding and war trips and had claimed to see a huge yellow snake that had spoken to him in a dream. But this had not been reason enough for him to become a medicine man in the opinion of the others.

Coyote was pleased with Alan's ambition to become a

medicine man. But there was a silent hurt in his eyes, because Never Still had not yet qualified as a full-fledged warrior. The warriors had gone on a horse-stealing raid shortly after Alan had been wounded by the mountain lion. Yellow Snake had distinguished himself by riding full tilt into a group of the enemy, thus spoiling their aim and helping some of the warriors to escape. Another boy, the son of Mule, had been wounded and cut off from the others. He had killed an enemy to make good his escape. It had been his fourth trip, and it had qualified him as a warrior, although he was a little older than Never Still. He had been given the name He-Goes-Out-to-Fight.

Never Still stayed much by himself. The shame of still bearing his boyhood name stuck in his pride like a barbed arrow. He had become known as "one who abides without moving." The expression could indicate either a thoughtful person or one who was calm and clearheaded in the face of events.

So the pattern of days and life went on. The boys began to separate into their future ways of life: Alan as a medicine man; Yellow Snake ambitious for power; He-Goes-Out-to-Fight as an upcoming warrior; Never Still as one who thought deeply. It was early in youth, as compared to the standards of white boys, but it was the result of a hard economy that was organized to hurry the boys into manhood so that they would be an asset to their people.

Soon they would travel south into the great Sierra Madres to avoid Ghost Face. Everything was ready. There were many horses and mules. The food had been prepared for the long journey.

There was no chance for escape now. Alan was still too weak to travel alone, and Never Still seemed always in the background if Alan wandered off a little. Bartolome Amadeo had been casually accepted into the band as one of them, due to his knowledge of their language and customs. He warned Alan repeatedly against attempting another escape. Alan looked forward to a long winter farther away from his people than he had ever been before.

The band of Chiricahuas left their summer camp one cold dawn, just before the sky was lighted by the sun. Mule went first, riding with five picked warriors, to act as the advance party. Then came Coyote with ten warriors. Behind Coyote's men came the women and young children, leading pack horses and mules. The older boys and the untried warriors drove the extra horses and mules. Then came the rear guard, led by Black Bear. To each side of the main party there were flanking scouts slipping through the underbrush away from the main trail.

They traveled all that day, reaching the lower slopes of the mountains at dusk. They went into camp. In the morning the women and girls would harvest the ripe fruit of the prickly pear cactus. Some of the children were dead tired that night, but there was no outcry from them. They knew better. The hands of all other men were against the Apaches, and speed was essential until the band reached the fastnesses of the Sierra Madre of the South.

At dawn, the harvesters left the mountain meadow where the brown-eyed Susans yellowed the drying grasses. There was a distant fairy bugling, and a great flock of wildfowl flew overhead, heading south for the time of Ghost Face just as the Chiricahuas were. Alan and some of the other untried braves went with the harvesters to watch for enemies. A few veteran warriors went along as well.

On the desert below them, a thin tendril of dust arose near a dried river course, many miles away. Dust-devils rose now and then, only to vanish as swiftly as they had come. The streamer of dust was too far away for the warriors to worry about it, but Alan knew he must warn them. The dust might be from the movement of horses and wagons. Perhaps they were his own people, yet he must warn the warriors.

Alan went to tell Antelope what he had seen. Antelope was counting the long brass cartridges from his ammunition pouch. He eyed the dust as Alan spoke to him. "The Enemy," he said quietly. "There is plenty of time to finish the gathering. The Enemy is riding away from us, not toward us. You should have known that, boy."

Alan went back to his post. He was fifteen now, almost a man according to Apache standards, and to many of his own people. If he escaped now, what could he do? He had no family of his own. But he could find some kind of work. Perhaps he could go on to California. Mexico, always mysterious, sprawled to the south. The mountains there were covered with trees and brush. They were sharp and clear to the eye. There was a deep curiosity in Alan about that country to the south, despite his eagerness to escape.

The band traveled south again after the fruit gathering. They crossed the border well after dark. Camp was made high on a naked ridge, and no fires were allowed. Warriors ringed the camp as guards, listening to each night sound and evaluating it. The wind rushed through the thorny vegetation. Coyotes wailed under the starlit sky.

They rested for four hours and then went on. The journey through the harsh land was already wearing on the children. Animals that could not keep up were slain for their meat. This was a land where water was found only in rock pans, many of them known only to the Chiricahuas. The water was brown with droppings and sometimes thick with wrigglers, but it was water. It was strained and poured into the greasy horse-gut canteens. Bartolome Amadeo, clad as a Chiricahua, gradually grew more melancholy as they progressed into his homeland.

In a week of hard travel, they reached a mountain

fastness high in rugged mountains. A stream danced and chuckled over the smooth stones of its bed. Tall pines filled the air with a winy odor. There were but two trails into the hide-out. Both of them were narrow and ideal for defense. In a short time, the winter camp was established. Low dwellings sprang up like great mushrooms. The horses and mules were herded into a box canyon. The squaws gathered huge quantities of dry wood. Coyote immediately left to scout the area. The Chiricahuas were now ready for Ghost Face.

Alan kept up his studies under the skilled tutelage of Looking Glass and some of the other medicine people. But there was plenty of time for hunting and games as they settled into their winter routine. Alan now handled his bow like a veteran. He learned more of the hunting lore. Women were not allowed to hunt. That was the prerogative of the male. Alan learned not to eat onions before he went after deer, so that the deer would not smell him. Yet many onions were cooked with the deer meat. It was necessary to cleanse himself thoroughly before the hunt. He must hunt with an empty stomach so that the gods would pity him. The appearance of a crow before a hunt was considered a good omen. The basis for this seemed to be the belief that all the animals had been kept hidden by the crows until Killer of Enemies, with the help of Coyote, freed them during the absence of their keepers. The crows had returned just in time to see their charges escape. This had so angered them that they had called out the names of the waste parts that now formed the principal portion of their fare. Killer of Enemies was another one of the supernatural deities of the Apaches, while the spirit Coyote sometimes helped the Apaches and at other times played tricks on them.

A hunter must be reverent before taking up the chase. A hunter must never be selfish. A basket must never be brought on the hunt, for this indicated selfishness. Alan learned to think about where he was going to hunt the night before he left. Some of the other boys poisoned their arrows before the hunt, but Alan did not like the idea, preferring to bring down his game with a skillful shot. The arrows were poisoned by taking animal blood and mixing it with the pounded-up sharp prongs of the prickly pear cactus. This mess was allowed to spoil and then was placed on the arrow points. Whatever was shot with such an arrow was sure to die, although it did not spoil the meat. The poison could also be used to kill humans.

Alan learned to shoot deer in the flank so that the shaft would work up into the vitals during the running action of the deer. He learned to use a leaf whistle to imitate the soft cry of a young deer, to attract the mother. If he made a kill, he must place its head to the east and never walk in front of it. He must never straddle it or walk across the carcass.

After he had skinned his deer, he must brush the carcass with the skin in the four directions. Then he must twice lay the hide on the carcass, reversing it with the front part of the hide on the rear part of the carcass. The formal talk was then given. "When you see me, don't be afraid," he would say. "May I be lucky with you all the time." That way, he would have good luck with the deer and see them all the time.

Offerings must be made to the crows. "This is for you, Crow," he would say. "Make me lucky, and we'll have this food all the time. I leave this for you every time."

There was one time when Belt hunted with Alan. They were caught by darkness far from the camp. The weight of the kill slowed them down. Belt placed the meat in a heap and covered it with the hide. The heavier parts of the carcass were strung up in a tree by a yucca string.

Belt always placed a slit piece of the entrails on the horns of a buck for good luck. Some of the other hunters had their own particular devices, but Alan satisfied himself with the simplest of rites.

One of the most important factors of the hunt was to be generous with the kill. The widows and aged people always received portions. The first man who came upon the kill was entitled to the whole deer if he so desired. Usually, only a part of the meat was taken by him. This was a rule that must be followed, for other men might not have been so fortunate in the hunt. Later, if the deer was being taken to camp on the back of a horse, this rule need not be followed. Alan sometimes thought that white hunters might learn some rules of behavior from the despised Apaches.

Alan kept busy with his hunting and his studies. His strength seemed to return greater than it had been before his wounding by the mountain lion. Never Still hunted with him now and then, but a deep unhappiness had overtaken the young Chiricahua. Yellow Snake and He-Goes-Out-to-Fight joined Mule on a horse raid, but Never Still was not asked to go. The raiders brought in fifteen fine horses, and Yellow Snake strutted about the camp, exhibiting the fine sliver-chased shotgun he had captured from a Mexican herder.

The winter days were taken up with hunting, an occasional raid or small scouting party, and the playing of the hoop-and-pole game. At night the people told the age-old stories of Coyote, the sly half-hero and half-villain of Chiricahua folklore.

CHAPTER NINE

It was the hoop-and-pole game that reopened the old wound between Yellow Snake and Alan. Alan had learned to play the game in the summer camp with a small set made especially for the boys. Now he was allowed to play where the men had their playing ground. Women, children, and dogs were barred from the playing place. It was strictly a man's game, just as the stave game was considered only for women and girls.

Alan's position in the band was a peculiar one. He had not finished his four times on the warpath and on raids, which would have given him the status of a man, but his past record among these people was good, far better than that of some of the other older boys. His so-called power from the lightning gave him prestige. His capture of Bartolome Amadeo had added to it. His killing fight with the mountain lion had raised him almost to man's estate. He was also respected as a good hunter. He had gone one day to watch the hoop-and-pole players and had been challenged to a game by He-Goes-Out-to-Fight. Alan had won in a close match. Thereafter he played often, although he had little to wager on the games.

Grass and stones had been removed from a strip of earth thirty feet long and a foot wide. The earth had been watered and packed down hard and smooth and then covered with slippery pine needles. The poles were almost as long as the playing field and had been made of three or four pieces of wood bound together with sinew. One of the two poles was painted red at the butt end. Both poles were notched and marked with different graduations. Each notch counted for so much in the game.

The hoops were about six inches in diameter and were also notched. A knotted string was tied across the middle of each hoop. The knots were called "beads". The biggest knot was in the middle. All the notches had names. The players agreed on how much each notch would count before the game started.

A rock was placed in the middle of the earth lane, and there was one at either end to show the field boundaries.

The long lane ran east and west according to custom. At either end of the playing field were ridges of grass. The lanes were called "that which against the pole is repeatedly thrown." The hoop could be rolled through these lanes or outside of them.

The object of the game was to roll the hoop with an underhanded motion toward the grass ridges. The pole was cast after the rolling hoop just as it was about to fall over. The object then was to make the butt of the pole fall under the hoop. Two men played from the center, first to the east and then to the west. Only the winning throw was kept, and only one score, that of the man who was ahead, was tallied. What he tallied was added to his score and what the other player got was subtracted from it.

Three prominent warriors acted as judges in the game. There was no appealing a decision once it was made by the judges. No weapons were allowed in the playing area.

Never Still was playing his first game since he had left the summer camp, and he was out of practice. The prize between him and Yellow Snake was a fine Mexican blanket. Alan had just defeated Bartolome and won a fine deer hide from the Mexican. It had been agreed that the winner of their match would play the winner of the match between Never Still and Yellow Snake. That game was almost over. Yellow Snake made an expert cast and won easily.

Never Still handed his pole to Alan. Yellow Snake smiled. "I will win easily," he boasted, "for an Enemy cannot beat a true Chiricahua."

Never Still turned quickly. "An *Enemy?* He is one of us!"

There was pure hate in the eyes of Yellow Snake. "You would say so! Has he slain any of the Mexicans? Has he slain any of the Americans? What manner of warrior would he make?"

"He captured Socorro! He fought the mountain lion with but a knife to save me!"

"Play!" shouted Black Bear. "You talk like women!"

The game began. For a time, Yellow Snake was winning. He glanced now and then at the Mexican blanket and a Sharps rifle that he had put up against the deer hide and the Mexican knife that Alan had wagered. In Yellow Snake's mind, he had already won, for he would never have offered such a fine prize as the rifle if he had not been sure of himself.

Yellow Snake rolled the hoop. The poles slithered after it. Alan gained points. In the next cast, he was slightly ahead. They cast again. Yellow Snake crept up on Alan. Then Alan made a fine throw and shot ahead. Yellow Snake flushed. In his haste he made a poor cast. Alan now had a good lead.

Alan rolled the hoop. Yellow Snake deliberately bumped his pole against Alan's, spoiling his aim. The judges did not see the cheating. But Coyote had seen it. His face darkened with anger.

There was tension in the air as they stood ready for the last throwing. Yellow Snake rolled the hoop and then drew back his arm to throw his pole. His foot slipped, and his pole slid completely off the field. Alan's pole slid fairly and came to rest with a high score.

"He wins," said Black Bear after getting the nod from the other two judges.

Alan walked toward the prizes. Moccasins slapped the earth behind him. "It was not fair!" protested Yellow Snake.

It was against all rules to protest. Black Bear looked up. "You have lost," he said. "Be still!"

Alan stopped beside the fine rifle. The warriors were scowling at Yellow Snake. The hoop-and-pole game area was always a place of good humor and fellowship.

"Look out!" yelled Black Bear to Alan.

Alan whirled. Yellow Snake had raised his pole. He brought it down with all his strength. Alan darted sideways and threw up an arm to protect himself. The pole cracked against his arm. The second blow slashed at his head. He went down on one knee as the warriors closed in. He came up from the ground like an uncoiling spring to grapple with the raging Chiricahua. He threw Yellow Snake back, measured him with a left jab, and then smashed home a hard right. The Chiricahua staggered. Alan stepped in close and grounded his enemy with a right hook. Yellow Snake sprawled on the ground shaking his head.

Two warriors stood over the fallen Yellow Snake. Coyote stopped beside them. "Go from the camp!" he ordered Yellow Snake sternly. "You have violated the rules. Come back when you are ready to make peace with your opponent."

Yellow Snake stood up, shaking in frustrated rage. "Knife and awl!" he spat as he walked away.

Alan picked up the Sharps rifle. It was old but had been well taken care of. Yellow Snake turned. He thrust out his right hand, thumb and little finger extended, then hissed like a snake between his lips. There was pure hatred in his eyes, but he had to go. There were no loopholes. He would go, but his hate would live within him.

Bartolome walked toward the camp with Alan. "I am glad you won," he said, "but you have made a bitter enemy."

Alan nodded. Yellow Snake had hated him ever since the day Alan had defeated him at wrestling.

That evening Bartolome came to Alan. "You must think again of escape," he said, "for Yellow Snake will never forget. He will have but one thought over and over again in his mind—to kill you for the shame you have brought upon him."

Yellow Snake had left the camp shortly after losing the game. In time, news trickled into the camp that he had allied himself with the Southern Band of the Chiricahuas, called in the native tongue the Enemy People. They fought constantly with the Mexican soldiery. It was also said that many of them wanted to move up north, across the border into the United States. They were inhabitants of the Sierra Madre and the Hatchet Mountains. There were many good war chiefs among them.

Alan wisely worked hard to perfect himself in his chosen field. Bartolome furthered Alan's knowledge of old Mexico, about which he loved to talk. He told of the great raids of the Apaches even beyond Durango, far to the south, and how some of the Apaches made unwritten pacts with some of the Mexicans who lived in the little villages scattered about Chihuahua and Sonora, promising not to attack and kill if the Mexicans allowed them freedom to take as many horses and mules as they liked. Thus, the Mexicans lost many fine animals, but at least they were safe from a massacre.

The Mexican Army fought the Apaches with varying degrees of success. Many of their officers were men in disgrace sent to the frontier as a sort of punishment. Some of the soldiers were more feared in the little villages than were the Apaches. Some regiments, such as the famous Sixth Infantry, were fine Indian fighters, asking and giving no quarter in the pitiless warfare. Bartolome himself had once served for a short time with the Sixth.

"Why are the Apaches so cruel to the Mexicans?" asked Alan of Bartolome one evening while they were making arrows.

Bartolome shrugged. "They are cruel to the *Americanos* as well. There is great hate on both sides. The white people have not always been kind to these wild people."

Alan flushed. "Speak of the Mexicans," he said hotly, "not of the Americans."

Bartolome waved a hand. "Have you ever heard of the man called Senor Johnsohn?"

"No."

"The *Americanos* invited the people of Red Sleeves to a great *fiesta* in Santa Rita, in what is now called New Mexico by your people. There was much to eat and drink. There was a great pile of maize, covered with green branches. Gifts of meat and grain were given to the Apaches. While they gathered up the gifts, they were fired upon by two cannons hidden behind the maize. The cannons had been loaded with stones, iron scrap, nails, and glass. There were two hundred Apaches in that crowd! Mostly women and children! That man, Senor Johnsohn, fired the cannon himself. Do you know why?"

Alan shook his head.

Bartolome lowered his voice.

"Because the scalps of the Apaches were worth many pesos to the governor of Sonora. He would pay one hundred and fifty pesos for the scalp of a man, one hundred for that of a squaw, fifty for the scalp of a child."

"Santa Rita was then part of Mexico! It was not part of the United States, Bartolome!"

"Senor Johnsohn was an *Americano*. It was *he* who fired the cannon."

Loyalty to his country surged up in Alan. "Things like

that could not happen under the government of the United States!"

Bartolome laughed bitterly. "Listen! Before your great Civil War, an officer came to Apache Pass, looking for a white child who had been kidnapped by Apaches. At that time, Cochise, the great chief of the Chiricahuas, had been at peace for quite some time with your government. He was even supplying firewood for the stage station in the pass. He came in under a flag of truce to talk to that officer. Cochise was accused not only of stealing the child, but also of stealing cattle and horses."

Bartolome looked at Alan. "Cochise offered to find out who had done these things. Cochise was an honorable man. He was called a liar. Cochise was angered as any man would have been. He escaped from the soldiers and was wounded in the leg. Then he went on the warpath. The officer retaliated by hanging three Chiricahuas who were relatives of Cochise, and three Coyotero Apaches as well. After that it was war to the death!

"Then war started between the North and the South in your country. The soldiers were withdrawn from Arizona. The Apaches went wild."

Alan straightened an arrow against a heated rock. "What happened then?"

"It was later proved that Cochise had nothing to do with the kidnapping and the stealing. By then it was too late. Cochise, once the staunch friend of your people, was now their deadliest foe in the Southwest. Because of that one foolish officer, hundreds of your people met bloody death at the hands of the Apaches."

"You talk like a real Apache!"

Bartolome bowed his head. "I am half Apache, it is true. Perhaps not even half, as my father was said to have Mexican blood in him. There are two sides to each story, Alan. It is only fair to hear them both."

"I still think the Apaches have been fairly treated in my country."

"Some years ago, an officer of your Army settled some Apaches on a reservation near Fort Grant. They were quiet and intent on learning how to farm. Some wild Apaches made a raid. While the soldiers were off chasing them, a band of white men and Papago Indians attacked the reservation Apaches and practically wiped them out.

"There are men in Tucson, now known as the Tucson Ring, who cheat your army on supplies of hay, lumber, and other things. It is to their advantage to keep the Apaches stirred up so that the army must keep many soldiers in Arizona Territory. Thus they make money because of war! Some Indian agents are as crooked as a flash of lightning. I have heard that some have even given smallpox-contaminated blankets to the tribes to get rid of them."

Alan put away his arrows and tools. The words of the Mexican turned over in his mind. Someday, perhaps, he might be able to clean up such conditions in his own country if he ever got back to it.

CHAPTER TEN

There came to Coyote one day a great desire for sweet mule meat, of which he was very fond. It was probably more than the thought of the meat alone that made him decide on a raid against the Mexicans. The winter had been long, and the warriors were tired and restless in their inactivity. Some of them had been quarreling among themselves. One day Keensighted, a fine scout, brought in word that the Mexican soldiers had left the village that lay to the south of the mountains and had traveled far to the west. There was no protection for the village. There were many horses and mules in the corrals. Coyote talked about a raid to his warriors, and it was agreed to go.

Only the warriors who were needed were to go, but some novitiates would be taken for experience. The party was small, as was customary for raiding parties, in comparison to the larger war parties. There was to be no war dance. Alan and Bartolome, out of sheer boredom, had agreed to go along. There were to be nine warriors and four untried young men.

There was no snow on the lower slopes and the lowlands as the raiders approached the village. They reached the village at night and hid in the nearby hills.

Bartolome agreed to act as a scout and asked for Alan to accompany him. Out of his scorn for the Mexicans, Coyote agreed, feeling that Alan would come to no harm.

The two of them went down the slope toward an arroyo that led up behind the village. A cold-looking moon had arisen and shone like a disk of yellow ice in the clear sky.

Alan studied the houses. They were well-built, colored salmon, pink, blue, and yellow. The walls were thick, and the windows were small. The windows had been set with mica and barred with iron. The doors were thick and studded with bolts. Bartolome whispered to him that sheets of iron were sandwiched in between the wood of the doors as protection against bullets and fire arrows. A covered well was in the center of the plaza. The corrals were high-walled and closed by heavy wooden gates. Yellow lamplight gleamed dimly through a few of the mica windows. The odor of bitter woodsmoke hung over the village.

There was no sign of soldiers as the two young men padded silently about the village, looking for all the world like true Chiricahuas with their long hair and buckskin clothing. Bartolome stopped behind a building. "What will you report to Coyote?" asked Alan.

Bartolome shrugged. "The people here are safe enough. They are used to the Apaches coming to take their horses and mules."

Alan looked to the north toward the unseen border. "Can we escape now?"

Bartolome rubbed his jaw. "We look like true Apaches. White men who live with the Indians are sometimes hated worse than the pure Indians. Even I would not be safe among the Mexicans now."

"We can steal clothing."

"Yes—but what if we are caught by Coyote?"

"We'll have a head start."

"We will see. Come. Let us circle the village. It is very quiet."

They padded about the town. A squat, rounded tower, set with loopholes, dominated one end of the plaza. "The tower," said Bartolome. "In the old days the people would go in there when the Apaches came. Now their fear is so great that they submit without a fight. It makes me sick!"

Alan gripped him by the arm. "*Tsst! Tsst!*" he hissed in warning.

A man had strolled out from between two houses. A large-bored blunderbuss hung from his back. He walked slowly about the plaza, singing softly to himself. He passed within a few feet of the two crouching scouts. He paused and looked about and then strolled toward a house. The door opened, outlining him in the lamplight. The soft notes of a guitar drifted from the house and then were cut off as the door closed.

"Do you know what he was singing?" asked Bartolome.

"No."

"*La raza de bronce que sabe morir.*" Bartolome looked back at the cold, brooding hills. "'The Bronze Race That Knows How to Die,' a song written by one of my people in grudging admiration for the Apaches, Yaquis, and Tarahumaras. Prophetic, is it not?"

"Let's get out of here. Perhaps we can slip away."

It was no use. As they left the arroyo, they saw the silent Chiricahuas rising from the brush. "There are no soldiers there," said Bartolome to Coyote.

Coyote shifted his heavy repeating rifle. His liquid eyes studied Alan as though he knew what thoughts had passed through his mind. "Good," he said. "We will enter at dawn."

The raiders hid in a hollow and covered themselves with the one blanket each of them had allowed himself. Alan had by now become used to the hard life. His body was well greased, and his blanket was warm. He fell asleep with the melancholy song of the Mexican running through his mind—"The Bronze Race That Knows How to Die."

They entered the quiet village just as dawn grayed the sky. Bartolome hammered on the door of the mayor's house. A shivering Mexican came to the door with a huge horse pistol in his thin hands. His face blanched when he saw the silent warriors standing in the street.

"We have come for horses and mules," said Coyote in fair Spanish.

The mayor hastily put the pistol out of sight. There was no chance against these feared raiders. It was useless to die for a few horses and mules. He bowed. "They are in the corrals," he said.

Coyote held up a hand. "We will take our pick, harming no one—unless there is resistance. It is understood?"

"Yes. Yes."

The warriors went to work swiftly. Some of them scattered through the village where they could cover the streets. Others opened the corral gates and walked in among the animals. They ran expert hands over the horses, looking for short tendons, deep galls, poor eyes, and teeth. It didn't take long. They took a few plump mules for a feast. Ten horses were also driven into the street.

The guards lolled about the plaza, their hands on their weapons, eying the few Mexicans who watched their animals being taken. Frightened eyes looked out at the Apaches through the small windows. Coyote dispatched warriors to get the Chiricahua mounts. He led his party from the village as the horses were brought in.

Alan looked back as they rode off. There was feral hate in the eyes of the mayor as he stood there in the wreathing yellow dust. That was one thing the Apaches could not stop him from doing—hating the raiders with all his soul. A silent warning seemed to come from him.

Later, as they drove the horses up the slope, Alan looked back to see a thread of dust rising on the western road. A lone horseman was riding hard. The soldiers had gone west.

There would be much feasting in the camp of Coyote, who had had the audacity to enter the village and take his pick of the stock. As they rode deeper into the canyon, Alan thought again of the little mayor. Trouble was brewing for the Chiricahuas; of that, Alan was quite sure.

Before dawn, the day after the raid, the warriors drove the horses and mules deeper into the mountains. The day was cold, but it was more than cold that bothered the Chiricahuas. Their way was to seek always the high ground, rather than to travel the easier routes as the Mexicans and Americans did. The mules and horses made a great deal of noise, and the dust pall above the party was a sure sign to anyone who might be interested in the whereabouts of the raiders.

Coyote called a halt. Alan and Bartolome were sent up on a high ridge to look over the land. Bartolome shivered in the cold wind that swept the exposed ridge. "Look," he said. A streamer of dust rose high in the air, dust from many horses. "Mexican soldiers," said Bartolome. "See how the sun shines on their ornaments and weapons?"

"We can outride them."

"Who sent for them, I wonder?"

"The mayor. I'm sure of that."

The sun was getting higher. Bartolome rubbed his lean jaw. "I do not like this."

Alan looked to the southwest. He stiffened. There was something indefinable against a low ridge. Then he knew what it was. More dust! The flashing of metal came through the dust.

"What is it?" asked Bartolome.

"See for yourself. Where are your eyes?"

The half-breed wet his lips. "There is a telegraph line

west of here. The line goes to the garrison at Quatro Jacales. There are many soldiers there. Good troops. They have been sent for."

Both of them plunged down the steep slope, ignoring the sharp thrusts of prickly pear and cholla. They cascaded down to the warriors. Bartolome gave his report.

Coyote looked at their prizes. "There are many of the soldiers from what you say," he said thoughtfully.

"If we leave the herd, we can outride them," said Bartolome.

Coyote scowled. "We will take them with us! There is a canyon leading toward the border. We will follow it and then cut back to drive the herd over the big mesa. By that time, it will be dark, and we will get away."

They rode swiftly back down the canyon, away from the camp route. Bartolome dropped back beside Alan. "This is madness. Coyote is a good warrior, but he has one great fault."

"So?"

"He despises the Mexican soldiers. He is also greedy. He will sacrifice us for these animals. You will see."

It was the middle of the afternoon when the raiders met Mule and Never Still. They had been out hunting. They were thin with travel and coated with dust. Coyote called a halt to rest the horses. "Why are you here?" he asked Mule.

"We were heading back to the camp when we met a Chiricahua of the Southern Band. He warned us that the Mexicans had long planned to strike our camp. Soldiers are gathering everywhere. We rode to see. It is true. Dust is rising everywhere. There is not much time left for us to escape."

Coyote spat. "I am not afraid of them!"

The warriors impassively eyed their fighting chief. They were thinking of their families back at the camp. Now and then one of them would look up at the lip of the canyon as though expecting to see the soldiers. It was not their way to stay on low ground when the enemy was about. If they abandoned the horses and mules, they could take off afoot and get high into the mountains where they would be safe. There were not many of the Chiricahuas; there never had been. They liked to pick their time and place for fighting. This was not good.

Mule sketched a map on the ground with a stick. He drew a line to mark the border and then drew a diagonal line across it to mark the canyon they were in. He marked two places to show where the Mexican troops had last been seen. "There is no time to waste," he warned. "We must leave the horses and mules and take to the high places as is our custom when pursued."

"We still have time," insisted Coyote.

The warriors were restless. They would not look directly at Coyote, but rather watched him when they thought he was not aware of their scrutiny. Fear hovered over them like a drifting buzzard. The sun was warm on Alan's back, but he shivered a little. There would be short shrift for them if they were caught.

Coyote stood up. "We are the quarry. Have you all thought of the camp? If we leave the animals and scatter, there is a chance the Mexicans might attack the camp. We can perhaps lead them away if we go on."

Mule snapped his stick in half. "They have never found our camp. The Mexicans have no stomach to go into the mountains and attack our people on their own ground."

"Enough!" snapped Coyote. "We ride on!"

Hoofs clattered on the hard earth, and the dust rose again. But now, the dust was more than a discomfort. It was a signal banner to the soldiers. Coyote led the way up a branch of the canyon. Alan wondered how close they were to the border. There was no way of telling.

The sun was sinking when Coyote turned his horse up a rough slope that led to the top of the mesa. He turned to look back. There was the sound of a stick being snapped. A puff of smoke pushed out from the canyon wall. A warrior hit the ground as his horse went down. He gripped the mane of one of the captured horses and easily swung himself up onto its back. Rifles spat from the rimrock. The growths seemed to have sprouted feathery blossoms of smoke. Two warriors went down. The horses and mules plunged about in confusion.

Alan hit the ground and rolled into a shelter of rocks as the brazen notes of a bugle echoed and re-echoed throughout the canyon. A man wearing a kepi appeared on the lip of the canyon. The dying sun glinted from his bugle. A rifle bellowed near Alan. The slug raised a puff of dust from the soldier's blouse and drove him back out of sight.

"Scatter!" yelled Mule. He lashed at the captured animals with his heavy quirt. The Apaches rode in among the stampeding animals, hanging alongside their own horses, leaving only an arm and leg exposed to the heavy rifle fire.

Alan mounted and urged his horse onward. The firing never faltered. Smoke and dust raised a thick veil in the canyon, making marksmanship difficult. But there was little need for good shooting. All the soldiers had to do was fire down into the mass of men and animals, reload, and fire again until their rifle barrels were misty with heat. Coyote, by his very stubbornness and greed, had led his warriors into the type of ambush they feared the most.

The floor of the canyon rose toward a place where the walls closed in. Here, one side of the canyon had collapsed, leaving a steep slope. Alan turned his horse up the slope, followed by Bartolome and some of the other warriors. The rest of the party stayed on the canyon floor. Alan dropped from his horse and headed for cover. He raised his heavy rifle and peered down the slope. Rifles began to crackle near him as the men with him began to fight back. Some of the warriors down in the canyon were trying to get under cover.

The Mexicans now appeared, lining the canyon rim, firing as fast as they could to cut off the retreat. There was little chance of the Chiricahuas getting away. Alan lowered his rifle. He would not shoot at the Mexicans.

The soldiers began to work down the slope toward the canyon floor. "Look!" yelled Bartolome to Alan.

A lone warrior had stopped and was facing the onrushing soldiers. Blood trickled from his scalp, and one leg was braced against a rock. In his right hand was a revolver, and in his left a knife. It was Never Still.

The trapped warriors dived into the brush. Never Still covered their retreat, firing steadily and accurately with the pistol. He held back the shouting Mexicans.

"Good!" yelled Mule. "The way is open!"

Never Still killed a Mexican. The warriors broke up the canyon, running swiftly. Some of them had cast aside everything but their breechclouts and moccasins. There was no chance for Alan to join them. He trailed his rifle and darted between huge boulders. The warriors had lost men and horses, but some of them had made good their escape, thanks to the heroic Never Still.

Rifle fire still crackled as Alan made his way through a thorny jungle. Mule, Bartolome, and Big Knife were close behind him. Alan wondered how many of the raiders had been killed. There would be no wounded left alive after the Mexicans got through. A ragged buzzard drifted high overhead. Alan looked at it with revulsion. He wanted to go back and help Never Still, but it would be hopeless. Never Still would be dead by now.

Just after the moon had risen, the survivors of the raiders met on a naked ridge overlooking the country to the north. There were but eight left of the fifteen who had entered the trap. Coyote limped from a leg wound. Another warrior had lost two fingers from his left hand. There was scarcely one of them who did not have a filthy bandage somewhere on his person. It had been a hard comeuppance for the Chiricahuas after their bloodless raid on the village. No word was spoken about those who had been lost. Coyote led the way back toward the camp, keeping to the high places. There would be much wailing in the winter camp. It was a terrible blow. Coyote had lost much face.

CHAPTER ELEVEN

Coyote had learned a bitter lesson. Something had changed deep within him. He was hesitant and wary as he led his men back toward the distant camp just before dawn on the day after the ambush. The sky was graying when they heard many horses. The Chiricahuas faded into the brush like so many phantoms.

Horsemen appeared up the canyon; at least fifty of them. Alan felt his heart thud against his ribs. They were Americans. Three of them passed within fifty feet of the warriors.

It was light enough to see them well. They were tall men wearing faded shirts and blue trousers. Battered campaign hats, shaped to the wearer's fancy, were on their heads. Carbines rested across their thighs, and their slitted eyes studied the canyon as they rode along. The strong odor of sweating horses and men came to Alan. They had been on the trail a long time. The three men passed from sight.

The main force was led by two officers. A big sergeant rode behind them with a guidon flapping above his head. This might be Alan's chance. But the hard eyes of several warriors were on him.

A squad brought up the rear. The troopers had yellow scarves across their mouths as protection against the thick dust raised by the main group.

Alan turned slowly. Bartolome shook his head. A few feet from Alan was Thin One, a young warrior. He had cocked both hammers of his double-barreled shotgun. It rested against a rock. Alan eased back and lay still. Then he shoved a foot against the shotgun. It clattered against rock. One of the barrels spat flame and smoke. Alan rolled into some brush and crawled behind a boulder.

The echo of the shot slammed back and forth between the canyon walls. Troopers yelled. Hooves clashed. Carbine fire broke out. Alan slid down the slope, ripping off his headband and dropping his rifle. He plunged through a thicket, skirted some rocks, and stopped short to look at the excited rear guard.

The main group had halted. Horses, four to a man, were led off into the brush. The troopers scattered for cover. A carbine cracked now and then. Alan looked back. A warrior was outlined against the sky and then vanished with bullets snapping at his heels. Lead splattered against the rocks. Smoke was sifted by the dawn wind. The firing died away as the troopers looked for targets. It was Alan's chance.

Alan ran toward the nearest troopers. "Don't shoot!" he screamed.

Taut faces peered at him from beneath hat brims. Carbines came up and steadied. "I'm a white boy!" yelled Alan.

"It's a trick!" shouted a lanky corporal. He fired. The slug whined eerily from in front of Alan. He stopped. "I was with the Warden party!" he cried.

The next slug burned across his left shoulder. It was no use. He dived into a clump of catclaw. The barbs ripped at his flesh. He floundered through as leaden missiles searched for him. He plunged into an eroded gully and ran up it.

The canyon wall was steep now. He turned and sprinted along a level space, hurdling rocks and crashing through brush. Bullets whipped past him. They were shooting better in the growing light. A bullet slashed through his loincloth. Some of the troopers had mounted and were spurring their big bays after him, holding pistols at the ready.

A draft of air swirled about Alan. There was a place where the wall had collapsed, leaving a gully that opened up toward the rimrock. He ran up it with his chest heaving like a bellows. He crawled over the rim with the last of the bullets whining up into the air past him.

He steadied down to a mile-eating lope. He could run for hours at that pace.

The sun was high when he halted. There was no sign of life other than a buzzard floating high overhead like a scrap of charred paper. Sweat streamed down Alan's body and stung the myriad cuts and scratches on it. He looked back at the rough country he had traversed. It was as deserted as the moon. He dropped in the shade of a boulder and lay there for a long time. After a rest he began to pick the cactus thorns from his flesh with the tip of his knife. That and the short reserve knife he carried in his loincloth were the only weapons he had. He had no food or water.

It had been a close call. His own people had nearly killed him. If the warriors suspected he had deliberately kicked over the shotgun, his fate would be decidedly unpleasant if he went back to them. Until he could get rid of his Apache clothing, he would be a target for every American or Mexican he might meet. There were few people in that silent land, but they would shoot first and ask questions later. Still, he couldn't part with his desert moccasins in that country of rough earth and spiked vegetation.

Which way could he go? To the south was the land of the Mexicans, who hated Apaches worse than rattlesnakes. To the north was the United States, and those people held no love for the Apaches either. He would have to survive by himself, living off the land, until he could act and dress as a white boy again.

He bound a strip of loincloth about his long hair and popped a pebble into his mouth to ease his thirst. He set off for the heights, which were smoky with haze to the east. He must find food and water.

It was late afternoon when he saw the thin veil of dust rising behind him. He set off in a steady lope for the broken country ahead of him. He was tired, and it seemed as though the dust was getting closer all the time. The sun glinted from metal. Soldiers again, although he had no way of knowing whether they were Americans or Mexicans. They were both enemies until he could pick a time and place to prove he was one of them.

Later he could distinguish the horsemen. They were Americans. Sun reflected from something. Probably field glasses. They had seen him. His legs ached as he drove on. There was no use in trying to hide from them on the barren slopes. He had to outrun them. He slogged on, planting one aching foot in front of the other in the deadly race.

The sun was a coppery ball to the west when he reached a hiding place. He looked back to see horsemen behind him. They had spread out into a wide crescent. He trotted up the coulee, climbed out of it to follow a knife-edged ridge, and then slid down a long talus slope to vanish into a wilderness of scrub trees and shattered rock formations.

He fell asleep, drugged by weariness. It was the scraping noise that aroused him. The moon flooded down in a cold, eerie light. Alan shifted a little, almost groaning aloud as his stiffened muscles took slight strain. The scraping noise had stopped. The night wind rustled the brush. The noise came again. Alan turned to look fully into the basilisk eyes of a thick-bodied rattlesnake.

The sinuous body began to coil. The flat, ugly head began to rise for the strike.

The place was rank with the snake smell. Then Alan realized he had blundered into a den of them, for he heard faint rattlings and the thin scrape of the scaled bodies all about him. The snake poised for the lightning-like strike.

Alan threw himself sideways, thrusting out his left hand to grip the scaly body just behind the wide head. He drew his knife and slashed deeply, cutting his own hand as the keen blade sank deep into the body. He stabbed again and again until he threw the writhing, dying body away from him in revulsion. Sickened, he jumped to his feet and ran away. Tears sprang into his eyes. He shook his head. This was no way for a man of the Chiricahuas to act, although they themselves dreaded the rattlers.

He followed the easiest path as he worked his way upward. The landscape was bathed in the silvery cold moonlight. Etched on the ground were the shadows of rocks and brush. It was late at night, with the moon on the wane, when he found a rock pan with a few inches of discolored water in it. He strained it thoroughly with a piece of his loincloth and drank the fluid thirstily, holding back a wave of nausea as he did so.

He slept on the open ground until the sun warmed his naked back. He sat up. He must be at the far southern end of the Big Mountain, the stronghold of the Central Band of the Chiricahuas, where he had spent last summer and fall. The summer camp was far to the north. Here he could stay and survive until he could get back to his own people. There would be food and water. He would make a bow and some arrows and establish a hidden camp until the time came. Right now, he needed food and rest above anything.

In the days that followed Alan's escape from the Chiricahuas, he kept himself busy establishing his camp. He found a narrow canyon through which a trickle of water worked its way into a big rock pan. He tied thick whips of brush together to form the frame of his little lodge and then thatched it with bear grass. He found a place alive with rabbits and placed snares of buckskin in their runways.

He made his fires of the driest wood, allowing just enough time to cook his meat before he put out the flames. He fashioned a bow of juniper wood and made the string of yucca. He found some dried canes and made arrows for hunting small game. He lost much weight but managed to keep strength in his body.

One afternoon he was patiently stalking a hawk for its feathers when he suddenly saw another hawk, which had been hovering high in the air, turn and fly rapidly away. Something had frightened it. He worked his way down the canyon and hid in the brush. He studied the terrain below him. Suddenly he grew tense. Stones had clicked not too far away from him.

He drew out his knife and thrust it into the earth beside him. There was a movement in the brush. Minutes drifted past. A man staggered out of cover, swaying wearily as he stood there. He came slowly toward Alan, supporting himself with a crooked staff. Alan raised his head. The bent figure wore the loincloth of an Apache.

Closer and closer came the limping man. Then he staggered and fell heavily. His stick clattered against the stones. Alan nocked an arrow and picked up his knife. He worked his way down the slope and stared at the prone figure. Then he began to run toward the fallen man. "Never Still! My brother!" he called out.

Never Still did not move. Alan rolled him over. The Chiricahua was bleeding from a gash over his left eye. Black blood encrusted the left side of his head. His eyes were hollow in his gaunt face. A filthy bandage was bound about his left thigh. His stench was sickening.

Alan picked him up. He was as light as a child. He

carried him up the canyon, pausing often for rest, until he placed the unconscious Chiricahua in the little lodge. After he had wet the swollen lips, Alan carefully cut away the dirty clothing and bathed the filthy, blood-encrusted, emaciated body. Never Still opened his eyes. "Brother," he said quietly as he gripped Alan's arm with weak fingers.

It was noon of the next day before the young warrior spoke again. He watched Alan roasting rabbit meat. "The Mexican soldiers thought they had me," he said. "A bullet scraped my head, and I went down. When I awoke, I was in their camp, bound to a saguaro cactus. They were very angry, my brother. Their eyes flashed, and they fingered their bayonets, but they did not strike.

"Some of the soldiers of your people were also there. Many of them, with loud voices. I understood enough to know that the soldiers of the White-eyes had seen a lone warrior. Somehow, I knew it was you. The white-eyed soldiers would not let the Mexicans torture me. They wanted me to guide them to our camp. The chief of the American soldiers protected me, although they were in Mexico. They wanted to make peace with our people. They promised me that I would not be killed if I took them to our camp. I trusted none of them!"

Alan cut the meat into small pieces and fed Never Still. "Do not talk too much," he said.

Never Still smiled. "I am safe with you."

"How did you escape?"

"Child of the Water was with me. My reserve knife was in my moccasin top. The white-eyed chief loosened my bonds so that I might eat. In the darkness, I cut my feet loose and stood there as though still tied. A Mexican came to guard me. I struck him down with my knife. It was dark and impossible for those dogs of soldiers to follow a Chiricahua. But I was weak from loss of blood. I do not remember much from then on, other than planting one foot ahead of the other for many hours."

Alan looked away. He could not desert Never Still, yet he had been getting ready to go to his own people.

"What is wrong, my brother?"

Alan shrugged. He began to feed Never Still.

"You did not answer me," said the young warrior.

"You must rest. We have water here and are safe from the soldiers. In time you will get back to your own people."

"Our people," corrected Never Still.

"Yes—our people. Rest now."

Never Still was very weak. There were times when he was delirious. His wounds suppurated. Alan cleansed them and bandaged them anew. A constant cough troubled the Chiricahua, but gradually he put some meat on his thin frame. The Time of Little Eagles, the spring, gave way to early summer, the Time of Many Leaves, and still the young Chiricahua was too weak to get about.

Alan seemed to gather strength as the days drifted past. His body was tough and wiry. His shoulders had filled out and already he was taller and heavier than most of the warriors of Coyote's band. He hunted daily and became deadly with his arrows. Deer, turkey, and rabbits fell before them. It became the Time of Large Leaves, the midsummer, before Never Still began really to recover. One day Alan returned from a hunt to find the Chiricahua sitting on a rock looking to the north with brooding eyes.

"What is it, my brother?" asked Alan.

"Our people are in the old summer camp many days by now."

"If the soldiers did not find them," said Alan dryly.

"They did not. Child of the Water appeared to me in a vision last night. All is well. We must go home. They need us both."

Something in his tone told Alan the young man was suffering from homesickness. His sickness was now of the soul rather than the body. It was time for them to part—Alan to go back to the white people; Never Still to go back to the Chiricahuas. "I cannot go with you, my brother," said Alan.

"Why not?"

His eyes haunted Alan. Slowly Alan told him how he had escaped from the raiding party by dislodging Thin One's shotgun, thus alerting the troopers.

Never Still looked down at his own gaunt body. "I cannot travel alone through the Big Mountain country," he said quietly.

"I will stay with you until you are strong enough."

Never Still shook his head. "You must go back with me. There is something we must do together."

"So?" Alan eyed Never Still. A subtle change seemed to have taken place in him.

"The Chiricahuas are few in number. The soldiers of the Mexicans and Americans are many. They have fine horses and weapons."

Alan leaned back against the rock. "They do have many more men than the Chiricahuas."

"In time we Chiricahuas will be driven from our homes or killed one by one. Do you think we might make peace with the Americans?"

"Yes."

Never Still gripped Alan's shoulder. "Then you must get me home so that we can talk with our people and show them that they must make peace. The old free days are gone. This I know, for I have given it much thought."

The Chiricahua was sincere, but Alan had no idea of going back to the Apaches.

"You will go with me then?" asked Never Still.

Alan stood up and picked up his bow and the turkey he had killed. There was nothing he could say.

The rest of the day Alan found many things to do. The sun was hot, and the winy odor of the pines drifted down from the heights above the camp. He had to reason out a plan to get back to his people. He glanced at the lodge. Never Still lay just outside of it. The Apache boy could never manage the trip back to the summer camp by himself. He needed the incantations and medicines of his mother to help him get well. Alan sighed and shrugged into his quiver strap. He picked up his bow. There was a long chance that he might round up a stray horse or mule. Never Still could not make it afoot. Alan struck off to the north in a steady, ground-devouring stride.

It was almost dusk when a faint noise came to him on the wind. He slipped into cover and nocked a shaft. The noise came again, the sound of hooves. Down a gentle slope was a stand of scrub timber. The sound came from there. Suddenly, as though materializing from the earth, there appeared a mounted warrior. A lance was slung across his back. A brass-bellied carbine was across his thighs. He rode easily, turning his head from side to side, eying everything in sight. Alan did not know him, so he sank into the brush debating as to whether or not he should show himself.

The warrior passed from sight. Moments later, there appeared ten more warriors, all of them well-mounted and armed. They were Chiricahuas, Alan was sure, but none of them were familiar. He was about to reveal himself when he recognized one of the braves. He wore a headpiece of fur from which protruded two yellow-stained cow horns, much like the headdress Coyote wore into battle. His face was broad and cruel. There was no mistaking Yellow Snake, who had been banished from the band of Coyote many months before.

Alan watched them pass from sight. They might soon camp for the night. He must steal a horse for Never Still, for he knew he would get no help and nothing but hate from Yellow Snake. There was no other choice.

CHAPTER TWELVE

It was almost midnight when Alan left his camp after seeing to it that Never Still had been fed and was asleep. Alan trotted up the canyon and stopped half a mile from the place where he had last seen the party of Chiricahuas. There was a faint moon in the sky, and a cool wind rustled the leaves.

He picked up the trail by finding a pile of fresh horse droppings. Then he found a rock with the heaviest side turned upward as though it had been dislodged by a horse. He climbed a slope and looked down into a small oval canyon, which was a branch of the bigger canyon behind him. He saw a faint spark of light below him, as though the wind had fanned a bed of embers.

The moon drifted out from behind the clouds. He could distinguish dark forms lying near the fire. There were nine of them. They were careless in their own country, lying around a fire. Two warriors were unaccounted for. They would be watching the horses. Alan worked his way down the slope and squatted in the brush, testing the night with eyes, ears, and nose. A horse whinnied from the far end of the small canyon.

He approached the far end of the canyon until he could see the horses bunched against a rock wall. He kept downwind, trying to locate the guards. Then he saw one of them leaning against a rock, muffled in a blanket. The moon shone dully on the barrel of his rifle.

Alan lay on the rocks. They were still warm from the heat of the day. If he could get in among the horses, he might be able to leap on one and ride it from the canyon. But he must also stampede the others, or the warriors would be after him. He studied the slopes until he spotted the other guard. The warrior was up high, looking to the west toward the great valley.

Alan crawled toward the horses. It was a game the boys had always played with old Jack Rabbit. One horse stood apart from the others—a blocky gray. The leader, if Alan knew horses. The gray was closest to him, shielded from the guard by the rest of the herd. Alan moved as noiselessly as a cat until he was high above the herd. He hooted softly. The guard did not move. Alan hooted louder. The guard looked about uneasily.

Alan shifted and then hooted again. The guard was getting nervous. Alan worked down the slope. The guard had moved away from the herd as though to get closer to the other guard on the ridge. Alan slipped up to the gray horse, speaking softly in Apache until he could place his hand on its neck. The gray nuzzled him. Alan felt for the hobbles and cut them loose. The other horses had drifted toward him. They saw that the gray was not nervous, and they stood quietly.

Alan looked over the gray's back. The guard was coming back. There was no chance to steal away with the gray. It must be done the hard way. He led the gray away from the herd into the shadows of a tilted slab of rock. His breath came harshly in his throat, and he was afraid the guard might hear it.

The guard was looking up at the place where Alan had played the part of an owl. Alan swung up on the gray and slammed his heels against its sides. The gray whinnied, reared a little, and then set off at a fast run. Alan turned toward the herd and slapped some of their rumps with the hobble strap he had picked up. The guard yelled. The horses milled about. Alan got in behind them, screeching like a demon and lashing at them with his strap. A rifle boomed behind him, and the slug whispered past his head.

The gray was fast. Alan had made a good choice. A rifle flared on the ridge, but Alan grinned despite his fear, for he knew the guard was shooting wild.

The herd was pounding down the slope. Their hooves rattled like pebbles in a gourd, and the bitter dust swirled up behind them. The warriors who had been sleeping were now racing for cover. It was not the Apache way to run to a scene of excitement as a white man would have done. First, they would hide, take stock of the situation, and then act. Alan had figured on that inborn caution of theirs.

A rifle flashed from the brush. Alan winced as hot lead creased his back, merely cutting the skin. Their shooting was good now; it was too good. An Apache cut into the herd, running like an antelope. He gripped the mane of a horse, but Alan swerved the gray against the warrior and knocked him head over heels to one side. The warrior rolled over and fired a wild shot from a pistol.

Alan shot through the canyon mouth, followed by a spatter of bullets. He lashed at the nearest horses and sent them pounding into the big canyon toward the valley below. He urged the gray up the other way and let him go full out. There was power and stamina in the horse. It was hard going on the rough ground, but the gray picked his way with uncanny accuracy. Alan wrenched his mane and forced him under an overhanging rock wall. In the dim moonlight he could see some of the warriors chasing down the canyon toward the stampeded herd. He grinned as he rode up the canyon.

The moon was almost gone when Alan reached the

camp after traveling a circuitous route over barren rock. He had carefully erased the hoofmarks on any softer ground he had been forced to cross. He picketed the gray in a rock cleft. He was a fine horse.

Never Still was awake when Alan returned. "My brother," he asked quietly, "where have you been?"

"I have a horse, my brother."

"From the Mexicans?"

"No."

"From the Americans, then?"

Alan hesitated. "No. From some of the Chiricahuas."

"They are coming to help us?"

"No."

"I do not understand."

"They were not of our band."

"Perhaps they were Red Paint People?"

"No. I think they were of the Enemy People, from far to the south."

Never Still stared at him. "They are our allies."

"I wasn't sure. I stole the horse and stampeded the others."

There was a deathly quiet, and then Never Still spoke softly. "You stole from a Chiricahua?"

Alan became angry. "That's what I said!"

"It is not good."

Alan stood up. He looked down at the sick Chiricahua. "Listen," he said. "You are my brother. I got the horse for you. Now shut up about it."

"Where were they going?"

"How should I know?"

"Perhaps to join our band or visit them at least. Do you know what that means? When you get back you will be called upon to explain this."

Alan shrugged. "I'll worry about it when the time comes."

"There will be trouble."

"Knife and awl! Get some sleep. We have the horse. We'll worry about trouble when the time comes."

Alan slept the rest of the night and before dawn he was up and about, getting ready for the trip to the summer camp. He had a small quantity of food, and he could hunt on the trip. It was not a long journey for two healthy young men, but Never Still had been having intermittent spells of weakness, which always laid him low.

Alan tore down the lodge and effaced the place where it had been. He dragged branches over the trampled area to erase tracks. He covered up the fire hole and brushed earth over it. Then he helped his friend up on the gray and led the horse from the canyon.

They made slow time the first day and camped that night in a thicket of scrub trees and brush high on the flank of the Big Mountain. They climbed steadily higher the next day until they entered the first of many mountain meadows. Never Still seemed to feel better when he saw the tall trees and the masses of flowers nodding gently in the warm wind. The grass was thick along the banks of a shallow, chuckling stream. A bear waddled off grumpily as they made their camp. "It is a good place," said Never Still.

The Chiricahua rested as Alan watered the horse. The air was thick with the odor of sun-warmed trees and the perfume of an infinite variety of flowers, which carpeted the meadow. A turkey gobbled from the brush. Jays chattered angrily at the intruders. A lone parrot, a visitor from south of the border, flew off in a brilliant flash of color.

Never Still was content, but there was a worm of fear in the back of his mind. Alan had changed a great deal. It would not be easy to guide him back to the old ways.

The slow journey through the mountains ended at last when Alan saw a wisp of bluish smoke, tattered by the fresh wind, drifting not far from the site of the old summer camp. Alan, ever suspicious as befitted a true Chiricahua, left Never Still in a brushy hollow with the horse and then scouted ahead. He strung his bow and nocked an arrow as he advanced.

A ridge afforded him a view of the camp. He dropped flat in the thick grass and studied it. Gradually he saw familiar things: a hulking warrior who might be Mule; a spotted mare he seemed to remember from the winter camp.

An hour drifted past. It was not until he saw the familiar waddling figure of Looking Glass that he was sure it was the camp of Coyote. There was no sign of the warriors from whom he had taken the gray horse.

He went back through the dappled glades and gobbled softly as he neared the hollow. Never Still answered him. Alan helped him to his feet. "They are there, Never Still," he said. "We will leave the horse here. I did not see the warriors from whom I took it, but we can't take a chance on that."

Alan cut a stick for him and held tightly to his arm as they walked toward the camp. Never Still was breathing hard, but no sound of pain came from him. It was Big Knife who saw them first. He ran forward with an expression of wonderment on his broad face. He silently gripped Never Still by the shoulders and then helped him walk toward the camp.

The boys and girls came from the surrounding forest. The women left their work, and the warriors hastened from the lodges. Looking Glass dropped an olla into the rushing stream, and heedless of the fact that it bobbed away on the current, she ran to her two sons.

The camp was full of excitement as Alan told the people of his adventures and how he had found Never Still. He was almost done when Bartolome Amadeo came into the camp carrying two rabbits. He smiled at Alan and then glanced warningly at Thin One, the warrior whose shotgun

Alan had knocked over to make good his escape. Thin One had taken no part in the excited welcoming of the two wanderers, but his smoldering eyes never left Alan.

Coyote nodded as Alan finished his story. "It is great medicine," he said. "There is a place for you in my lodge forever, Son of the Thunder People."

Alan shook his head. "Never Still needs quiet and rest."

Bartolome came forward. "There is a place for him in my lodge," he said quickly.

Alan went to the Mexican's lodge. Bartolome came close to him. "Thin One has been in disgrace since his carelessness with his shotgun. Luckily none of the warriors were killed by the Americans. I am not sure whether or not he knows that you did it deliberately."

Alan felt cold all over. "But you know."

Bartolome began to skin a rabbit. "Yes. You could have escaped forever. Why did you come back?"

"Never Still needed my help," Alan said simply.

Bartolome pointed his bloody knife at Alan. "You are loyal, but you are a fool! You'll never get another chance like that to escape again."

"I'll take the chance."

Bartolome grunted. "They watch us like circling hawks. Yet it is a good life—provided the soldiers do not come into these mountains."

"Has there been any sign of that?"

"A half-breed trader told us that troops are being gathered at Fort Huachuca and at Forts Grant and Bowie. Apache scouts have been enlisted to fight against their own people. It is said that Goyathlay, called Geronimo by the Mexicans and Americans, is again on the warpath. Victorio, a great warrior, has one hundred braves and has raided through Texas, New Mexico, Arizona, and Mexico. There are many American and Mexican soldiers being concentrated to run him down.

Everywhere the Apaches are rising against the whites. It is a bad time."

"We must escape soon, then."

"Yes! Yes!" Bartolome said excitedly. "But how? There is a rumor that a band of strange warriors has been seen in these mountains. Men from the Enemy People. They are fierce and bloody men. The Mexican soldiers have been harrying them until now, they are drifting north into the United States. Geronimo himself was born a member of the Enemy People."

Alan felt uneasy. He had stolen the horse from them. He told the Mexican what he had done.

Bartolome shrugged. "Perhaps they did not recognize you. In any case you cannot leave now. If they do recognize you, you must speak up and tell the truth. You should have asked them for help, Alan."

"Yellow Snake was with them."

Bartolome whistled. "You have many friends here, but he speaks with a forked tongue. Be careful, my friend."

Never Still took the name Nanogohn, which meant "coming home weak with wounds and privation". He was now recognized as a veteran warrior, but to Alan he would always be Never Still, the boy who had befriended him when he was all alone.

In the days that followed Alan's return to the camp, he put on weight. He hunted regularly but made no attempt to escape, for Bartolome had told him to wait for a good chance, and he would go along. The two of them would have a better chance for success. Alan resumed his studying under the patient teaching of Looking Glass. There was no sign of the strange warriors. Coyote, Mule, and Big Knife departed on some secret mission down into the lowlands.

Late one afternoon, as Never Still lay on his pallet near the stream, he spoke of what was in his heart to Alan. "We have many enemies, my brother," he said. "The Mexicans have many soldiers. The Americans are strong and getting stronger. Many of them are now making their homes in lands that once belonged to my people. It gets harder to steal horses and raid the ranches. Our people are too few in numbers to face the enemies we have. We do not have the fine weapons or the wagon guns that speak loudly and kill many warriors with one shot. It has been in my mind that we will all die or go to prison before long."

Alan slowly sharpened his knife. The steady *wheesht-wheesht* of steel against stone kept time to his low voice. "The Americans might not kill you or send you to prison. They would give you a place to live, cattle, seeds, and tools with which to make a living in peace."

"We are hunters and warriors. Must we hide behind walls on the hot lowlands? Must we raise stinking cattle and sheep and grub in the hard earth like the Pimas and the Papagos?"

"Yet you take the animals and food of other people. You could raise your own animals and grow crops."

The Chiricahua shook his head. "No! We will live as our ancestors did."

"Then some of you will die, and others will go to prison. You do not know how strong my people are. Some of their towns have more people living in them than all three divisions of the Chiricahuas. They have thousands of trained soldiers."

"We will live as we always have."

"Every day more people come out to this country."

"Why do they not stay in their own part of the country?"

"Because there is freedom in the United States. There is land for the asking. Here a man can stand on his own two feet and become as good as the next man."

"By killing or imprisoning the Chiricahuas?" asked Never Still bitterly.

Alan began to whet his knife on his naked thigh. It was impossible to explain such things to the simple primitive beside him. How could he understand? He had been raised in ignorance of how great a country the United States was and of what it could become.

Never Still touched Alan's shoulder. "Perhaps what you say is true, my brother. But my people will fight to the death, and I must fight with them!"

Alan stood up and slipped his knife into its sheath. He placed the whetstone on the top of one of his moccasins. "Rest now," he said as he walked away. There was a sadness in him. He had to escape. There was no other choice. Yet with all his heart, he wished that he and Never Still could be brothers forever.

CHAPTER THIRTEEN

Late one afternoon, Alan returned from a hunt to see a long file of mounted warriors urging their tired horses up the trail. He sank into hiding and watched them. There were twenty of them. Yellow Snake rode with them, holding a fine repeating rifle in his hand. The words of Bartolome came back to Alan: "Everywhere the Apaches are rising against the whites. It is a bad time."

Alan had turned loose the gray he had taken from the strange Chiricahuas. It would have been better to kill it in some remote place, but he had not been able to do so. Despite his Apache training, he had never been able to treat horses with the callousness they did. Now he was sorry that he had not killed the gray.

There were great fires going in the camp when Alan returned. The camp was crowded with the people of Coyote's band and the newcomers. Horse and mule meat was being roasted. There would be maize, honey, nuts, *atole, penole,* and berries in plenty. The firelight reflected from the greased bodies of the warriors. The strangers were all well-armed with revolvers and repeating rifles. A few of them also carried bows and arrows.

Their leader was a surly-looking, brawny man. He

wore the traditional desert moccasins, breechclout, and loincloth. His upper body was clad in a blue cavalry jacket with sergeant's chevrons on the sleeves. The jacket was filthy and smeared with grease. His headdress was made of cloth and fur and was horned. But it was his face that arrested attention. There was an inborn cruelty to the thin, down-drawn mouth and the hard eyes.

Bartolome was in the lodge. "It is as I told you, Alan. These warriors have come to ask Coyote to join them in all-out warfare against the Americans. Their leader is One Who Yawns, better known to the white people as Geronimo!"

Alan nodded. He could have guessed who it was.

"He was hated by Cochise, whose power he tried to usurp. He is much feared because he is a shaman and claims to get messages from the supernatural. He is always in trouble. He is a real *bronco*—a wild one."

There had often been talk of him in the camp. He was treacherous, bloodthirsty, and infinitely cruel. Yet some of his bloody career might be traced to the fact that his wife and three children had been slaughtered by Mexicans. A chilly feeling came over Alan as he looked out at the surly warrior.

When the feasting was over, the men and women danced in turn, and then the warriors formed a dancing ring, which in turn was ringed by dancing women. In time, Coyote and Geronimo came to sit upon folded blankets and drink coffee.

At last, Geronimo arose and spoke in the measured formal speech of the Apaches, accenting and supplementing his words with motions of his hands.

"I have come, my brothers," he said, "to ask you to join my warriors against the Americans and the Mexicans. Is this not our country? Why do they act as though we are encroaching on their land?

"Our ancestors were here long before the White-eyes came with their fine rifles and wagon guns. They are strong, but so are we. We have never been defeated in a fair fight! We are hunted through our mountains as though we were mad dogs! Yet we have struck back, capturing horses, guns, and children from them. My camp is rich with their blankets, food, weapons, and clothing, yet there is much more that can be taken by brave men.

"I walked away from the camp of Cochise long ago because he would not fight against these strangers. May a coyote eat him! I, Goyathlay, will fight against them as long as I live!"

Geronimo sat down and looked at Coyote. Coyote waited politely and then stood up. "The words of my brother are good. He is a great raider. Yet we are safe here in the Big Mountain country. We raid the Mexicans for food and horses. The mountains are full of game. We are but few in numbers compared to the White-eyes. I ask for peace at this time, as long as they leave us alone."

Geronimo's hard eyes swept the circle of warriors. He had evidently expected a quite different answer. He stood up. "Yes, my brothers, you are safe here in the Big Mountain country. I agree that the Mexicans have much food and many horses we can take. The mountains are full of game. We are few in numbers compared to the White-eyes. Coyote speaks for peace as long as they leave us alone.

"But they will not leave us in peace! Already they make many new roads for their wagons throughout our lands! They bring in many soldiers and build new forts. Some of our former brothers of the Tontos, Mescaleros, and Arivaipas are penned on reservations as some of us once were, grubbing in the dirt like Pimas and Papagos. Are we not men? The Hopis, the Houses on Bocks People, the Opatas, the Strings Coming up Between the Toes People, the Maricopas, and the Wood Under the Feet People—all are afraid of the White-eyes and have allowed themselves to be penned up on reservations. Are we not men? I say we fight them to the death! I speak for war!"

Many of Coyote's warriors nodded their heads as they listened to the inflammatory words. Bartolome leaned close to Alan. "He is stirring them up. He is a great talker, that one. Coyote's deeds are greater than his words. Geronimo is like an empty olla, which when kicked, makes more noise than a full one. Watch him. He is not through."

Geronimo turned to Coyote. "One of our brothers, who once rode with you and now rides with us, will speak to you."

Yellow Snake stood up with great pride. He was the true warrior now, despite his youth, with confidence in his skill. He held up his fine repeating rifle. "From the White-eyes," he said loudly, letting the firelight dance on the polished metal. He dipped his fingers into his ammunition pouch and cast cartridges on the ground. "From the White-eyes. I have many of these and can get many more. Why do you sit here like women in your mountains? Come with us against the enemy! We will leave a trail of bodies and burning houses from the mountains to the place the White-eyes call Tucson! Here is our new leader! He will lead you against them! Come with us!"

The poison was working up into a froth. The greedy eyes of the warriors dwelt on the rifle and the many cartridges. It was a crucial moment.

Suddenly a horse neighed from beyond the camp. Every warrior raised his head. Two boys went to get the stray. Hooves thudded, and a horse appeared in the firelight. Alan stood up as he recognized the gray he had turned loose.

Yellow Snake stared at the horse. "My horse!" he said. "Stolen from me days ago. How did it get here?"

Never Still looked across the fire at Alan. Thin One eyed Alan also. "Perhaps our brother can tell us," said

Thin One. "I saw him with this horse just before he brought Never Still back home."

"Don't move," whispered Bartolome to Alan.

"What have you to say?" asked Coyote of Alan.

"I have never seen that horse," lied Alan.

"He lies!" snapped Thin One.

One of the warriors who sat near Yellow Snake began to study Alan. "It is he," he said. "The one who stampeded our horses in the canyon south of here. I was closer to him than any of the others."

In the silence that followed, Alan looked from face to face. There was hardness on the faces of Geronimo's men. There was suspicion on the faces of Coyote's braves. Thin One strode dramatically into the cleared space before the fire. "There is something else," he said loudly. "He was close to me when we were hiding from the American soldiers. My shotgun went off, alerting them. It was he who kicked it over. This I know. Big Knife will tell you so too!"

"Speak," said Coyote to Big Knife.

Big Knife was a friend to Alan. But he must tell the truth. There was nothing else he could do. "It is true," he said quietly.

Alan whirled and tried for the gray. Thin One blocked the way. Alan turned toward the trees. Yellow Snake closed on him. Alan whipped out his knife. The blade cut a terrible gash down the face of the young warrior. Alan threw a shoulder against Yellow Snake, who was blinded by his own blood. He went down.

Other warriors closed in. Bartolome jumped up and gripped his rifle. "Run!" he screamed at Alan.

Bartolome fired as Alan sprinted into the woods. The shot galvanized the rest of the warriors into terrible action. Bartolome reversed the empty rifle and crashed it down on the head of a brave. "Run, my friend!" he screamed. "I can't return to my own people, and I will live no longer with these bloodthirsty savages!"

Alan darted around a big tree. He glanced back at Bartolome, but it was too late to help him now. Alan crashed into thick brush. As he raced through the night, he hoped the young Mexican was dead, for his fate, if he lived, would be too terrible to think about.

Alan bounced from a tree, went down on one knee, then leaped into the cold stream. He splashed across, sick with pain and fright, and pulled himself out on the far bank. Guns flashed behind him. There was no moon to light the way as he floundered out of the brush into a meadow. All he had was his knife and short reserve knife, while behind him, the woods were full of some of the greatest trackers in the world.

Half an hour dragged past as he raced through the woods, slid down a rocky ridge, and plowed along a talus slope beneath a bald peak.

Sounds of pursuit had died away long ago. It meant nothing. They would travel silently, sniffing the night air like hounds and listening to every sound as their knives thirsted for his blood. He could not stop. His short lead on them was all the advantage he had, and he had never been known as a speed runner. He glanced back as he ran. There was no sign of life.

He rested for a few moments and then fear drove him on as he fancied he heard a faint sound in the darkness. He shot a glance back over his shoulder. Suddenly his right foot met nothing but air. He fell forward, turning three times in midair, and then struck hard on a gravelly slope. Then he knew no more.

It was the clattering of hooves against stones that awoke him. He opened his eyes and winced as the sunlight seemed to lance into his very brain. The sky was dotted with cloud puffs. He lay on a rough bank between rows of sharp rocks. Above him, the scrub trees had taken root in shallow pockets of soil, screening him from sight. He rolled over, almost shrieking aloud as he felt the agony of his bruised body. He crawled beneath a rocky overhang and lay still.

The clattering stopped. The silence was broken by the occasional stamp of a hoof. A low murmur of voices drifted down to him. He felt for his knife. It was gone. He drew the short, curved reserve knife and waited tensely, momentarily expecting the noisy descent of someone from above. A hawk flew in toward the cliff and then veered off on the wind.

The clattering resumed and then died away. There was no doubt in his mind that it was a searching party of the Chiricahuas. They would not give up easily. He felt his body inch by inch. There were no broken bones. His long hair was matted with drying blood, and the skin was scraped from his right forearm. There was a deep gash in his right knee, and two fingernails had been ripped a little. His mouth was dry and sore, and his head throbbed. He crawled out and found his long knife. He shuddered as he eyed the sharp rocks. Ten feet either way and he would have been smashed to a pulp. He had fallen at least seventy feet from the ledge. He looked down and felt sick. There was a sheer drop of over two hundred feet below him.

Patiently he stuck it out until dusk before he attempted to climb the cliff. Battered as he was, he thanked God for the fall that had saved him from the searchers. He avoided known trails and struck off down the mountainside, picking his way carefully in the darkness. Hours after he started, a faint moon arose and he made better time. He wanted to eat and rest, but there was no time. He took a Spanish supper by tightening his breechclout and then kept on his way. At dawn, he hid in a sheltered hollow and found a little water in a rock pan. He fell asleep as soon as he finished drinking.

He stayed in the hollow all day, listening for sounds of pursuit, but they never came. He struck out again after dark, staggering now and then in his weariness. The

moon came up to light his way. He camped in a thicket at
dawn and managed to knock down a cottontail rabbit
with a stone. Despite his fear of discovery, he kindled a
small fire of dried wood and quickly roasted the rabbit.
The meat was half raw, but nothing had ever tasted so
good. He forced himself to save a little of the meat for
his journey.

It took him another night's travel to reach the desert
country. Often, he looked back at the towering Big
Mountain but saw no signs of humans. It seemed as
though he was the only living thing in that vast and silent
land.

He traveled for part of the day through cut-up land,
watching a buzzard that hung high above him. The
ragged bird of prey was sure he had a fine meal waiting
for him. Alan went through gullies and hollows, often
going out of his way to stay in the rough areas, safe from
prying eyes on the heights.

Sweat ran down his body and stung his cuts as he
slogged along. A swift shower of gentle rain filled some of
the rock pans to afford him water.

Late that night, he was far below the mountains, and
he managed to surprise and kill a huge jackrabbit. He
made his camp that night beside a shallow watercourse
that was dotted with pools of water like beads on a
string. At dawn, he made a smokeless fire and cooked the
rabbit. He tore into the stringy meat as though it were
the finest steak.

CHAPTER FOURTEEN

Alan was beginning to feel better when he saw the dust rising far behind him. He kept on his weary journey, driving himself with his reserve stamina.

In the middle of the afternoon, he saw dust ahead of him, drifting on the hot desert wind. Tired as he was, he kept on, hoping that this dust was made by the horses of white men. As he trotted along, he hacked off his long hair until there was nothing left of it but a ragged shock atop his head. He threw away the headband and the medicine cord that had been given to him long ago by Looking Glass. He was about to throw away his amulet of a charred oak twig struck by lightning, but something made him keep it. It was then he saw the thin file of horsemen riding south of him. He needed no field glasses to identify them. Apaches!

He crouched in an arroyo and watched them. They were moving stealthily as they approached a gully. They hid their horses in it and spread out along the lip of a low swale that covered the approach to a rutted, winding road that cut across the sandy earth. A mile to the west the dust was still rising. Then the sun shone on metal and on the white tilts of wagons. The white men were outnumbered by the hidden Apaches and obviously unaware that they were there.

Alan wanted to yell, but it was no use. There was not much chance of reaching the wagon train without being seen by the warriors. An agony of indecision swept over him as he saw the distance shorten between the unsuspecting white men and the painted death which awaited them.

He could distinguish the white men now. They were dusty troopers. The thud of hooves and the jingle of trace chains came to him on the wind. He could wait no longer. He tightened his breechclout, pulled up his moccasin tops, and leaped from his hiding place to race toward the soldiers.

He dared not look at the warriors. He began to yell at the top of his voice. Two men who were riding ahead of the wagons stopped and then stood up in their stirrups to stare at him. He waved his arms and yelled. Hooves thudded behind him. He looked back to see half a dozen mounted warriors closing in on him. He knew where the others were. Most of them were still in hiding, waiting for the wagons.

He slammed his feet hard against the earth. His breath came harshly in his throat. One of the lead troopers yelled and thrust up an arm. The wagons ground to a dusty, brake-shrieking halt. The troopers fanned out and raised their carbines. The racing Apaches were only a hundred yards behind Alan now. A rifle spat thinly. Suddenly he tripped and fell, cutting his face on the flinty earth. He ripped his knife free and rolled over, bounding to his feet. Carbines flatted off, and an Apache went down. He rolled to his feet from his dead horse and was swung up behind a hard-riding warrior with no pause in the headlong flight of the horse.

Carbines and rifles crackled. Suddenly the earth to the south seemed to sprout a wave of mounted warriors who bore down on the exposed flank of the troopers.

Some of the soldiers wheeled to meet this new threat. Alan plunged into a jungle of prickly pear as the warriors swept past him. He saw the hate-contorted face of Yellow Snake and the grim face of Mule. They wheeled to get at him, but fifty yards from them, a white man raised a repeating rifle. It spat, and Mule shuddered with the impact of the bullet. He went down. Yellow Snake flung himself on the far side of his pinto and veered off, but not before Alan saw the fresh scar running from ear to jaw on the left side of his face. It was the mark of Alan's knife.

Two Chiricahuas pulled their mounts to plunging halts. One of them was the warrior who had pulled the dismounted brave up behind him. They fired at the tall man who had dropped Mule. The white man coolly forced his buckskin horse to the ground and dropped behind it. His rifle spat three times. The double-mounted horse went down, spilling his riders. The third Apache slid silently from his gray.

The flats were a hell of pounding hoofs, crackling gunfire, and hoarse yelling. The marksman behind the buckskin killed another warrior and then got to his feet. He urged his horse to its feet and looped the reins about his left arm. He came forward. Alan ran toward him. The marksman raised his rifle to fire. A trooper wearing sergeant's chevrons kneed his horse in front of the man. "Don't shoot, Jim!" he yelled. "He's only a kid! Capture him!"

"He's an Apache, isn't he, Murphy?" roared the man. "Nits breed lice!"

Sergeant Murphy rode his horse hard against the marksman. Then he rode close to Alan, leaped from his bay, and slammed a rocky fist against Alan's jaw before the boy knew what was intended. Alan dropped his knife as he went down. Before he could get up, his wrists were tied securely together. He was jerked to his feet and thrown up on the front of the soldier's saddle. Then the trooper swung up behind him and set the steel to the big bay. They raced toward the wagons.

Teamsters were firing steadily from beneath their wagons. Their long rifles took a heavy toll on the screaming warriors. A dozen troopers closed in on the Chiricahuas, firing their heavy revolvers in an attack that broke the heart of the warriors. They went for cover, followed by whining slugs. An Apache rose from the brush and turned to run, but the tall man was too quick for him. His rifle spoke and dropped the Chiricahua.

Soon there was nothing left to fire at but a cloud of dust as the Apaches scattered across the flats in their flight to safety. Alan was roughly dumped to the ground. The sweating troopers gathered near him, reloading their smoking revolvers. One of the troopers was staring stupidly at a shattered hand that dripped blood. Another moaned on the ground, gripping his thigh with bloody hands. Beyond him was a dead man, staring up at the sky. Alan squirmed up into a sitting position. There was hate on the faces of the troopers beneath their dusty hat brims.

One of the troopers flipped open the breech of his Springfield and loaded it. He snapped the breech shut and cocked the carbine. "Get out of the way," he said thickly. "They got my bunkie, Calhoun. I'll take care of this Apache."

"Lay off, Sweeny!" yelled the sergeant as he jerked his Colt from its holster. He twirled the cylinder. The whirring of the steel sounded loudly in the stillness. "I'm in charge here! Put up that carbine! Get back to your horse! On the double now!"

"What about it, scout?" asked a teamster of the tall marksman who sat his buckskin." Them 'Paches gone for sure?"

"They got a bellyful, Schmidt. They won't be back."

Alan stared at the scout, realizing now that he couldn't be more than nineteen or twenty years old. The scout dashed the sweat from his handsome tanned face. "Sergeant Murphy has a prize," he said quietly. "I wonder how long he'll be able to keep him alive?"

Murphy spat. "Do you have to kill all of them, Jim Warden?"

"Jim!" yelled Alan. "Don't you know me?"

Jim Warden came close. "Apaches got my kid brother," he said thinly.

"I'm Alan! Your kid brother!"

Jim dropped his rifle. He pulled Alan to his feet. "I don't believe it," he said over his shoulder to the gaping troopers. "He was captured at Apache Pass about a year ago!"

Jim wiped the dust from Alan's face and looked down at him. "It's Alan, all right! What have they done to you!"

Alan's throat went dry. He fought hard to keep the tears back. "I'm going home," he said brokenly. "At last, I'm going home."

———

THE WARDEN PLACE was situated not far from Tucson. Bill Warden had gone into the freighting business and had twelve wagons rolling every day. Jim, big and more than capable for his age, had traveled to California with Gila Simmons, and then had returned with him to Tucson. He had absorbed much of Gila's knowledge of the frontier and had added a few licks of his own. In time he had been hired as a civilian scout for the Army.

Bill Warden was much the same, industrious and ambitious, talking always of the fine farm he would have someday after he had made his pile in his freighting business. His wagons worked out of Fort Lowell, which was the big supply center for the forts in the southeastern part of Arizona Territory. He was under contract to haul Army supplies. He hadn't said too much about Alan's captivity, but now and then, Alan caught his father studying him when he thought his son wasn't looking.

Alan's mother had changed. Her hair had been dark when she had left Illinois, but now it was shot with streaks of gray and there were lines on her face. She couldn't do enough for Alan, treating him almost like a child, hanging onto the last of her children, for Jim Warden was a man already, and Bill Warden was absorbed in his new business.

Alan was allowed to keep what was left of his Chiricahua apparel only after an argument with his mother. He hid the fine Mexican knife in the shed and kept the short reserve knife in his pocket.

It was a strange experience for him to wander about the rambling adobe house his father had bought near Tucson. The family had arrived safely. The attack in Apache Pass had been fought off with only one settler killed and two wounded. His mother told him of their first days in Tucson and of the strange ways of the people who made Tucson, the Old Pueblo, their home.

Alan spoke very little of his life with the Chiricahuas other than to say he had been treated well enough. He knew they didn't believe him, for they had seen the mountain lion scars on his chest and the other lesser scars on his lean body. In time, Jim became a little short with him, and it was only old Gila Simmons who seemed to understand him.

One day Gila asked Alan if he would like to ride into Tucson with him. They rode slowly toward the town. Gila glanced at Alan. "Appears to me yuh ain't too happy, son," he said.

Alan shrugged.

"Yuh was with Coyote, eh? A good warrior."

Alan nodded.

"I expect yuh traveled some with the band?"

"Yes, to the winter camp."

"Yuh stayed in the Big Mountain country most of the time, though?"

Alan nodded. He watched a road runner scuttle awkwardly down the middle of the dusty road with a lizard dangling from its beak. He wished he were running with the ungainly bird rather than having to listen to Gila.

Gila shifted his chew and spat. "I suppose yuh know all them trails up there?"

"You probably know as many of them as I do."

"No. Not the real secret trails."

"What do you mean, Gila?"

"Yuh know what I mean! The secret trails. The ones they use when they're jumpin' up dust to git away from the soldiers."

Alan flushed. "I know the Big Mountain country," he said, and let it go at that, hoping Gila would shut up.

Gila shrugged. "Useta live with the Indians myself. Spent some time with the Utes and later with the Mescalero 'Paches in New Mexico Territory. Made friends with some Tontos but never with the Chiricahuas."

The remainder of the ride was spent by Gila in the telling of his life in the great Southwest—of how he had scouted for the Union troops when New Mexico had been invaded by the Confederates of Texas. He told of being chased by the Mohaves and saving his life by swimming the raging Colorado. He went on and on until they reached Fort Lowell, which was situated some miles outside of Tucson. The well-built adobes were shaded by trees and vines. The sun glinted from the polished buttons of the soldiers who went about their business.

CHAPTER FIFTEEN

Big Bill Warden was waiting for Gila and Alan at the entrance to the fort. "Come on," he said shortly. "The major is waiting."

Alan shot a look at Gila. "I thought you said we were just going riding," he said.

Gila rubbed his bristly jaw. "I didn't want to tell your mother where we was goin', son. The major wants to see yuh."

Alan's father nodded. "She wouldn't like it. Let's go on in."

They walked into the inner office of headquarters. A gray-haired officer was waiting for them. Jim Warden was leaning against a wall, toying with a braided-leather quirt. Bill Warden placed a hand on Alan's shoulder. "This is my boy Alan, Major Steele," he said.

Major Steele gripped Alan's hand. "You raise big sons, Bill. Have you recovered from your experiences, Alan? I understand you had a rough time."

"I feel fine, sir."

"Good. Sit down, everyone." The officer turned and drew a large roller map down against the wall. Alan recognized it as the area of the Big Mountain country. The sites of several forts were marked upon it.

The major leaned across the desk. "Now, Alan," he said quietly, "your father and your brother have told me some of your adventures. I'd like to have you elaborate on some of them."

"I don't understand, sir."

"Tell me what happened after you were captured."

"I was taken into the Big Mountain country by some of The People."

"The People?"

Gila grinned. "That's what they call themselves, sir."

The major looked queerly at Alan. "I see. Go on, young man."

"I was taken to the camp of Coyote, our 'smart one.'"

Gila leaned forward. "The 'Paches call their chief that, Major."

Alan continued. "They fed me and let me have a place to sleep."

"Later you were tortured, of course?" said the major in a kindly tone.

"No."

"He's lying," said Jim. "Look at the scars on his body."

"Shut up, Jim," said Bill Warden.

"Go on, son," said Gila.

"There was a little ceremony. They called me 'Son of the Thunder People' because I had been saved by the lightning arrows when Mule was about to kill me with a lance at Apache Pass."

They all looked queerly at Alan with the exception of Gila. "Stands to reason," said Gila, "'cause lightnin' is considered to be the arrows of the Thunder People. Alan has a *power!*"

Alan shifted uncomfortably. He almost wished he were back with the Chiricahuas. It seemed to be a much freer life than the one he was now forced to live. "I was adopted by Coyote and Looking Glass, his squaw. I was sent to school."

Jim Warden laughed.

"School?" queried the officer.

"Untried braves' school," said Gila, "where they learn how to hide, track, hunt, use weapons, find food, and raid for horses."

"Ummm—" said the major.

"I was a brother of Never Still, the blood son of Coyote and Looking Glass. Never Still and I hunted together. We shot bobcats for our arrow quivers. Jack Rabbit taught us the ways of a true son of Child of the Water."

"But you were tortured?" insisted the major.

"No! I was treated as one of them. No better and no worse."

"Keep talking," said Major Steele. He began to toy with a letter opener shaped like a miniature saber.

"We raided the Mexicans for horses. We went south in the Sierra Madre at the time of Ghost Face, the winter, and camped in the mountains there. I began to study to be a medicine man."

"Why?" asked Bill Warden.

Alan looked at his father. "It was thought I had *power.* I had been saved by the arrows of the Thunder People. I had captured a grown Mexican on my first raid. I had saved the life of Never Still, my adopted brother, when he was attacked by a mountain lion. Besides, if I did not become a medicine man, I would have to continue my training as a warrior and in time I would have to kill Americans and Mexicans."

Major Steele wiped his dragoon mustache both ways. "This is hard to believe, but I don't think he is lying."

"Chiricahuas don't lie!" said Alan. "Which is more than I can say for many Americans."

The men looked at each other and then at Alan. Alan flushed. Jim stepped forward angrily, but Gila held him back. "Let him be, Jim!" he said.

It was hard for Alan to think as a white boy should. Too late, he realized that his training with the Chiricahuas had branded him far more deeply than he had thought.

"How did you escape?" asked Major Steele.

"Warriors from the Enemy People came to our camp and wanted Coyote to lead his warriors with them against the Americans. The Enemy People are from the Southern Band of the Chiricahuas. The Mexicans have made it hard for them to live and raid in Sonora, so they are coming up here. Coyote did not want to go to war. There was some trouble at the meeting because I had taken a horse from some warriors of the Enemy People. I had to escape, or I might have been killed."

"You see?" blurted Jim. "They meant to kill him!"

The major stood up and looked at the map. "Now, Alan, I want you to come here and locate the camp of Coyote and the trails that lead there."

Alan studied the map. He mentally clothed it with trees, rock formations, peaks, and streams as he remembered them. It was a good map. He wondered how it had been made.

"Well?" asked Steele impatiently.

"Why do you want to know?"

"Because we must close in on that area. The Apaches are cutting a swath of fire and murder throughout the southern part of Arizona and northern Sonora. If we can strike them in their own country, we will put an end to it. A good part of it, at any rate."

Alan thought of patient Looking Glass; of brave Coyote; of wise old Jack Rabbit; of Never Still. It would be a bloody war of extermination. Perhaps it was right to show the major the hidden trails, but he could not do it. "I can't show you on the map," he said, "because I don't understand it."

"Then you can guide us there," said Jim.

"I won't go."

Major Steele stepped in between Alan and his angry brother. "Listen, Alan," he said, "many white men and women have been murdered by those bloodthirsty fiends. Ranches, stage stations, wagon trains, and travelers have been wiped out with hardly a trace left of them. The troopers cannot catch them in the open country. They scatter if they are followed and are gone like the wind. We must strike them where they have their food supplies and their homes. Do you understand?"

Jim gripped Alan by the shoulders. Then he raised his right hand and struck him hard across the face. "I wish they had killed you," he said. "You're nothing but a renegade!"

Bill Warden pushed his eldest son aside. Alan touched his stinging face. "May I go home now?" he asked.

Bill Warden struggled to keep his dislike from showing. "He isn't himself as yet, Major Steele. Later, perhaps."

The major nodded. His gray eyes studied Alan. Gila took Alan outside. He placed an arm about Alan's shoulders. "Take it easy, kid," he said. "Jim is rough. He's all horns, hoofs, and rattles. He'll be a great scout if the 'Paches don't kill him. He hates 'Paches like they hate rattlers. Yuh understand?"

"He's my only brother," said Alan brokenly.

"Yeah, but yuh'd never know it. I useta think he was hot on killin' 'Paches because of what they had done to yuh. Now I ain't so sure. I'm beginnin' to think he just likes killin'."

"That isn't true!"

Gila grinned. "Take it easy, son."

They mounted their horses and left the post. "I'll race yuh to the junction," said Gila.

They thundered up the dusty road, followed by the angry shouts of the gate sentry who was shrouded in their dust. Alan won easily, and they jogged along the home road. Alan felt better. Yet he knew he was a stranger in his own family. It seemed to him he had left his real brother and his friends high in the hazy Big Mountain country.

After Alan's experience at Fort Lowell, he saw very little of Jim. The sparse news about him came from Gila, who always stopped by the Warden house when he was in the vicinity. There was an active campaign against the Apaches. Many of the so-called "reconstructed" Apaches had left the reservations and had gone to join the free life of the wild ones.

Victorio, a fighting chief, refused to stay on the San Carlos Reservation and cut loose on a whirlwind campaign that left a bloody path of terror throughout the Southwest. Old Nana, seventy years old and rheumatic, fought beside Victorio. Nock-ay-del-Klinne, a medicine man, spoke with such persuasion that he managed to turn some of the loyal Apache scouts against their white officers. There had been a hard fight at Cibecue because of his treachery.

Jim was serving with the troops who were chasing the will-o'-the-wisp Geronimo and his wild warriors. There had been little success, for when pursued, he would fade into the Big Mountains or across the border into Sonora. Jim had been wounded in a fight in the Swisshelms and would be home soon for a rest. Troops were concentrating at Fort Lowell for a campaign against Geronimo, and Jim was needed.

"There will be hard fightin'," prophesied Gila on one of his visits.

After Gila had left, Bill Warden spoke to Alan. "You'll change your mind, son?" he asked.

"No."

"It's for the best," urged his mother.

Alan left the house. He would be sixteen in another month, and he had been thinking for some time of leaving home. But he knew it would break his mother's heart. He saddled his roan mare and rode into the hills. He liked being alone. Miles from the house he let the mare graze while he lay down to look across the great valley of the Santa Cruz.

He was still daydreaming when he heard the clop-clop of hoofs. He turned to see two boys riding toward him. They were the Switzer brothers, whose father owned a ranch not far from the Warden place. The boys were big. Fred was seventeen and a half years old and a head taller than Alan, while Oscar was about Alan's age and size. They drew rein and looked down at him.

"It's the renegade," said Oscar with a leer.

"Mebbe he's waitin' for his Apache friends," suggested Fred.

Alan got up and walked toward his mare.

"What's the matter, 'Pache?" called out Oscar. "Don't you talk to white folks?"

"When they've got sense," said Alan quietly.

"Meanin' what?" asked Fred ominously.

Alan tightened the mare's girth and ignored the brothers. Oscar dismounted and came toward him. "How come yuh won't tell the soljers where yuh useta live?" he asked.

"I'm riding home," said Alan.

"No, yuh ain't, renegade," said Oscar. He grinned. "Not until yuh tell us what we want to know."

"Meaning?"

"Yuh can tell us where they live, and we can tell the soljers."

"It's none of your business."

"Don't seem to be anybody's business but yours."

"So?"

Oscar tightened his belt and swaggered forward. "I'll make it our business, renegade." He placed a hand on Alan's shoulder and spun him about. Then he slapped Alan across the face. "Well?" he asked. He looked back at his brother with a grin.

Alan was in for it now, but he wasn't going to take it lying down, despite the odds. He caught Oscar on the jaw with a wild right and followed through with a left that swept over Oscar's head. Oscar ducked and jolted Alan with an uppercut that brought blood into his mouth. He staggered back. Oscar closed in, battering at him with both fists. Alan went down hard.

Oscar spat. "Get up," he said. "I ain't done yet."

Alan got up, ducked a vicious right, and then caught Oscar flush on the chin. Oscar went back. Alan closed the gap between them and sank a left into the boy's middle. As Oscar bent forward, he was grounded by a hard right jab.

Fred slid from his dun. "Go get him, Oc," he said. "I'll help yuh make him talk when yuh whip him."

Alan wasted no time when Oscar got up. He rushed in, gripped his opponent about the waist, and threw him sideways. He butted him with a shoulder, driving him down. As Oscar got up, he was met with a smashing right that grounded him again. He shook his head and spat out some blood.

Fred whirled Alan about and hit him twice. Alan fell over Oscar's legs and hit hard. Fred gripped him by an ankle and dragged him about on the rough ground. "Give him the boot, Oc," he said. "We'll teach him to attack us Switzers."

Oscar got up. There was hate in his muddy eyes. Alan's hand closed on a rock. He threw it. Oscar was clipped on the jaw and went down for the long count. He lost all interest in the fight.

"I'll get yuh for that!" Fred yelled. He dropped Alan's leg and reached down to grip him by the shirt. Alan grabbed Fred's scarf and pulled down, while at the same time, he shoved both feet into the big boy's stomach. Fred was hurled over Alan's head, and he smashed against the ground. Alan jumped to his feet as Fred tried to get up. Alan kicked out. His boot heel caught Fred on the jaw. His head snapped back. He clawed for his sheath knife, but Alan stepped on his wrist and ground down hard with his boot. Fred yelled in pain and let go of his knife. Alan snatched it up. The wild killing craze was on him now, but he threw it off and stepped back, breathing hard.

"Let me alone," Fred moaned. "Let me alone."

Alan threw the knife into the brush. "*Ahagahe!*" he said. "You come after me again, and I'll kill you!"

Alan swung up on his roan and spurred it down toward the road. The fat was in the fire now. He would hear a lot about this.

He didn't have long to wait when he reached home. Jim was there, wearing a sling to support his left arm. He ignored Alan. Bill Warden was cleaning up at the water barrel when he looked up to see Amos Switzer ride into the yard with his two battered sons. Ben Switzer, Amos' brother, and a noted rough-and-tumble fighter, was right behind him. Oscar's jaw was swollen, and there was a bloody lump on Fred's head.

"Warden!" yelled Amos, "I want to talk to yuh!"

Bill Warden dried his face. "Go ahead, Switzer."

"That renegade kid of yours attacked my two boys and look what he has done."

Bill Warden looked at Alan. "What about it, son?"

Alan couldn't help but grin. "I'm not such a fool as to jump two of them, Dad."

Old Man Switzer spat. "Tricky, he is. Ambushed my two boys with sneaky 'Pache tricks. Liked to kill Oc here."

Bill Warden flushed. He glanced at Ben Switzer. "Be careful what you say, Amos. What about it, Alan?"

"They called me a renegade," he said. "Oc jumped me, and I beat him. Then Fred tried it, and I beat him too."

"He's a liar!" roared Switzer. "He couldn't lick *one* of them at a time!"

"I'll do it again," said Alan quietly, "with someone to see that I get fair play."

Ben came forward. "Yuh dirty little renegade," he said

thinly. "Livin' with white folks and turnin' against 'em! Yuh know where them 'Paches hide out. I got a good mind to drag yuh to Fort Lowell and beat the tar outa yuh until yuh talk."

Bill Warden dropped his towel. "That's enough out of you, Ben. You lay a hand on that boy, and you'll wish you'd stayed home where you belong."

Ben spat. He dropped his right hand to the butt of his pistol. "Take them words back, or I'll draw!"

Jim moved so swiftly, his motions seemed a little blurred. When he raised his right hand, it held his Colt, cocked, and aimed at Ben's belly. "Crawfish, Switzer," he said softly.

Ben flushed. For a moment it looked as though he would draw, and then he looked away. "Yuh got no call to get in on this, Jim."

Jim smiled, but there was no friendliness in the smile. "You threatened my father, Ben. Now get on that cayuse of yours and pull leather out of here. The rest of you can jump up a little dust too."

The Switzers mounted. They rode to the gate. Amos turned and rested a hand on his cantle. "We'll see about this!" he yelled.

"Git!" called out Jim.

"We'll make that renegade kid talk, Warden!" yelled Ben. "He won't always have yuh watchin' over him."

Bill Warden looked at Alan. "Was it a fair fight, son?"

"I used a rock."

Alan's father looked away to hide a smile. "Fair enough," he said as he put on his shirt. "You see how it is now, Alan? I've had trouble about you before this time. Won't you reconsider and tell Major Steele what you know?"

Jim holstered his Colt. He gripped Alan by the shoulder. "Dad's right, kid. You've got guts. You must have, to face those two bullies and lick them. What about it?"

Alan looked down at the ground. They were right. In

order to live peaceably with his own people, he'd have to help them. "All right. I'll do it under one condition."

"So?" asked his father.

"That the soldiers will give Coyote's band a chance to surrender and come into the reservation."

Jim looked over Alan's head at his father. He nodded. Bill Warden rubbed his jaw. "Fair enough. We'll see the major first thing in the morning."

CHAPTER SIXTEEN

It was early in the morning of a clear fall day when the field column formed at Fort Lowell for the campaign against the Chiricahuas. The officers were almost all veterans of campaigns against the Apaches, Sioux, and Cheyennes. The troopers were, for the most part, seasoned men. There was a platoon of Apache scouts, loyal men who had eaten the bread and salt of the Government. Tough mule packers stood by their long-eared charges. Escort and Dougherty wagons were loaded with reserve ammunition and supplies, and there were two ambulances in charge of a medical sergeant.

Events had moved swiftly in the weeks preceding the departure. Scouts, both white and Apache, had brought in news, which had been sifted and evaluated. It was almost certain that Coyote's band was still in the Big Mountain country and that they had been joined by Southern Band Apaches as well as wild Apaches from the San Carlos Reservation. There were many of them. A message had been received at Fort Lowell from the colonel of the famous Sixth Mexican Infantry that the regiment was ready for the field and would maneuver south of the border should it be necessary. Members of the tough Guardia Rurale, or Rural Guard, of Chihuahua and Sonora, were already in the field watching for movements of the enemy.

Alan stood beside his mare, equipped for the field. His father had bought him a Winchester rifle and a Colt pistol. The column was to ride to the San Pedro, join another column there from Fort Huachuca, and then converge with other units already in the field. Jim Warden had already left for San Pedro with Gila Simmons.

The late summer had been a madhouse of slashing Apache raids, and it seemed as though nothing could stop them. Alan's father had given permission for him to accompany the column. Alan had told Steele quite a bit about the Big Mountain country, but he had reserved some of his knowledge. It was part of the secret plan that had made him hide his desert moccasins and other Apache gear in his cantle pack. There was nothing definite about his plan. He'd have to know the military situation first. He had determined to save Never Still if he could, as well as the others of Coyote's band. Time was running out swiftly for the Chiricahuas. They must either submit or die fighting.

Alan's mother and father came over to him. Bill Warden gripped his hand. "I started out from Illinois with two boys," he said, "and find I've ended up in Arizona with two young men. It seems as though there is little time for boyhood in this country."

"I'll be all right, sir," said Alan.

His father's gray eyes were troubled. "This is not a picnic excursion. You, probably more than the others, must realize how the Apaches feel. You've lived with them and have been part of their life. You're in a bad spot, son. You know that, don't you?"

"Yes, sir." Alan held his mother's hand. No one but Alan Warden, Son of the Thunder People, knew exactly the spot he was in.

"You'll come back, Alan," his mother said. "You must come back this time!"

"Boots and saddles" rang out across the parade ground. The troopers moved out to the stamping of hooves and the jingle of chains. Dust curled up and wreathed troopers and wagons.

Alan did not look back as he fell into place beside big Sergeant Murphy and the men of C Troop. The guidon snapped in the dry wind. Alan eyed the troopers. They were tough fighters. He wondered how many of them would come back if his plan failed.

They reached San Pedro in good time. The troops from Fort Huachuca were already in bivouac when the Fort Lowell column arrived. The area was noisy with the work of farriers replacing or tightening horseshoes, and of artificers checking the running gear of the wagons.

The long column took the road at dawn, heading toward the Big Mountain. Alan felt better than he had for weeks, riding with the troopers who kidded him a lot but who treated him like a man instead of a boy.

The column halted a half-day's march from the mountains. Alan took care of his horse and then walked to the limit of the bivouac area to look at the looming mountains, purple-hazy in the hot air of the late afternoon. A thread of dust rose slowly from the earth, miles to the east.

Sergeant Murphy stopped beside Alan. "That might be Jim and Gila. They were to meet us here today."

"How many other columns are closing in?"

"One from Fort Bowie, although they're only watchin' the northern end of the mountains in case the 'Paches drift that way. Another column from Fort Bayard is patrollin' the eastern side of the mountains. The Mexicans are maneuverin' along the border to close the southern trails. I'm thinkin' we have a sack about old Geronimo. It won't be long before we pull the drawstring tight and bag the old devil."

"There are still a lot of holes left."

"Aye! But we have parties of scouts, both white and Apache, pluggin' some of those holes. It will be a wily fox that outwits our hounds, me boy."

That evening, as Alan chewed his hard bread and crisp bacon, he was glad to see Jim and Gila ride into the bivouac. They swung stiffly down from their dusty, foam-flecked mounts, and went into Major Steele's tent. Moments later, an orderly came for Alan.

The tent was warm and close from the heat of the day. The major was studying a sketch map. Alan nodded to Jim and Gila.

Steele looked up. "Your brother and Gila have been farther into Apache territory than any other scouts to date, Alan. Look at this map. Tell us where the camp of Coyote is."

Alan studied the map and then placed a finger on the mesa where the summer camp had always been.

"How close did you get to that area?" asked Steele of Jim.

Jim placed a finger on an area where Alan and Never Still had often hunted. It was a good ten miles from the summer camp.

"Beyond that," said Jim, "the country is rough, cut up, and full of blind canyons. We poked about in there but couldn't find any well-traveled trails."

"Did you try in any farther?"

Gila grunted. "Yeah. But we came back."

"Why?"

Gila shifted his chew. "We found Josh Matson in there."

"What did he know?"

"Nothin'," said Gila laconically. "He was dead. Looked like a pincushion with 'Pache airers stickin' in him. Later we run into Steve Boswick. Steve had been scoutin' with Josh. Steve said him and Josh was jumped by Geronimo and his boys."

"He was sure it was Geronimo?"

"Yup. Seen him once at San Carlos. It was him all right."

"How many warriors?"

"'Bout a dozen."

Steele rubbed his lean jaw. "Which way did they go?"

"Steve said they was headin' south the last time he seen 'em."

Jim Warden rubbed his healing arm. "That didn't mean much. They travel like the wind. They could be anywhere now."

Steele nodded. "Let's hope the Mexican troops are in position. If Geronimo gets past them, he'll hole up in the Sonora mountains for the winter. One thing puzzles me: where are the rest of his warriors?"

Jim shrugged. "Gila and I figure there are still quite a lot of them in the hills and mountains east of here. We spotted a long file of them riding east up a canyon."

"That was after you met Boswick?"

"Yes."

Steele leaned back in his chair. "Of course, our main objective is to get Geronimo. However, if he gets away, we'll have to settle for smaller fry."

Gila glanced at Alan. "I figure the warriors we saw were from Coyote's band. I recognized two of them I saw at Fort Bowie some years ago when things was real quiet."

"Well," said Steele, "getting Coyote will be worth the trip. We have information that he reinforced Geronimo with some of his warriors. If we can corral Coyote, we've done a good job. It will be up to the Mexicans to nail Geronimo when he heads south, although I wish we could bag him."

Alan looked at the map. He could easily lead the troops into Coyote's camp. If they went in without his guidance, they'd be cut to pieces, for the warriors of the band, outnumbered though they were, had the advantage of position and knowledge of the terrain.

"Coyote didn't want war," said Alan as though to himself.

Jim turned quickly. "His hands are as bloody as Geronimo's!"

Alan looked at Major Steele. "Will you give him a chance to surrender?"

"Yes, of course. But I'll not sacrifice a mule to make him come to reason. If he wants a fight, he'll get it! General Crook's orders are explicit. Hang onto the trail; follow them into their own territory; don't come back until they are run down. Gentlemen, that means we stay in the field until we haven't a horse fit to ride or a cartridge to shoot!"

"Perhaps someone could go in there and talk with Coyote," said Alan quietly.

The three of them looked at Alan. The officer shook his head.

"I'll go alone," said Alan.

"Don't pay any attention to the kid," said Jim.

Steele drummed his fingers on the table. "I'll not let him go. Nor will anyone else go. If Coyote wants peace, he must come to us."

Alan shrugged. "Then you will lose many men, sir."

"I'll have to take the chance. Get some sleep, son. We break camp at midnight and close in on the hills."

Alan went to his bed under an escort wagon. The sun had gone, dying in rose and gold to the west. He watched Jim and Gila eat and then bring their blankets to the wagon. Jim stripped to the waist, and Gila inspected the puckered bullet hole in Jim's forearm. "A good rubbin' will help it," he said. "Wisht I had some Volcanic Oil for it."

Alan had already secreted his cantle pack containing his Apache gear in the wash a hundred yards from the camp. He closed his eyes.

It was an hour before midnight when Alan sat up.

The camp was quiet. A faint new moon was rising. There was a ring around it, prophesying possible rain. Now and then, the boots of a sentry grated on the earth. A horse nickered. The blanketed forms of the troopers covered the ground between the wagons and the horse lines. Gila was snoring. Jim lay still, his healing arm wrapped in his extra shirt.

Alan slid out of his blankets. He had his Winchester and Colt and a full canteen. There was hard bread and beef in his cantle pack. He crawled from beneath the wagon and under some mesquite bushes. Foot by foot, he worked his way toward the dry wash. The sentry turned at the end of his beat and came back toward Alan. Alan rolled silently into the wash.

The sentry passed. Alan got his gear and headed east along the wash. A quarter of a mile from the camp he stripped off his clothing and pulled on his desert moccasins. He put on his breechclout and swung his gun belt about his lean waist. He hooked his canteen to the gun belt. The food he wrapped in his shirt and tied to his back. He was about to leave when he heard a soft footfall up the wash. He crouched behind some brittlebush.

Jim came toward him. He stopped ten feet from Alan. "Come on, kid," he said. "Get back to camp."

Alan stood up.

Jim bent his head forward. "So! You're turning renegade," he said harshly.

"Let me alone," said Alan.

"Where do you think you're going?"

"Into the mountains. Coyote can be talked into peace. I'm sure of that."

Jim's face tightened. "You little fool! You'd go to their camp and tell them our plans!"

"No! If the troops move in, there will be bloodshed. Maybe it can be stopped."

"You care more about those red devils than you do about your own people."

Alan turned to run. Jim moved swiftly. He gripped Alan by a shoulder and whirled him about. Alan ducked under a slashing backhanded blow. Jim grunted as Alan rammed his head into his stomach. He jerked his Colt free to buffalo Alan with it. Alan swung his rifle and brought it down on Jim's wounded arm. Jim yelled in pain and gripped his arm.

Alan sprinted up the wash, hurdled the bank, crashed through a clump of catclaw, and broke into the clear. Jim yelled again. The camp awoke. Troopers bawled questions into the night. Alan set off at a steady mile-eating pace that would cover much ground before dawn. He was sorry for what he had done to Jim, but his plan came first. If he failed, it might not make any difference to Alan, for his Chiricahua friends might kill him long before the troopers made contact with the warriors. There was no turning back now. If the troopers caught him, he would be placed under arrest.

Alan looked up at the dim mountains, mysterious under the soft light of the new moon. What lay ahead of him only God, and perhaps Child of the Water, knew.

CHAPTER SEVENTEEN

Alan reached the hulls before dawn. It was cold on the desert, and only his steady exertion had kept him warm. Somewhere behind him the sleepy troopers were probably already hidden before the coming of daylight. But Gila and Jim might be tracking him. They were as wily as Apaches. They had to be to live in that country.

Alan squatted in a gully and ate his bread and meat, washing it down with water from his canteen. He had no idea how he would reach the camp of Coyote without being discovered, for the Chiricahuas must know that troops were operating in the area. They would shoot first and ask questions later. They would be "spooked," as Gila might have said.

He forged on until suddenly, he was traveling in the eerie light of the false dawn. Ahead of him were many draws and gullies still deep in shadow. He would hole up for a time. He chose a place where he could watch the trail that led up into the mountains, and where he could still see the lower land to the west. He carefully effaced his tracks and dropped to rest in a hollow formed by two huge slabs of rock that leaned against each other.

The heat awoke him. The sun was lancing down from

high overhead, baking the rocks around him, but he felt good as the sweat broke from his body when he moved about. There were no signs of life to the west. The troopers had probably moved ahead of their supply train and carefully hidden themselves.

The long day drifted past. He left his hideout after dusk. He made slow time until the moon rose, silvering the desert and plunging into deeper shadow the hollows of the silent land. He reached a familiar place at the foot of a trail. He had no choice but to follow it, for there was no other way to go.

The wind was blowing gently, rustling the brush and keening through the pass above him. It set alive the mountain night, peopling it with whispering phantoms. It was late when Alan stopped to rest. Then he saw signs of man close to him—a pile of fresh horse droppings. He padded on with his rifle across his left forearm ready for action.

He was full out into an open area when he saw the dark object ahead of him. He faded into the brush at one side of the clearing. It was a man, lying on his belly, with one arm outstretched. He did not move. Alan waited, but there was no alien sound in the night.

Alan crawled out and walked over to the man. He hooked a foot beneath the body and rolled it over. The arms were stiff. Sightless eyes stared up at him. The mouth gaped open as though the man had died screaming at his fate. Blood stained the earth beside the body. One hand was twisted in the stained folds of the shirt. The other hand held a piece of hardtack from which a piece had been bitten. The man had been dead for many hours.

To one side of the area Alan saw faint hoof tracks. Unshod ponies. An empty cartridge case lay on the ground. He eyed the dead man. He wore cavalry trousers, but many scouts and discharged men wore them, so there was no assurance that he was a soldier.

Alan left the place to its ghostly guardian. Fear seemed to gain control of him. The wind chuckled evilly from the dark places and gibbered at him from the heights.

He reached a cold canyon through which the wind moaned. He listened for a time and then went on. The place was quiet except for the wind. It was too quiet.

Slowly his confidence came back to him. He placed his feet carefully so as not to dislodge any stones. He looked back and kicked one of them accidentally. It rattled sharply in the stillness. Alan heard a soft slapping noise. A shadowy figure grew out of the brush. There was no mistaking the thick mane of hair bound by a headcloth. Apache!

Alan reversed his rifle to meet the attack. He could not risk a shot. The warrior fended off the first blow of the rifle and then drove in hard with his knife. Alan sucked in his belly as the blade swept past. He swung his rifle, but the warrior leaped back.

Alan dropped his rifle and closed in, gripping his opponent about the waist, driving a shoulder up into the right armpit to keep the knife arm up high. They swayed back and forth. Alan managed to free his knife and held it, blade uppermost for a quick thrust below the ribs as he had been taught by old Jack Rabbit. A knee came up into his groin. He gasped and staggered back. The moon had passed behind the clouds, and it was too dark to see whom he was fighting.

They circled warily. The Apache's blade flicked out. Alan retreated. The warrior came on again, stamping his feet hard. The blade swept out. Alan jumped back.

The warrior circled and came in fast. His knife shot out for a hard thrust. Alan dropped his knife and gripped the outstretched wrist of his opponent. He dragged the man close and then thrust out his left leg. The Apache fell across the leg and lost his knife. Alan snatched up the knife for the quick killing thrust.

The moon sailed out from behind the clouds. Alan looked down into the tense face of Never Still. "Brother!" he said, sick at the thought of what he might have done.

Never Still sat up. "I did not know it was you, my brother. I thought it was one of my people who scouted for the White-eyes."

"What are you doing here?"

Never Still smiled. "It is better for me to ask you that question."

Alan squatted beside the young warrior. "Are you alone?"

"Yes. I left the camp because I could not stand it any longer."

Alan wiped the sweat from his face. It had been a close thing.

"Where have you been, my brother? With the enemy?" asked Never Still.

"I have been with my people."

"Why have you returned?"

"You must take me to your father. I must talk with him."

Never Still stood up. "My father is gone."

Alan stared at him. Coyote dead! Alan had not figured on such a situation. "Who is the 'smart one' now?"

Never Still spat. "Yellow Snake claims the leadership."

There was little chance of dealing with him, thought Alan.

Never Still bowed his head. "Many warriors are gone. The women and children are afraid. Geronimo left us to flee to Sonora, but my father would not leave these mountains. When we needed the warriors of Geronimo to help us, as we had helped them, they left us to run away and hide because of the soldiers. Geronimo thinks always of himself."

An owl hooted from the rocks. Never Still cast pollen toward it. "The owls hoot in the woods every night. They call to us with the voices of those who are gone. I, myself, have heard the voices of some of the bad ones."

"Why do you not surrender? You will be treated well. The Gray Fox, General Crook, is an honorable warrior. He will protect you."

Never Still spoke wearily. "I tried to tell the warriors that. Some of them were convinced, but Yellow Snake spoke words of honey, promising them many rifles, horses, and blankets if they would raid the soldiers who even now are hiding below us in the desert."

"You know of that?"

"Yes."

"So?"

"Yellow Snake has gained power. He leads the people in the war dances. The drums beat every night. By dawn, the warriors will be heading down to wait for the soldiers as they come up from the lowlands."

"You must go with me to the camp!"

"I would be safe enough. Yellow Snake would not dare to touch the son of Coyote, but you would not live to see the dawn."

"I think I still have friends in the camp. They will protect me. Many of them are afraid of the power I have from the Thunder People."

"You are mad!"

"Listen to me, my brother! Help me get to the camp. Stand by my side as I speak to the warriors. I can help your people find the trail of peace with the Americans."

Alan was drawn close to Never Still. "I will do it, Son of the Thunder People. I believe you. It is our only chance."

They followed the familiar winding trail. It was several hours before dawn when they reached the sleeping camp. They walked boldly to one of the fires and threw wood on the embers. A guard came swiftly out of the darkness with a ready rifle. He stared at them. "What is this?" he asked coldly.

The people awakened and came out of their lodges. Yellow Snake loaded his rifle and pushed his way through the crowd.

Never Still raised a hand. "Here is my brother," he said. "He has come back to us to talk of peace with the White-eyes."

"He is no longer one of us!" snarled Yellow Snake. His scarred face was contorted with hate.

Jack Rabbit hobbled to Alan. "You have always been his enemy," he said to Yellow Snake. "But some of us remember him as a friend. Remember also that he has a power from the Thunder People."

Yellow Snake looked at the warriors. Jack Rabbit had spoken words of wisdom. Alan's long shot had paid off so far. He breathed easier. He must talk with the silver tongue of persuasion or he and all of them might die. He prayed to God as he stood there, and added a little prayer to Child of the Water. He would need all the help he could muster.

Looking Glass brought food to her two sons. Her large eyes held Alan's for a moment, and then she turned away. He had evidently hurt her deeply.

All the warriors were there now. Yellow Snake strode imperiously into the center of the clearing, ignoring all protocol. Jack Rabbit was beside Alan. He was an old man wise in council. Black Bear, a great storyteller and a courageous warrior, was there. Antelope bore fresh scars on his gaunt body. Keen-sighted, who could read a trail like an open book, had also been recently wounded. Thin One, whose hatred of Alan was plain to see, leaned against a tree by himself. There were many old faces missing. Coyote was gone forever to the House of Spirits. Alan had seen Mule die. Bartolome Amadeo was missing.

There were too few of the wiser heads left. Most of the remaining warriors were those with little war experience who could easily be swayed by Yellow Snake's wild promises of loot and glory.

Yellow Snake raised a hand. "The enemy is within our reach. A great victory will give us many horses and weapons. We can defeat the Americans and then ride south into the land of the Mexicans. There we can join Geronimo and his brave warriors. In the spring, we will be stronger. We will sweep the enemy from our lands forever. I have spoken!"

There was a long silence. Then Black Bear stood up to speak. "You are very young and very brave," he said to Yellow Snake, "but we are few in numbers. Perhaps we warriors can escape to the south, but what of our families? We cannot outride the Americans and Mexicans if we have them with us."

Keen-sighted spoke, "Black Bear is right. Many of us are weak with wounds. We have only a few horses left. I have only a few cartridges for my rifle."

Thin One stood up and walked into the circle. "You talk like women! Yellow Snake will show us the way. We can cut the Americans to pieces before they get very far into the mountains."

Antelope was next. "He speaks well," he said, pointing at Thin One, "but there are far too many of the enemy. It is true we know these mountains better than the white men, and with Geronimo's help we might have defeated the enemy. But he has left us to save his own skin. We are alone. We must make wise council before we decide on war or peace."

Yellow Snake spat. "May a coyote eat you!"

Antelope's face went taut at the cutting insult. He dropped his hand to his knife. Then he withdrew it and sat down.

"Yellow Snake is mad for power," said Never Still to Alan. "Geronimo left us because we were of no further use to him after we gave freely of the blood of many good warriors. See? Even now, Yellow Snake is positive that the men of this band will join him on the war trail."

Alan stepped into the circle.

"He cannot speak!" yelled Yellow Snake. "He deserted us to go to his own people. Can a boy speak to warriors?"

Never Still stepped forward. "He is a man! He is protected by the Thunder People. Did he not kill a full-grown mountain lion to save me? See his scars? Did he not save my life when I was almost dead and bring me back here? Let him speak!"

Yellow Snake was not too sure of his control over the band. He might make enemies by refusing Alan the right to speak. He must bide his time.

"It is true that I have been with the Americans," said Alan, "therefore, I can speak with a straight tongue of what I have seen. To the north are many soldiers. To the east there are others. Many of them now approach from the west. Yellow Snake speaks of riding into Mexico. Does he know that the Mexicans are in great force on the other side of the border? Does he know that men of the Tontos, Arivaipas, Mescaleros, and Yavapais have eaten the bread and salt of the white men and are now serving with them against you?"

"He lies!" yelled Yellow Snake.

Alan spoke on. "The Gray Fox, General Crook, has given orders that the soldiers must stay on the war trail until all of you are on a reservation or are dead. He promises amnesty for any of you who will come down from these mountains in peace. There will be clothing, cattle, food, and medical help for you on the reservation. Already there are many of The People on reservations. You also can go there. It is for you to decide."

A cold wind blew through the trees. It was now late fall, the time of Earth-Is-Reddish-Brown. Soon Ghost Face would be upon these people. As Alan stepped out of the circle, rain began to sift down through the trees.

Each warrior spoke in turn, revealing his thoughts on the subject. Now and then the angry voice of Yellow Snake broke in on them. In the time of Coyote's rule of the band, he had been driven from them because of his rudeness. But now he seemed to be of a new breed that scorned the old ways.

Alan leaned close to Never Still. "How can we reach the Americans?" he asked.

Never Still looked up at the sky and then at the ground. "I will go to them."

"Will they believe you when you say that the band might counsel with them?"

"I do not think so."

"Will you go with me then?"

Never Still clasped his hands together. He had ridden with Geronimo. It was dangerous to go to see the white soldiers. "I think I must go," he said at last.

The warriors were still undecided. The cold rain ran down their greased bodies. Some of them wanted peace, but others wanted war. Many of them were in the middle, wanting war, yet afraid of what Alan had revealed to them.

Yellow Snake was speaking again. "I speak for war! Who is with me? Many of our old friends and relatives are no longer with us. Why? I will tell you! Because of the Americans! They have killed them!"

His point was good. War parties usually avenged deaths; they were for revenge. If loot would not tempt the warriors, then the thought of revenge, sweet to a Chiricahua, would surely sway them to his way of thinking.

"Tonight we can again have the fierce dancing," said Yellow Snake.

Alan walked into the circle. The issue was between him and Yellow Snake. Yellow Snake shifted his rifle. There was death in his cold eyes.

Suddenly there was a loud crash of thunder. Lightning forked across the streaming sky into a peak. The air was filled with the odor of the electrical charge. Warriors quailed in fear of the "lightning sickness."

Jack Rabbit gained his voice at last. "See? The

Thunder People have spoken! Son of the Thunder People has power from them! It is an omen! We must do as he says!"

The warriors shouted in agreement. It was the second time that nature, or some force greater than nature, had come to help Alan. Yellow Snake spat. He turned and stalked away into the dripping brush. Thin One followed him.

CHAPTER EIGHTEEN

"What shall we do?" cried Black Bear to Never Still. The warriors crowded about the young warrior, seemingly acknowledging him as their new leader.

Alan spoke for Never Still, "All of you must take the trail to the canyon that meets the desert west of here. Wait there, undercover, until my brother and I can contact you. Do not shoot if you see the soldiers. Remember—do not shoot!"

Alan and Never Still rode swiftly from the camp. It was dawn when they reached the lower slopes. Alan looked for signs of the troops. They must have sought shelter from the hard-driving rain.

"*Tsst! Tsst!*" hissed Never Still.

Alan halted his horse. A man moved behind a rock. A trooper. He stared at them through the rain. "It's young Warden!" he yelled back over his shoulder.

"Ride closer!" called the trooper. "Tell that buck to hold up his hands!"

They rode beneath a huge rock overhang out of the cold rain. Major Steele came out of his little tent. Gila Simmons followed him. He grinned as he saw Alan.

"Where have you been?" sternly asked the major.

Alan slid from his wet horse. "Settling a war, sir."

"You had us worried sick. Where's Jim?"

A feeling of foreboding came over Alan. "Isn't he here?"

"No. He trailed you."

Steele led the way to his tent. Gila, Alan, and Never Still crowded in behind him. Steele turned. "Start talking," he said to Alan."

Alan told of his experiences. "This warrior is Never Still, son of Coyote. Coyote is dead.

Steel rubbed his bristly jaw. He thrust his head out of the tent. "Sergeant Murphy! Tell the men they can light fires for coffee. As long as we know the Apaches want peace, we can take a chance on the fires."

The major sat down on his camp chair. "I'll take half a troop to meet them. Alan, you ride ahead with what's-his-name here. I want three of the older warriors to counsel with me. Unarmed. I'll give them every chance. You've done a fine job, Alan."

Alan and Never Still went to the mess tent, which was a wagon tarp stretched between two high boulders. They drank coffee and ate issue bacon.

It was early afternoon when the rain stopped. Sullen clouds drifted over the wet terrain. Alan and Never Still rode ahead of Major Steele and his detail of twenty men. Gila Simmons, Lieutenant Banning, and Sergeant Murphy rode with the major. The troopers were nervous, although Major Steele rode as though he were going to a review rather than to a meeting with some of the deadliest guerrilla fighters spawned on the North American continent.

They were far up the canyon when Never Still raised an arm. The command halted and eyed the forbidding walls of the canyon.

"What's the matter?" asked Major Steele.

"They are just ahead," said Never Still to Alan.

Alan translated to the major. Steele turned to the lieutenant. "Mister Banning," he said, "dismount your men. Keep them under cover. Make no suspicious moves. I'll give the order to fire if necessary."

Steele spurred his horse forward. "Tell your red friend to relay this information to the warriors, Alan. They are to meet us at the bend of the canyon. Unarmed. We will not carry arms."

Never Still listened to Alan and then nodded. He rode ahead and disappeared around the bend of the canyon.

"I hope you know what you are doing, young man," said Major Steele to Alan. "I don't mind admitting that I'm scared, clean through."

An hour drifted past. It was getting darker. Just about the time Alan was ready to give up, he saw Never Still riding slowly around the bend followed by Jack Rabbit, Black Bear, and Antelope. They halted a hundred yards from the white men, dismounted, and squatted on the wet earth.

Major Steele unbuckled his pistol belt and passed it to Lieutenant Banning. He rode forward, followed by Alan, Gila, and Sergeant Murphy, who had left their weapons with the troopers.

There was an uneasy feeling as the white men and the Chiricahuas faced each other. Alan saw Never Still sitting to one side. There was a tense look on his face.

Jack Rabbit, through Alan, invited the White-eyes to palaver. The council moved a little awkwardly. Gila understood a little Chiricahua. Alan supplemented with his knowledge of the tongue.

Major Steele spoke at length on the reservation system. It was well known to Jack Rabbit and Black Bear, because they had once spent some time at San Carlos. Outwardly the conversation went steadily, but the warriors were prone to weigh each sentence in their minds, evaluating it, sucking the juices from it. Then Black Bear spoke about having their families live with them on the reservation and assurances that the band would not be separated. Antelope asked whether they would be protected against lawless whites if they lived on the reservation. He also wanted to know if they might be able to hunt.

Major Steele said that troops would be near the reservation to protect the Apaches. He did not say for sure whether they would be able to hunt or bear arms of any kind.

Jack Rabbit, the oldest and craftiest of the three warriors, spoke in weighted words, trying to probe into the major's mind. Would they be allowed to practice their old religion? Would they be free to practice the ancient rites of their people? The windy old man went on and on while the skies grew darker.

Alan became bored. He drew off to one side and sat on a rock, half listening to the words of the old man. He was worried about Jim. If Jim blundered into the waiting warriors of the band, there might be a real fracas. One shot and the whole parley might break up in gun smoke.

Time drifted past. Alan watched a ragged buzzard sweep down the canyon, spot the men, and then veer off toward the northern cliff. Suddenly it veered again and flew swiftly away from the rimrock. Something had startled it.

Alan eyed the rimrock. The wind was still blowing from the north. Then he saw a clump of bear grass move against the wind. He watched it. It might be a crouching mountain lion. But they were timid of the man smell and would not stay around an area if they noticed it.

A faint metallic sound carried down to Alan. He could have sworn he saw something move in the bear grass. He worked his way up the slope. The canyon wall loomed above him. He edged his way up a fault. The others were too interested in their talk to miss him.

A stone clicked beside Alan. It had dropped from the canyon rim. He climbed slowly until he reached a ledge ten feet below the rimrock. It was then he saw the Apache, crouched in the brush, staring fixedly at the group far below him. Alan's throat went dry. It was Yellow Snake. His rifle was in his hands.

Alan eased himself over the canyon rim and then lay flat. One shot would trigger bloody action down in the canyon. Yellow Snake could kill either a white man or a Chiricahua. It would make no difference. The results would be the same. War!

Alan crawled through the brush. He slid into a hollow and saw two horses. They were Chiricahua mounts. Yellow Snake had left the camp with Thin One. Thin One must be somewhere near the two horses.

Alan drew out his short reserve knife. He might have to kill, but the deaths of the two wild ones would be worth the risk to prevent further bloodshed. Alan used all the craft he had learned from Jack Rabbit as he stalked Thin One. Then he felt, rather than saw, a movement in the thick brush. He crept closer and saw a pair of boots protruding from beneath a bush. Alan inched forward. It was Jim. Jim held a cocked pistol in his right hand and was looking at something just beyond him. That something was a man. Thin One.

The Chiricahua held a double-barreled shotgun. He was looking toward the canyon. Jim raised his pistol. Alan squirmed forward. "Jim," he called softly, "don't shoot!"

Jim turned swiftly. His face was tense. "Stay down!" he hissed.

"You can't shoot!"

Jim wiped his dirty face. "I followed you," he said coldly, "to bring you back. My horse broke a leg. I was working my way back to the column when I spotted these two horses."

Thin One moved closer to the canyon brink. Alan crawled closer to Jim. "Listen! Major Steele is palavering with the leaders of the Chiricahuas down in the canyon. There's half a troop down there. Up the canyon are the rest of the warriors. If you shoot, you'll start a real fight."

"How did it come about?"

Alan eyed Thin One. The warrior was intent on what was going on down in the canyon. He explained everything to Jim.

Jim grinned. "You've got more than your share of guts, kid. You used your head. Better than I usually do. I'd have gone in there shooting rather than try to reason with them. But a lot of good men would have been killed. What do we do now?"

Alan tested the edge of his knife. "Thin One has to go first," he said, indicating the warrior with a jerk of his head.

Jim nodded. "I thought I was the bloodthirsty one. I'll take care of that bird." He let down the hammer of his gun and holstered the weapon.

"Watch him. He's stronger than he looks."

Jim spat scornfully and then crawled through the brush toward Thin One. He was close to him when Thin One suddenly whirled. Jim rushed in, wrenching the shotgun away from the Chiricahua. Jim struck at him with the barrels of the shotgun.

Thin One ducked out of the way. He ripped out his knife and went into a crouch. Jim dropped the shotgun and took out his knife. They circled warily. Jim lunged. Thin One avoided the blow and countered with a slash that raked Jim's chest. He grunted in sudden pain.

Jim retreated. Thin One followed confidently. Alan grasped a rock. Thin One thrust hard. The blades clicked together and rose high. They stood there, chest to chest, straining against each other. Then the spell broke. Thin One weakened and gave ground. Jim drove his blade home. Thin One went down.

Jim glanced back at Alan and smiled. He bent over the fallen brave. Thin One freed his short reserve knife.

It ripped upward into Jim's right side. Jim coughed thickly and fell over the dying warrior.

Alan ran to his brother. Jim held his wounded side.

"Forget about me," he said thickly. "I'll be all right. I've been hurt worse than this before. Go get that other devil."

Alan snatched up Jim's knife and darted into the brush. Yellow Snake had vanished. Alan tripped, and his knife clattered into a cleft. Then he saw Yellow Snake. The Chiricahua had rested his rifle on a rock and was taking careful aim down into the canyon.

Alan closed in on the warrior. Yellow Snake turned. Alan was almost on him. Yellow Snake jabbed his rifle muzzle at Alan's face. Alan gripped the rifle barrel and jerked it hard. Yellow Snake was off balance. Alan cut his right hand hard at the base of the warrior's neck. Yellow Snake grunted and released the rifle. Alan tried to turn the rifle for a butt stroke.

"Ahagahe!" snarled Yellow Snake as he felt for his knife.

Alan smashed at him with the rifle, not daring to shoot for fear of exciting the men down in the canyon. Yellow Snake slashed at him. The knife tip raked Alan's fingers. He dropped the rifle.

Yellow Snake closed in on Alan. Alan went down before the savage rush. Yellow Snake dropped on top of him, striking wildly with the knife. It missed a stroke and snapped against a rock. Alan remembered a wrestling trick taught to him long ago by Jim. Yellow Snake's strong hands closed about Alan's throat. Alan swung up one of his long legs against Yellow Snake's throat. The warrior gagged and loosened his grip. He reared backward.

Alan smashed at the contorted face above him with both fists. Yellow Snake rolled free and jumped to his feet. One of his legs sank beneath him. A soft spot at the edge of the canyon gave way. For an agonizing second, he stood poised on the brink and then he went down with a shrill, wailing scream that awoke the canyon echoes. A dull thud came up from far below.

Alan walked wearily back to Jim and helped him to one of the horses. He swung up on the other one and led Jim's horse to a place where a faint trail went down into the canyon.

The rain drizzled down as they reached the canyon bottom. They rode slowly toward the group of white men and Chiricahuas. Jim raised his head. "Major Steele," he said, "you can thank Alan. The kid stopped him from putting a bullet into one of you to start a bloody war." Jim jerked his head toward the fallen Yellow Snake.

Steele wiped his pale face. "It almost broke up the parley," he said. "They've agreed to come into the reservation. We owe Alan a great deal."

Alan dismounted and walked over to his Chiricahua friends. Never Still embraced him. "I wish I had been up there to help you," he said.

"My other brother was with me," said Alan proudly.

The rain streamed down. Thunder pealed in the gorges. A shaft of lightning lanced high overhead. The Chiricahuas cast pollen toward it and said quick prayers.

Hours later, in the wet darkness, the troopers left the canyon, followed by a long line of Chiricahuas. Jack Rabbit and Black Bear had gone with Never Still to bring down the women and the children.

Alan looked back at the warriors. There was finally peace for them. In time there would be lasting peace between white man and red.

Gila kneed his horse close to Alan. "What do yuh aim to do now, son?" he asked.

Alan looked up at the flashing lightning. "I'd like to go to school," he said simply.

"Sounds good. What do yuh aim to be?"

Alan placed a hand on the cantle of his saddle and looked back at the Big Mountain. "I'd like to work for the Government, Gila. To work with Indians. I think we owe them something for taking their land away from them."

"Amen to that," said the scout.

They rode west through the rain. It was good to ride the trail of peace.

TUMBLEWEED TRIGGER

CAST OF CHARACTERS

MATT TURLOCK
Many men had died looking into the muzzle of his Colt;
now it was his turn.

MORGAN ENGELS
Behind his slick mouth was the mind of a man who
would let nothing get in his way.

JIM STURTEVANT
The one argument that convinced him was a bullet
through his head.

CATO SEMMES
He wasn't sure that he was faster on the draw than
Turlock—and there was one way to find out.

BENNIE OSGOOD
Would he be able to back up his bunkhouse brags with
hot lead?

LESLIE STURTEVANT
The spirit in her shone as brightly as her golden hair...but
was it enough to tame a wind-devil?

CHAPTER ONE

The wind had shifted, and the cold rain was being driven in through the shattered windows of the low adobe house. Matt Turlock did not move to escape from the rain. The feeling of it on his taut face was a mercy he had not expected. He edged closer to the window, making sure he did not silhouette himself against the lighter background of the white plastered wall behind him. Far to the west there was an eerie flickering of staghorn lightning, softly lighting the rounded naked hills that edged the valley. There was no one to be seen out there amid the tumbled boulders, the sagging fence line, the collapsed outbuildings, nor along the ragged, brush-stippled rim of the dry creek.

The lightning abruptly vanished, plunging the valley into wet darkness. Matt passed a hard hand across his bristly jaws, wiping the dust and stale sweat from his face with the help of the blessed cool rain. He closed his eyes, and a feeling of despondency crept over him. This was not the way Matt Turlock had expected to go, lying in a stinking and musty adobe, long abandoned by man.

Maybe they had left, figuring they had taken care of him, but there was no faith in that thought. He waited until the lightning flickered again, then raised his hat from the floor, moving it back and forth in the window. There was an instant blossom of red-orange light near the creek bed, followed by the sharp crack of a rifle. The battered Stetson jerked a little in his hand. He should have known they'd still be waiting.

He fingered his Winchester, then thought better of replying to that shot. He was low enough on brass as it was. Matt looked back over his shoulder, then he took his sweat-stained scarf from his neck and held it for the rain to soak.

He bellied across the filthy floor, feeling the empty brass hulls rolling beneath his belly and legs. There were a lot of them.

He worked his way into the little room behind the room where he had been holding the fort. The lightning etched itself sharply across the sky, illuminating the white-drawn face of the tall man who lay there, staring up at the fly-specked ceiling with eyes that did not see anything except perhaps the Angel of Darkness. "Jim," Matt said in a low voice. There was no answer from the badly-wounded man. Matt thrust a hand inside the bloodstained shirt and placed it over the heart. For a moment his own heart seemed to skip a beat or two until he felt the faint, almost indistinguishable beating of the stricken man's heart. "Jim?" he repeated.

The head turned ever so slowly. The sunken eyes seemed to hold the vague shadow of a smile deep within them; that and something else; something Matt did not want to see. "Matt, old boy," said Jim Sturtevant softly. He wet his dry lips. "I heard that last shot."

"They're still out there," said Matt. He began to wipe Jim's face with the wet scarf.

"Thanks." The wounded man let out a full breath, and his chest sank. Then his breathing became harsh and dry. "Can you make a break for it, old boy?"

"No."

Jim moved a little. "They want me, not you, Matt."

Matt grinned wryly. "Not the way they've been shoot-ing, Jim. Reminds me of Berdan's Sharpshooters at Gettysburg. You remember, Jim?"

"Those Yankees sure could shoot all right. Same kind of shooting my ancestors faced at Bunker Hill."

The rain slashed down heavily, pattering on the earthen roof. Trickles of muddy water began to seep through and patter on the dirt floor of the adobe.

Matt teetered on his boot heels. The Englishman was far gone. A doctor might just save him. It would be a long shot at that.

"I'll never leave here alive, Matt," said the Englishman.

"No use in asking them for favors. This is an execu-tion, Matt."

A cold feeling came over Matt. It was almost as though Jim had read his mind.

"You can make it though, Matt," said Jim quietly.

"I'll stick, Jim."

A rifle flatted off, and a searching slug whipped through the front window and pitted the adobe wall, scattering hard chips of plaster throughout the room. Matt winced as one of them cut his lean neck.

Jim gripped Matt's wrist with surprising strength. "Make your break. I have a loaded pistol. Don't worry about me."

"I wouldn't get fifty feet," said Matt dryly.

"You can if you use your head. Go on."

Jim raised his head a little. "They know you by repu-tation. A mercenary."

"What the hell is that?"

Jim smiled a bit, then his breathing grew labored again. After a moment, he looked at Matt. "A hired gun. A paid fighter."

"I never felt I was working for you on that basis, Jim."

"I know that. Do they?"

"I don't know."

"They'll kill you to shut your mouth, Matt. On the other hand, they can always use a fighter like you."

"I wouldn't work for Morgan Engels for half the money in the sovereign state of Texas!"

"Then they'll kill you."

Matt shifted his head and looked toward the front window. "I'll take a few of them along as payment, Jim."

It was no idle boast. Jim Sturtevant drew Matt close. "I haven't long, Matt. I always had a feeling they'd get me sooner or later. It isn't myself that I am thinking about now, but rather Leslie."

"Your kin?"

Jim nodded. "The only one of my family left now, Matt, Les needs your help. Thank God we ran into each other so long after the war. Fate, I think. A kind fate, I hope. I'll be gone in a little while. When I am gone, dicker with Engels. He's always looking for hired guns. Good hired guns. The best. Men like you, Matt."

"And if it works?"

"Go along with them to the Valley. Keep your mouth shut and your eyes open. Guide yourself accordingly. You'll do that?"

"It's probably the only way I'll get out of *this* damned valley alive."

"Then do it."

"You think I can fool Engels?"

There was a long silence and then Jim spoke softly. "You'll *have* to fool him, Matt. Otherwise, there'll be two graves here instead of one."

"There'll be others as well."

"Don't be a damned fool!"

Matt looked down at the Englishman. His voice had sounded as it had been when he was an officer in Hood's Texas Brigade. There was no need for Matt to feel for the wounds that were slowly draining away the life of Jim Sturtevant. The two of them had been caught just as they reached the adobe to get water for the long ride northwest into New Mexico and Jim's ranch in Bonito Valley. Jim's first wound had been enough to cripple him for life and the others had assured his death. By the grace of God, Matt Turlock had gotten through a hail of lead unscathed. Since then, four hours before, he had held the fort alone.

"Engels knows of you by reputation. He probably doesn't know we served together in the Confederate Army, Matt."

Matt half closed his eyes and wet his cracked lips. "Yeh," he said softly. He grinned like a hungry lobo. "Yeh..."

Jim's breathing began to race, erratically and harshly. A rifle spat flame and smoke through the slanting rain, and the slug rapped into a door frame. Close, that one; too damned close. It was four inches from Matt's head. He raised his Winchester.

"No, Matt," said Jim. "Play it smart. Play it cool. Your life may depend on it. Go on now. Start dickering with them."

Matt stood up and placed his back against the wall.

Jim smiled. "I know why you're hesitating. Go on. I won't be here long. They can't hurt me now, Matt." He reached up and gripped Matt's hand. "Once you're out of here alive, you can do as you like. If you don't..."

"What do I have to dicker with? My reputation as a hired gun? Engels won't take a chance on that alone."

Jim fumbled with his shirt and opened it. He slowly unbuckled the money belt he wore. He pulled it free from his body. "There's five thousand dollars in here, Matt. It was enough to keep us going in the Bonito Valley. Engels knows I went for money. He's probably sure I have it with me."

Matt grinned. "You think he'd let me get out of here with a load of *dinero* like that?"

"No. But you can hand it over to him."

Matt's eyes narrowed. "You loco? Les will need that *dinero!*"

Jim grunted in savage pain, doubling over. When he spoke again it was between dry, racking gasps. "Your life...is worth...more to me...than this money... Les can't... face Engels and ...his *corrida* alone...but you could help...if you wanted to...but you...have...to...get out of...here alive...Matt..."

The Englishman was right. Matt took the heavy belt and carried it into the next room. He peered through the window. The night was as dark as the pit. There was no sound of anything except the steady drumming of the rain against the ground and the adobe.

Matt stepped aside and leaned against the wall. He wanted a smoke, God how he wanted the solace of tobacco, but to make a light in that room would be to invite a dozen slugs. He listened to Jim's labored breathing, then suddenly it stopped. Matt raised his head. "Jim?" There was no answer.

Matt wet his lips. He fumbled with the heavy belt. Five thousand dollars! A man could buy a nice spread for that kind of *dinero,* or have a time seeing the elephant, say in El Paso or Fort Worth. But that money would pay his way out of this trap if he was lucky.

He waited until the lightning flickered again. "Hey, Engels!" he yelled.

A gun cracked, and a slug rapped into the wall.

The lightning died away.

"Hey, Engels! This is Turlock! Sturtevant is gone! I want to talk business."

There was a long silence in the rainy, hissing darkness.

"Engels?" called Matt.

"Start talking, Turlock!" came Engels' dry, precise voice from the darkness near an outbuilding.

"No shooting?"

"For a *while.*"

Someone laughed near the creek.

"Sturtevant was shot to dollrags," said Matt. "Wasn't that what you wanted?"

"*You're* doing the talking."

"Well, he's gone. I was paid to side him from Texas up here to New Mexico. I did my job."

"You sure as hell did! Killed one of my boys and wounded another. You thinking of talking your way out of that 'dobe? If you are, you haven't made any tracks yet, man."

Matt wet his lips. "Hell, Engels, it was a business deal. You ought to understand that."

"Keep talking."

"My deal is off with him. Let me get out of here and I'll hightail it back to Texas and keep my *boca* shut."

The same raucous laughter came from near the creek. Matt fingered his rifle trigger. One shot at that laughing jackass would almost be worth the trouble it would cause.

"How do I know you won't talk?"

"If I did, you'd damned well see to it that I never talked again. *Los muertos no hablan,* Engels!"

"You ain't dead right now, Turlock, and you've got a big mouth."

"You want to come and take me?"

There was a long silence. Then Engels called out. "Fair enough. Come out with your hands up. Unarmed!"

"I'm not that big a fool."

"Then the deal is off."

Matt rubbed his jaw. His mind was tired, and he wasn't getting anywhere. He hefted the money belt. "Engels?" he called.

"I've had my say."

"I have Sturtevant's money belt."

"You ain't going anywhere with it."

The laughing jackass sounded off again.

"No," said Matt, "but I can sure as hell burn it to ashes before you can rush this place."

"He's got a point," said another voice from behind a

boulder. "Besides, Mister Engels, it ain't getting any drier out here, and that sonofabitch can shoot like a buffalo hunter."

"Ain't nothing wetter than rainwater," agreed another seemingly bodiless voice.

"All right, Turlock," said Engels. "It's a deal. What do we do?"

"Come on in."

There was a long pause again. Then a tall man came from behind an outbuilding, etched in lightning glow, and walked toward the adobe. Whatever else one thought of Morgan Engels, he was no coward, or else he was absolutely sure of himself.

Matt stepped back, fumbled with the money belt again, then unbarred the front door. He could hear boots squelching in the pasty wet *caliche* outside as Engels's boys passed on either side of the adobe to come in from the back. Matt opened the door. He leaned his rifle against the wall. Morg Engels came in, took off his flat-brimmed hat, and shook the rain from it. He wrinkled his nose. "Place stinks worse than ever," he said wryly.

"You've been here before?"

"Yes." Engels's cold gray eyes held Matt's blue eyes. "I happen to own this place. I own this land. I own this whole damned valley."

"Sorry the place was messed up," said Matt dryly.

"Where is he?"

Matt jerked a thumb over his shoulder.

Engels peered through the doorway. "Dead?"

"Far's I know."

"You sound damned cool about it."

Matt smiled thinly. "Like I said, I was paid to side him up here from Texas. He's gone. My job is done."

"Merry Christmas," said Engels dryly. "As a matter of fact, I understand your type very well, Turlock."

"Gracias."

A door at the far end of the room opened, and a little

man came into the bigger room trailing a rifle. "All clear in there, Mister Engels," he said. His bright, birdlike eyes flicked at Matt.

"All right, Carnes."

A leg came through a window at the north side of the room. A big thick leg, followed by a big thick body, and a big thick head. The heavy rifle in the man's huge hands looked like a child's toy by comparison. "All right out here, Mister Engels," he said. The eyes were ludicrously small for the huge build of the man, but the light in them was as cold as the electrical discharge flickering across the streaming sides.

"Keno, Monk," said Engels.

Monk's hands tightened on the rifle. His eyes flicked toward Matt's rifle, then down to the low, tied-down holster that Matt wore.

"Make a light, Carnes," said Engels. "Where's Cato?"

"Heah, Mister Engels."

Matt looked toward the front door. A man stood there, wet with rain, looking hard at Matt. His eyes were gray, but so light in color that Matt had the odd impression they were almost white against the man's darkly tanned face. As the man had spoken, his teeth had shown, sharply white against his thin lips and the Mexican dandy mustache he effected, hardly more than a thin line on the upper lip.

"Youah quite an *hombre* with the long gun," said Cato in a low metallic voice to Matt.

"I do my best," said Matt casually.

"Youah quite a shot," insisted Cato. "Hit my partnah Clay in the head at sixty yahds with thet gun in the dahk. Killed him, Mistah."

"That's our business, ain't it, Mister?"

The eyes widened. "Listen to him," said Cato. "A funny man. Youah quite a cahd, Mistah. Yuh got some bones and a tambourine mebbe? A little burnt cork for the face, Mistah Bones?"

Matt's face broke into a slow, tantalizing smile, but the eyes were as cold as floe ice. "*You* got the accent and the name, Mistah *Cato*. My pappy had a cullud boy name of Cato once."

"For Christ's sake, Mister!" snapped the little man named Carnes. "That's Cato Semmes!"

"Pleased, Mister Semmes," said Matt. He wasn't quite as cool now. He had not associated the name Cato with the name Semmes. Separately they meant nothing; together, they named one of the fastest and deadliest guns in the Southwest.

An odd change had come over the smooth-faced gunman. His thin lips parted in what was intended for a smile. "This ain't the time and place, Mistah Turlock," he said, all politeness and gentility now, "but those words yuh spoke, youah going to eat when this business is ovah. *Eat,* yuh heah me?"

"For God's sake, Cato!" said Engels. "If you are so damned good, why didn't you get *both* of them instead of just Sturtevant when they got here?"

"Yuh wanted Sturtevant, didn't yuh, Mister Engels? Yuh got him, didn't yuh?"

Engels waved a hand. He took the money belt from Matt as Carnes lighted several candles. In the uncertain flickering light, the man thumbed through the compartments in the belt. He whistled softly. "Nice," he said.

"We goin' to stay here tonight, Mister Engels?" asked Monk. He wrinkled his ridiculously small nose.

"No. Go get the horses, Monk. Put Clay's body in the shed and block the door against the coyotes. Can Norm ride?"

"Only got a flesh wound," said Carnes.

Monk brought up the horses when he was done placing the dead body of Clay in the shed. He brought Jim Sturtevant's black as well, but Matt's sorrel was nowhere to be found. Engels jerked his head at Matt. Matt walked outside into the rain. Carnes took Matt's

Colt from its holster, and a cold feeling came over Matt. Maybe he wasn't as smart as he thought he was. "Maybe you'd better put Mister Sturtevant's body where it will be safe from the coyotes too," he suggested.

"Yeh," said Monk. He grinned.

They all mounted except Cato Semmes. He leaned in the doorway rolling a cigarette, his cold eyes on Matt.

"Take a look at Mister Sturtevant, Cato," said Engels.

"Yes, suh." The gunman vanished from the doorway.

They all looked at Matt.

Suddenly a shot rang out from inside the adobe. Smoke drifted from the doorway. Semmes walked casually from the building and swung up onto his bay. "All right," he said easily.

They rode toward the creek. Matt looked back at the adobe. An iciness had settled within him. Maybe Jim Sturtevant had still been alive when Cato Semmes had gone in to see him at Engels's orders. Maybe...

They splashed through the rising waters of the creek and headed up the grassy slope, Matt riding Jim's sleek black. He reached back to get Jim's slicker and saw the eyes of Cato Semmes on him again. The lightning flickered sharply, crackling across the streaming valley. Matt wasn't sure what they meant to do with him. If they had intended to kill him, it would have been easier to do it back there. Morgan Engels had something else within his devious mind.

Had Jim Sturtevant still been alive when Semmes had gone in to see him? Engels had given the order; Semmes had carried it out. Those two names were now etched in acid on Matt Turlock's memory, and anyone who knew Matt Turlock at all knew how long and sharp that memory could be.

The lightning forked into a naked butte, and the valley was brilliantly illuminated in eerie, bluish light. When the storm stopped, the coyotes would come out to bay at the moon and to look for food. They could not get at the body of the man named Clay, but there was nothing to protect the body of Jim Sturtevant. Matt Turlock's hands tightened, ever so slowly. Blood pays off blood. There was no other way in his code, or theirs for that matter. *Blood pays off blood...*

CHAPTER TWO

The wind-devil, or dust-devil, as it is sometimes called, is a trick of nature seen in the West. A slowly spiraling column of dust picked up from the flat desert floor by the vagrant wind, to be carried as a manifestation of the mad rigadoon of that wind, until the wind tires of it and deserts it, then it vanishes as quickly and magically as it appeared, perhaps to reform again miles away, to repeat the same senseless performance. It serves no useful purpose, coming and going as it pleases, creating nothing, establishing nothing, but it is there for some unfathomable reason of God.

So it was with Matt Turlock. His family had come from Missouri to Texas when he had been a child. His two sisters had died of fever, and his brother had been killed by a fall from a horse. Before Matt had hardly begun to shave, his mother had died, and his father had been killed by Lipans in the Big Bend country. There had been no need for Matt to have responsibilities. The ranch was hardly worth the powder to blow it to hell. Then the war had started, and a big fifteen-year-old boy had enlisted in the Fifth Texas, to fight throughout the war. At nineteen, with four years of war behind him, he had stood ragged and gut starved in the rain at Appomattox to see his tattered, smoke-stained regimental colors turned over to the Yankees. At that moment, Corporal Matthew H. Turlock, Missourian by birth, Texan through chance, and Confederate by choice, had decided to fight only for pay. A hired gun; a mercenary, as Jim Sturtevant had called him. In the ten years since the war, he had made it his living on the great cattle drives north from Texas to Hays and Abilene, Dodge City and Wichita, fighting rustlers, depredating Indians, and the hated Yankee Jayhawkers as well as the Yankee gunmen who kept law and order in the trail towns, the so-called 'Fighting Pimps'.

If there had ever been a man to whom the orphan named Matt Turlock owed any allegiance, it had been Jim Sturtevant, the Englishman who had been cashiered from his Guards regiment for some unknown reason, unknown at least to Matt, and it did not matter. For Jim Sturtevant had fought Yankees as well as any Texan or Arkansan in Hood's old brigade. He had also fought his way up from high private in the rear rank to command of Matt's company at Gettysburg. He had treated a seventeen-year-old kid as an equal although their every characteristic, except perhaps for one, seemed to be at odd ends. That one characteristic was a fighting heart; no quarter given or taken.

Now Matt rode with the men who had killed Jim Sturtevant in cold blood. All of them were to blame. They would pay the blood debt, one way or another, each of them in turn, or all together, it mattered not to Matt Turlock. Beyond that achievement in bloody violence, he did not care to look. *Wind-devil...*

They had reached Morg Engels's ranch house in the intense darkness before the dawn, cold and wet, silent and morose, for killing is a hard game on a man unless he is nothing but a killing machine. Each of the men who rode silently about Matt Turlock had the killing stamp upon him; the mark of Cain. But each of them also had a weakness in addition to his skill at killing.

Matt entered the ranch house with Morg Engels, followed by little Shorty Carnes, who had his rifle loose and ready in his brown hands. A fire was lighted in the huge stone fireplace. "Go make coffee, Shorty," said Morg.

Carnes jerked his head at Matt. "What about him?"

Morgan dropped into a chair and hefted Sturtevant's money belt in his hands. "Make the coffee," he said. "Mister Turlock won't do anything wrong, will you, Mister Turlock?"

"Like I said: Sturtevant is gone, and my job was done. I've got no axes to grind."

Engels leaned back in the chair. "I would have had you killed back there if I hadn't known more about you than you may think I do, Turlock."

"So?"

Engels smiled. "You see the men I have. These are the cream of my fighters. The rest of the *corrida* are run-of-the-mill. They take care of the cattle and the ranch."

"And the others?"

"They take care of me."

"And your enemies."

"You have the general idea."

Matt slowly rolled a cigarette. "How do you figure on explaining away Sturtevant's death?"

"Simple enough. He fired on me from ambush, killing one of my men, and wounding another. By great good fortune I escaped. In the return gunfire Sturtevant was killed."

"By a shot in the head."

The hard eyes lifted and held Matt's eyes. "Yes, by a shot in the head. So you see, it is purely a matter of self-defense."

"Unless I talk."

Engels smiled. "Now, Mister Turlock."

Matt lighted up. "Why did you want him out of the way?"

"It doesn't concern you."

"I suppose not." Matt blew a smoke ring.

"Did you know him before?"

Matt eyed the drifting smoke ring. "Yes," he said.

"Where?"

"In the army, the *Confederate* Army, Mister Engels."

"In what way?"

Matt looked directly at the rancher. "He was my company commander in the Fifth Texas, Hood's Division."

"So? Very interesting."

Matt knew intuitively that Engels had known those facts all along. If Matt had lied about his service with Sturtevant in the war, Engels would have been intensely suspicious. But Matt was not off the hook as yet.

"You saw him after the war?" asked Engels.

"No." That was also truth.

"Then how did you happen to ride with him, Turlock?"

Matt blew out another smoke ring. He had to think quickly. "I met him in Fort Worth. Found out he was there to borrow money. A lot of money."

Engels tapped the belt.

Matt nodded. "I suggested I ride with him as a hired gun, because of our service in the war together."

"And?"

"He never got wise to me, Mister Engels."

Engels's eyes narrowed. "What do you mean?"

Matt smiled slowly. "You didn't think he was actually going to get home with all that *dinero,* did you?"

Engels was closely studying Matt. "Go on."

"Jim Sturtevant had me bucked and gagged after Antietam. The reason isn't important. I never forgot it."

"It isn't a pleasant experience."

"It might have been better if he had killed me," said Matt slowly. His face was as hard set as granite.

"So we killed him for you."

Matt eyed the money belt. "That was only part of the idea I had."

Engels grinned. "I have to have *something* for my troubles with the deceased."

"Is that the only reason? Jim Sturtevant went to a lot of trouble to get that money, Mister Engels. He said he'd probably lose his ranch if he didn't have it."

"That is true."

"He thought a lot of that ranch."

"Have you ever seen it?"

"No."

Engels fingered the money belt. "Jim Sturtevant had a genius for selecting exactly the right place for his ranch, Turlock. There is no finer locale for cattle in the whole Territory of New Mexico. Shelter, water, grazing, *everything* a rancher could want, or hope to have. That was Sturtevant's J Lazy S."

"Was?"

Engels patted the money belt. "The note against the ranch can hardly be paid off now, can it?"

Matt tried to keep his face expressionless. Engels had the J Lazy S with its tail in a crack for sure.

The pungent odor of brewing coffee drifted out to them. The gray light of the pre-dawn shone against the rain-streaked windows. The wind had shifted, and it moaned softly down the big chimney.

Shorty Carnes brought in a tray with a coffee pot and cups. He placed it on the table and poured a cup for Morgan Engels. "Give Turlock a cup," said the rancher.

"Let him serve hisself."

Matt grinned. He helped himself. "Thanks, Shorty," he said. "Smells good anyways."

"Tastes good too!"

The little man had a touchy vanity. Matt filed that fact away in his memory.

"Beat it, Shorty," said Morg Engels casually.

"You aim to stay alone with this lobo?"

"I think Mister Turlock and myself can have a nice sociable little chat without fear of gunplay."

"Considering the fact, Shorty," said Matt easily, "that I have no gun on me."

"By God you was lucky Cato Semmes didn't draw on you!"

"He's fast?"

"Fast as lightning and eleven claps of thunder! I mind one time in Tascasa we was—"

"That's enough," said Engels sharply.

The little man grumbled his way into the kitchen and a moment later the door slammed behind him.

"He's right, you know," said Engels. He looked at Matt. "You were lucky."

Matt glanced down at his empty holster. "Oh, I don't know."

Engels narrowed his eyes again. He steepled his slim fingers. "I just wonder," he said. "According to Shorty, Cato is the best there is. Better than Courtwright, Allison, *or* Hardin."

"Covers some territory there."

"That's what Shorty thinks. All I know is that Semmes *is* fast, does his work, and gives me a certain amount of loyalty, for pay, of course."

"I heard him at work," said Matt dryly. "A shot in the head. He's fast, all right."

"It's said that *you* also kill for pay, Mister Turlock."

It was very quiet in the room now except for the soughing of the wind down the chimney.

"I can use you, Mister Turlock."

It was almost too easy.

"What do you say, Mister Turlock?"

He'd never leave that place alive if he said no.

"Mister Turlock?"

Matt drained his coffee cup and refilled it. "News travels fast," he said quietly. "People know I left Fort Worth with Jim Sturtevant and that he had a lot of money with him. We were seen here and there on the trail west and at the Horsehead Crossing of the Pecos. We were seen only this morning by a cavalry patrol. Now his body will be found in that 'dobe, the money gone, and Matt Turlock shows up working for his enemy. *You,* Mister Engels."

"Jim Sturtevant ambushed and killed one of my men, wounded another, fired at me, and died from wounds inflicted by my men. Self-defense, as I have already stated. I have some influence in this territory, Turlock. I have witnesses. There are none for Mister Sturtevant. Except you, that is. Go on.

"In my present version, Sturtevant died under the gunfire of men hired to protect me. You were nowhere around at the time. You are well known as a hired gun. Come and go, drift here and there, working at your trade. You possibly left him once he was safely in the area of his ranch."

"Possibly."

"No one will bother you if you come to work for me."

"And if I do not?"

The eyes were half closed. "I have five witnesses, including myself, that you murdered James Sturtevant and that we found this money belt upon you."

"And your price for me to work for you is your silence?"

"That is correct." Engels smiled a little. "Of course, you get pay and found, Mister Turlock. I want no slaves here on the E Bar E."

"Certainly not."

"Then it is agreed?"

"Agreed."

Matt stood up and emptied his cup. He placed it on the tray.

"You will not regret it, Turlock," said Engels.

"Thank you, Mister Engels."

"Not at all!" Engels waved a hand.

Matt walked to the door and took his hat from a hook. He turned. "Any orders, Mister Engels?"

"See my foreman, Jack Vance. Get some rest, Turlock. I may need you later on today."

Matt left the room and walked across the porch. He was halfway across the area between the house and the bunkhouse when he knew instinctively that Engels was watching him through a window. What he did not see was the secretive smile on the man's face as he gently hefted the heavy money belt up and down, up and down.

Jack Vance was all gray. Gray of hair and eyes, gray of face and clothing, and he walked with an awkward sort of a limp. There was no warmth about the man; his face was expressionless and his eyes lackluster, but there was hidden strength in the man, and Matt knew well enough he had not gotten to be ramrod of the E Bar E by political pull. It would take a man to handle such men as Monk, Norm, Shorty Carnes, and Cato Semmes.

Vance stood at the window of his room, looking out across the west valley to the east, talking almost in a monotone. "Ain't much ranch work for *hombres* like you to do, Turlock. The *vaqueros* do all of that. You work directly under Mister Engels's orders."

"Is there much to do?"

"Depends." Vance turned. "I know your stamp, Turlock. That doesn't matter to me. Mister Engels hired you; that's good enough for me. I don't question what he does. I just see that his orders are carried out. *To the letter*... I got good men here on the E Bar E. I got no trouble with them. We get rid of troublemakers in one helluva hurry. *Comprende?*"

"*Yo comprendo.* One big happy family, eh, Mister Vance?"

There was no answering smile on the foreman's face. "Yeh. What do you need?"

"A bunk. Bedding. A horse."

"Where's your horse?"

"Lost."

"You came in riding a black. Looked damned familiar, that black. You didn't steal him, did you?"

"Hardly, Mister Vance. He belongs, I mean *belonged,* to Jim Sturtevant."

"What do you mean?"

"You haven't heard about Jim Sturtevant?"

"I ain't been up but twenty minutes."

"He's dead, Mister Vance."

The face was as flat and expressionless as that of a marble statue. "So? At last, eh?"

"I wouldn't know about that."

"I guess you wouldn't. Who did him in?"

"I didn't say *how* he died."

Vance slowly cut a chew and placed it in his mouth. He worked it into pliability, then spat into a big can. "No, you didn't, did you? But that was the way he'd go. Shot down. I knew it, sure as thunder! Right?"

"Right!"

"Who done it?"

Matt walked toward the door.

"I asked you a question, *Mister.*"

Matt turned. "I wasn't there to see it," he said, giving Engels's fabricated version of the story. Let Morg Engels brief the foreman. The whole business made Matt Turlock more than a little sick.

"By thunder! I knew it would happen!"

"When did you know it would happen?" asked Matt, trying to sound casual.

It was almost as though a veil had dropped over the flat gray eyes of the man. "Forget what I said, Turlock."

Matt closed the door behind him. A watery sun was beginning to show over the eastern hills. The air was fresh and clear, but there was a foul stench of evil about the place. God had made a beautiful country for man; man had befouled it. It was almost beyond understanding.

Matt rolled a cigarette and walked to a nearby fence. He rested his elbows on it and looked out across the valley. Smoke drifted up from a ranch house almost as far as the eye could see. It was quiet and peaceful, but it would not stay that way long. Matt Turlock was damned well going to see to that. But there was one thing he must do, one way or another, and that was to contact Leslie Sturtevant and sound him out. It wouldn't do for Matt to let anyone know just yet what he had in mind. One wrong word, one slip, and he'd be as dead as Jim Sturtevant, having accomplished absolutely nothing.

He closed his eyes and again saw the pain-wracked face of the only man who had ever mattered to him, after the deaths of his brother and his father so long ago. Their memories were dimming through the years, while the memory of Jim Sturtevant would never die within Matt Turlock. He'd made a memorial for Jim Sturtevant; a memorial bathed in the blood of the men who had slaughtered the only man who had ever really mattered to Matt.

CHAPTER THREE

Three days had passed by and in that time the people in and around the Bonito Valley had learned of the death of Jim Sturtevant. There were those who believed the story created by Morg Engels, and there were others who did not believe it, but no one would talk publicly about their doubts and suspicions. But if there had been doubts and fears, tensions and suspicions in the Bonito Valley before the news of the death of Jim Sturtevant, they had doubled and quadrupled, and naked fear settled in the valley along with the intermittent rains that had started the night of the death of the Englishman.

It was Shorty Carnes who had been delegated to take Matt Turlock around the E Bar E and show him the lay of the land. The little man didn't care much for Matt but talkative as Shorty was, any audience was welcome. It was late on the afternoon of the third day at the ranch when Shorty drew rein at the top of a ridge and turned in his saddle. "West Bonito Valley," he said.

Matt drew rein and felt for the makings. He whistled softly as he mechanically rolled a quirly, his eyes studying the valley spread out before them. The far side of the valley was steep, rising from the lower slopes of the hills, over the timbered hills to the low mountains forming a huge backdrop. The dying sun was still touching the mountains and the hills with a wash of rose and gold. Down the center of the valley flowed a swift and shallow river, tinted golden by the sun. A soft wind rippled the thick grasses, giving the valley the look of a huge oval lake.

"How much of this is the J Lazy S, Shorty?" asked Matt as he lighted up.

"The whole south end."

"And the north end?"

"Belongs to the boss."

"Seems to me he has enough with that, the home range, and the land where Jim Sturtevant was murdered."

"Killed, dammit!"

"Killed then," said Matt dryly.

Shorty leaned on his pommel and spat casually. The boss has big ideas, Turlock. Mighty big ideas. Come in here a little too late to take the whole west valley. Tried to make a deal with Sturtevant, but Sturtevant was bull-headed. Wouldn't listen to reason. Figgered he had something good, I guess."

"He sure did."

Shorty waved a hand. "Didn't know much about handling money. Not like the boss."

"He knew how to pick out a place for a ranch, though," said Matt in admiration. He had never seen anything quite like this.

Carnes nodded. "He beat the boss out by a matter of days. The boss had always had his eye on this property, but he was negotiating for it when Sturtevant slipped it right out from under his nose."

"Made the boss unhappy, eh?"

Carnes grinned wryly. "That ain't quite the word, *hombre.* Come to think of it, I don't think the boss was as mad about losing the property as he was about *how* he lost it."

"Hurt his ego, eh?"

"What's his ego?"

"Him. Himself. Like Cato Semmes has an ego that makes him think he's the best draw in the territory. Monk thinks he's the strongest man in the territory. Jack Vance thinks he's the best ramrod. So on and so on."

"You must of read a book."

"One or two," admitted Matt. It wasn't the time or place to give credit to Jim Sturtevant, who used to teach his semi-illiterate men around the campfires in Virginia. He had always said that Matt's mind was as yet untapped of its knowledge. Matt had always thought he had been joshing, but Jim Sturtevant usually didn't josh about such matters.

"Anyways, Sturtevant ain't around now to hold onto the place."

"Les is, though, ain't he?"

There was an odd look on Carnes's wizened face. "Yeh, he is." He laughed shortly.

"Not much of a man, eh? Like his brother?"

"No, he ain't much like his brother." Carnes grinned widely.

Matt leaned on his saddle horn and rolled another cigarette. He passed the makings to Shorty. "I can see one bad feature about this place."

"Go on."

Matt jerked a thumb toward the hills and the mountains. "Sticky loopers could hide in them hills, slip down in the dark of the moon, snap up some heads, then slip back into them hills, through the passes out to the other side and find a market over there, no questions asked."

Shorty rolled a smoke. "Yeh. Well, Sturtevant always wanted isolation. He got it. He also got the sticky loopers. Used to have a thousand head on this place. Hardly got five or six hundred now."

"We'd call that a dairy farm back in Texas."

"Don't make much difference now. Between the

rustlers and the note against this place, Les Sturtevant will be out of business before too long anyways."

"And the boss moves in."

"You got the picture."

"Supposing someone else beats him out, like Jim Sturtevant beat him out?"

Shorty turned slowly and took the cigarette from his lips. "Ain't no one going to beat the boss out this time," he said flatly.

There was no need for Matt to go any further. No one around the Bonito Valley was going to buck up against Morg Engels for the J Lazy S. He had already committed murder and robbery to cinch his claim and after the first murder the rest are not so difficult, or so they say. In this case Morg Engels probably listed Jim Sturtevant somewhere down the list, for what Matt had heard around the bunkhouse in the past few days had convinced him that Morg Engels had already dabbled his slim hands in the blood of other murdered men.

The sun was almost gone when Matt's quick eye caught a movement across the valley. A small knot of cattle being driven by men toward the darkening hills. "Boys are working late on the J Lazy S," he observed.

Shorty hastily flipped away his cigarette and reached into one of his saddlebags for a pair of field glasses. He raised them and focused them. "I'll be damned," he said.

"Rustlers?"

"Sure!"

Matt drew in on his cigarette. "What do we care?"

Shorty lowered the glasses. "That ain't J Lazy S land! That E Bar E land and E Bar E cattle! And them ain't none of our *vaqueros!*"

"Maybe they're Sturtevant's boys?"

"No! Those are some of them Mex rustlers from the far side of the range there."

Matt stood up in his stirrups. "Maybe we'd better get some of the boys."

"No time."

Matt rubbed his jaw. "If a couple of men cut across the J Lazy S, through them hills there, and come out in that notch, would they be in front of the rustlers?"

"That notch is the central pass into the mountains, Turlock."

Matt looked down at Shorty's horse. "Can that plug move?"

"Sure as hell can!"

"Then what are we waiting for?"

They set their steel to their mounts and shot down the grassy slope, riding full out, quirting on the horses. It was too dark for the rustlers to look back and see anyone coming from behind.

The two E Bar E men reached the shallow river and splashed across in showers of spray. They raced across the flat land toward the dark lines of the hills. Far to their left were faint yellow lights. "Ranch house of the J Lazy S," said Shorty, jerking a thumb toward the lights.

When they reached the first rising ground, Shorty took the lead, guiding Matt through at a breakneck pace, but the little man knew his way, and he could ride like a jockey. At the top of a hill, he drew rein. "Breathe the horses," he said.

"Have we got time?"

"Listen!"

Faintly on the wind they heard the hoarse bawling of cattle from the north, and *behind* them.

"We got ten minutes," said Shorty.

"You aim to keep on at the same pace?"

"Why not?"

"Some ride," said Matt dryly.

A proud smile crept over the little man's face. "Ain't no one around here can beat Shorty Carnes on a horse," he said.

"I'll buy that."

If Shorty swelled up anymore, he'd plumb bust,

thought Matt. The little man's vanity was bigger than he was.

Shorty led the way on, riding slower this time, higher and higher, leading his horse now and then, threading his way with uncanny knowledge through the tangled brush and scrub trees that clothed the rocky slopes. There was a faint hint of moonlight in the eastern sky when at last the little man halted. He stabbed a thumb downward. "The pass," he said.

Matt ground-reined his sorrel and walked to the brink. It was a deep and twisting slash through the area, half hills, and half mountains, rugged and treacherous. "This the only way through, Shorty?"

"Yep. They either come through here or way north, but that's too damned close to the ranch headquarters. South, they'd be too close to the J Lazy S. This is the place, all right."

Matt cocked his head. The wind had shifted, and it brought to him the almost imperceptible sound of hoofbeats. "They're on the way," he said quietly.

"You can *hear* 'em?"

"Sure thing."

Shorty shook his head in admiration. "You got ears like an Apache."

"Better." Matt looked up and down the pass. Anyone to the west would be in thick darkness while travelers from the east would be coming up a rugged slope, with the moon behind them. "How do we get down there?" he asked over his shoulder.

"What do you figure on doing?"

"Get down there and block the way."

"Just two of us?"

"There's only half a dozen of them, Shorty."

"*Nine,* Turlock."

"Four for you and five for me."

"You talk big."

Matt grinned irritatingly. "Well, of course, if you're *afraid...*"

Shorty spat. He led his horse along the brink of the pass, then down a steeply angled trail, hardly perceptible in the darkness. Matt's heart was in his throat all the way down. Shorty turned at the bottom and looked at Matt. "You look a little green," he said dryly.

"I am."

They led the horses up the pass and picketed them in a small box canyon, took their Winchesters, and removed their spurs, to walk silently back to the very top of the pass, now faintly illuminated by the rising moon. It was now that Shorty looked to Matt for leadership. Matt pointed out a flat-topped boulder. "Get up there. Take off your hat and shoot between two rocks so you're not silhouetted. But don't shoot unless I do."

"Keno!"

Matt squatted behind a rock and levered a round into his Winchester. There was no desire in him to fight for the cattle of Morg Engels, but in common with most men of his stamp, he hated rustlers damned near as much as he hated horse thieves. Besides, he was still on trial with Morg Engels and his *corrida*. He had to set himself in solid, and if the blood of a few two-bit rustlers would help cement his relationship with the E Bar E, it was all to the good.

Matt took off his hat and loosened his Colt in its holster. Shorty was not to be seen, but he was up there in position. The noise of approaching horses and cattle could be plainly heard. Then three horsemen appeared, urging their mounts up the slope, steeple hats silhouetted against the faint light of the moon. Mexes, or men wearing Mex hats. They were talking excitedly, and it was in Spanish. New Mexico was a bilingual territory, and it was quite likely that these men were American citizens, for most of the sticky-fingered Mexicans south of the border kept pretty close to the Rio Grande when they raided into the States.

The cattle were bawling hoarsely as they were driven up the pass by the unseen vaqueros behind them, hidden in the darkness and the dust.

Matt waited until the leading trio of men were within fifty yards, then he pointed his rifle upward and pressed the trigger. The Winchester exploded into flame and smoke and the report of the rifle shot slammed back and forth between the narrow walls of the pass. Matt instantly reloaded the rifle and stepped quickly behind a high shattered boulder, looking through a wide split in the rock.

The horsemen had tried to swing their mounts, but the bawling cattle were too close behind them, and they were forced closer to Matt and Shorty. Shorty raised his rifle and fired, following suit with Matt.

Two of the Mexicans rode back against the trotting cattle to hold them while a tall man rode slowly toward the unseen riflemen. *Tor dios!* Why do you shoot?" he called out.

"Whose cattle are those, *hombre?*" called out Matt.

"I have bought them."

"From who?"

The man hesitated. "Who are you? How many are there up there?"

"Wouldn't you like to know?" said Matt. He grinned.

The cattle had halted. The other two men were sitting their horses in front of the small herd. There were no other horsemen to be seen.

"What is it you want?" asked the tall man.

"Just turn those cows back, Mister. Ride along behind them nice and quiet until you reach the valley."

Two minutes ticked past. Shorty shifted, and a rock fell from his perch. It was then that Matt saw a faint, furtive movement on the far side of the pass, almost on a level with Shorty's position. Suddenly the shadow moved quickly. "Shorty!" yelled Matt. He raised his rifle and fired. His shot was echoed instantly not only from the far side of the pass but from the tall Mexican as well. A man screamed. Shorty cursed. Matt swung and fired again. His shot struck the tall man's horse, and as he went down, Matt jumped to one side, peered through the smoke, and fired three times down his side of the canyon. A man grunted in savage pain and staggered out from cover, clutching his guts, letting hat and rifle fall to the ground. The tall man fired as he rested on one knee, and Matt dropped flat, firing from the ground. The man pitched forward. "Mother of God!" he screamed.

The echoes chased each other down the pass, and the thick smoke drifted in the wind. The cattle had turned in on themselves and were moving back down the pass. A man yelled hoarsely as his mount went down in front of the stampeding cattle, and they stamped him and his horse into a mass of blood and battered flesh.

It was hell in that narrow pass. A hell of bawling, panicky cattle and bawling panicky men, crashing downward through the swirling guns moke and acrid dust. A wounded man raised his head, saw horned and hoofed death pouring down on him, then dropped his head and covered it with shaking hands an instant before the stampede ran over him, grinding him to death.

Then the cattle vanished around a bend, leaving behind battered and dusty death. Matt padded out from behind his shelter and grounded his rifle, holding it with his left hand. He looked up toward Shorty. "All right, Shorty," he called. At that instant a man moved from behind a boulder, holding a nickel-plated six-shooter in his hand, aiming it at Matt. "Look out, Matt!" yelled Shorty.

Matt hurled his empty rifle at the man's face, crouched, drew, and fired in one fluid movement. The slug hit the man in the guts, doubling him up. His pistol went off as his hand closed in a reflex action. The slug struck the hard earth and rebounded, screaming thinly through the smoky air. Matt raised his head and lowered his smoking Colt.

"Jesus God," said Shorty in an awed voice as he came up to Matt. "I never seen the like of that! He had you cold, Matt, but you drew and killed him. God, you're a good man!"

The hard eyes studied Shorty. "As good as Cato Semmes?"

Shorty shrugged. "Mebbe. Mebbe not."

"You ought to be a good judge of that, Shorty."

The little man tilted his head to one side. "Only one way to find out, ain't there, Turlock?"

Matt opened the loading gate of his Colt and replaced the cartridge he had fired. He snapped shut the loading gate and spun the cylinder. He sheathed the gun, then began to reload his rifle. It was then he heard the tall man groan. Matt padded over to him. "Round up a horse for him, Shorty," he said over his shoulder.

"Let the rustling bastard die here," said Shorty coldly.

"I said get a horse!"

The little man cursed beneath his breath and rounded him up a stray horse. Matt examined the harshly breathing man. He found a bullet hole in the man's right thigh, but the bone had not been broken. He bandaged the wound and gave the man a boost into the saddle. He looked up at him. "You the head man, *hombre?*"

"*Si.*"

"You can just ride ahead down there after them cows and your *amigos* then."

The dark eyes studied Matt. "I do not know you."

"Makes us even then, don't it?"

"I am Bartolomeo Sanchez."

"So?"

The man's dark face tightened. "You have not heard of me?"

"Nope," said Matt casually. "Should I have heard of you?"

"You are new here?"

"*Si.*"

Shorty spat. "Sanchez is called by his people 'The Robin Hood of New Mexico,' Turlock."

Sanchez took off his heavy hat and bent his head. "At your service. I rob the rich and help the poor."

Shorty guffawed. "Yeh, like Robin Hood done. Only Bartolomeo takes his pick of the young girls of the people he's supposed to be helping. Hawww!"

Sanchez frowned. "*Bazofia,*" he said harshly. "What will you do with me, *hombre?*" he asked Matt.

"Take you to the ranch."

Sanchez's face paled. "To the E Bar E? Morgan Engels's ranch?"

"That's the general idea."

Sanchez wet his lips. "Please! Let me go. Turn me over to the law. Do not, I beg of you, let Morgan Engels get hold of me!"

Matt walked to his horse and swung up into the saddle, resting his Winchester on his thighs. "Ride," he said.

"Please, *amigo!*"

"Ride!" said Matt flatly.

A change came over the bravo. His face worked and cold sweat broke out on it. He bent his head. "*Senor,* shoot me here then."

Shorty grinned. He looked at Matt. "Go on," he said.

Matt stared at the little man and then at the rustler. "Act like a man, Sanchez," he said. "Ride, damn you!"

The rustler turned his horse and rode slowly down the pass like a man riding to his execution.

Most of the others who had fought were dead now, dead by lead or trampling hooves. Far down the face, a wreath of dust arose, and the bawling cattle could be heard. The moon was already flooding the hills east of the mountains. A cold wind blew through the pass.

"What's he so scared about, Shorty?" asked Matt curiously.

Shorty rolled a cigarette and lighted it. "You'll find out," he said mysteriously. "The boss warned Sanchez a long time ago not to get caught with E Bar E cattle. Sanchez ignored the boss. Sanchez pays the price."

"What price?"

Shorty drew in a deep drag of smoke and expelled it through his nostrils. "You'll see before too long," he said.

Matt felt for the makings. He had done his job. He had earned his pay for that day. He would be in solid with Engels now, but there was something about Shorty's words and manner he did not like. Something hidden and evil. But Bartolomeo Sanchez would have to pay the fiddler. It was his risk. He had been warned, and he had been caught. It was a rough country and a rough way of life. Pay the price or get out.

CHAPTER FOUR

The moon was up high, flooding the West Bonito Valley with cold silvery light as Matt Turlock and Shorty rode behind the now quiet cattle, heading them toward E Bar E range. Bartolomeo Sanchez rode with bowed head, just in front of Matt. There were only two of his men left, one of them wounded, riding unarmed with their wrists tied together, and naked fear painted upon their dark faces. Shorty Carnes seemed to be enjoying some vast and secret joke to himself.

On a ridge overlooking the moonlit range was a small group of horsemen. They moved down the slope. The moonlight showed on the dull metal of rifles. "It's the boss and some of the boys," said Shorty.

"Go tell 'em what happened, Shorty," said Matt. "Make a hero out of yourself."

Shorty looked angrily at Matt. "It was you who done most of it."

"Go on." Matt grinned. He watched the little man ride swiftly toward the others.

Bartolomeo Sanchez turned in his saddle. "Once more I beg of you, Senor Turlock! Let me go! Do not let me fall into the hands of Morgan Engels!"

Matt felt for the makings. He rolled a cigarette, rode

forward, and thrust it into the man's mouth. He snapped a match on a thumbnail and lighted the cigarette. "No," he said at last.

Sanchez drew the smoke in deeply. He straightened up in the saddle. "I am riding to my death," he said.

"Be a man!"

The dark eyes studied Matt. "It is not the thought of dying, *hombre,* it is the *way* of dying I do not like."

It was too late now for Bartolomeo Sanchez to get away. The E Bar E men took over the care of the tired and dusty cattle and bunched them near a waterhole. Morg Engels rode swiftly to where Matt waited with his prisoners. One of the rustlers looked quickly at Engels, and what he saw on that cold, hard face was enough to make him drive his spurs into his horse and race back toward the hills. A man raised his rifle, sighted almost casually, then fired. The flat report echoed from the hills. The man fell sideways from his saddle and lay still. Smoke drifted off before the night wind. Cato Semmes lowered his rifle. "I make it eighty yahds," he said.

"More like sixty," said Monk.

Shorty Carnes shook his head in admiration. "Sixty or eighty, it was a helluva good shot at a movin' target in this light!"

Engels drew rein ten feet from Sanchez and the other prisoner, who was hardly more than a boy, slim as a girl, but with head held proudly high. The rancher looked at Matt. "Thanks," he said. "Shorty told the whole story."

Matt nodded.

"How many of them?"

"Cattle? I don't know. Thirty or forty, I'd say."

Morgan Engels shook his head. His eyes glittered. "I meant rustlers. *Dead* rustlers."

Matt took his cigarette from his mouth. He looked back at the dead man lying in the moonlight beside his grazing horse. "He makes seven," he said. He looked at Engels.

"Bueno!" Engels eyed the tall form of Sanchez. "Well, Senor Sanchez, we meet again."

"It is not to my liking," said Sanchez quietly. He looked from one to the other of Engels's *corrida*. Big Monk, Cato Semmes, Shorty Carnes, Jack Vance, and Matt Turlock. There was no sympathy on their set faces.

Engels took a cigar case from his coat and selected a long nine. He bit the end from it and lighted the cigar. He eyed Sanchez over the flare of the match. "Damned near got away with it this time," he said.

"It was a good ambush, Senor Engels."

Engels nodded. "Six men lost out of nine up there. Two E Bar E men made the ambush. You're losing your grip, Sanchez."

Matt leaned on his saddle horn and studied Engels and the rustler. There was something going on between them he could not fathom.

"You remember my price for the next rustling job you did on the E Bar E if you were caught?" asked Engels.

Sanchez nodded. "I am ready to pay," he said. He looked at the boy beside him. "This one is young. He does not know much. He supports his crippled mother. Eusebio is young enough to reform, Senor Engels. Let him go."

Engels shook his head.

"I am not afraid to die, Bartolomeo," cried the boy.

Engels smiled. "A fighting cock," he said. He looked back at his men. "A hero, this one!" They all grinned except Matt.

Monk grinned. Cato Semmes was rolling a cigarette. He eyed the boy with amused eyes.

Engels took out his watch and snapped open the cover. "I'm late for an appointment," he said. He closed the cover and looked at Cato Semmes. "You and Monk take over. Jack and Shorty drive those cows further north. All but two of them. You understand?"

Vance nodded.

Engels turned to Cato Semmes. "Bring the beef up to the ranch, Cato."

The gunman nodded.

Engels waved a hand to Matt. "Ride with me," he said.

Matt touched his sorrel with his spurs and followed the rancher. He looked back curiously. Jack Vance and Shorty were driving the small herd north. Two steers had been left behind. Even as Matt looked, he saw Cato Semmes draw his Colt and fire twice. The two steers went down as though pole axed. The man *was* incredibly fast. Big Monk was out of his saddle and was already starting to skin one of the still-quivering steers.

Engels reached the top of the ridge and stopped to relight his cigar. He seemed to be waiting for something. Suddenly a thin scream of intense terror came from down on the flatland. It was the boy Eusebio. His screaming echoed and reechoed, then was suddenly cut short. Engels looked at Matt with an odd expression on his face. "The hero," he said dryly. He turned his horse and rode on. They were well on toward the ranch before Matt spoke. "What are they doing to them?" he asked.

"You'll find out tomorrow."

"I want to know."

Engels turned quickly. "Don't talk that way to me!"

"Sorry," said Matt. He began to roll a cigarette, but his mind was on those two prisoners.

Engels looked at the moonlit sky. "Will it be hot tomorrow?" he asked.

"Damned hot, Mister Engels."

The man nodded in obvious satisfaction. "I figured it would be." He spoke no more on the way back to the ranch.

Hours later, Mat Turlock awoke with a start in the quiet bunkhouse, cold sweat beading his forehead. He could have sworn he had heard a thin scream come to him on the rising pre-dawn wind of the valley. He looked at the others. Monk, Cato Semmes, Shorty, and all the others were sleeping soundly. The sleep of the just, thought Matt bitterly.

It was noon the next day when he was ordered to acquaint himself with the fence line area between the E Bar E and the J Lazy S. It was all right with him. He wanted to get away from the others. He rode south through rolling range country, east of the long ridge that formed part of the eastern wall of the main Bonito Valley. It was a fine, clear day but hot and showing promise of getting hotter.

By midafternoon, he had stopped at a waterhole shaded in a bosque, and from there, he could see through a wide notch in the ridge clear to the distant group of ranch buildings of the J Lazy S. He wanted to ride there and talk to Les Sturtevant, but it was hardly possible he could do so without being seen by some of Engels's men. Even now he had a feeling he was being watched.

He rode northerly along the ridge looking down into the quiet West Bonito Valley and he was even more impressed than he had been upon first sighting it. There was a sickness within him as he realized that Jim Sturtevant would never see it again. A thin thread of dust was rising from the valley floor on the western side of the river where the valley road trended north, to cross the river on E Bar E land, then rose to top a ridge, beyond which was another wide valley at the far end of which was the town of Roca Blanca, the local supply center. Someone was in a hurry. Someone probably from the J Lazy S.

Matt rode north on the ridge. The sun was beating down now, raising heat waves from the baking earth. Here and there a lazy wind-devil arose, swirled aimlessly about, then vanished as suddenly as it had appeared. Low clouds moved slowly across the bright blue skies, their shadows fleeting up hill and down dale ahead of them.

He was near the bridge, not far from where he had

left his prisoners to the tender mercies of Cato Semmes and Monk, when he saw something lying on the ground under the full glare of the sun. Two humped shapes. He stared at them. It was hard to tell just what they were, but beyond them were two other humped shapes. High in the sky were several hawks, wheeling and dipping, and beyond them, over the shimmering hills to the west, hung a lone buzzard like a scrap of charred paper floating in the sky.

Matt threw down his cigarette stub and spurred his sorrel. He never took his eyes from those four shapes upon the dun earth and an eerie, uncomfortable feeling crept up inside of him as he remembered horrible stories of certain practices of the Yaquis. But this was the Territory of New Mexico, in the United States. He tried to cast the thoughts from his mind.

When he was within two hundred yards of the four shapes, there was no longer any doubt in his mind. He rode slowly forward, bent forward a little in the saddle, eyes riveted on two of the four shapes. He already knew what the two farthest shapes were; the skinned and butchered carcasses of two steers.

At one hundred yards the sorrel shied and blew. Matt got down from the saddle and walked on, his tongue thrust between his lips, until he was sure of what he saw, and then a green sickness welled up within him as he knew well enough the horrible fate of Bartolomeo Sanchez and the proud boy named Eusebio who was, or had been, the sole support of his crippled mother. Green cowhide under the hot sun constricts a great deal with unyielding pressure, and anything inside of it, particularly a pinioned man, is slowly, very slowly but inexorably crushed to death within the unyielding embrace of the shrunken hide.

Matt Turlock had seen much of blood and horror in his twenty-nine years of life. Since the age of fifteen he had been fighting one way or another, against Yankees,

Indians, or anyone he was paid to fight against, so horror and blood had always been part of his life, callousing his soul so that he might live with himself. But this was sheer horror, the like of which he had never seen practiced, by white men at least.

Nothing but the boots and the heads protruded from the crushing envelopes of shrunken hides. The dusty boots looked much the same, although the ornate spurs had been removed from them. There was a hole in the right sole of the boot of young Eusebio, and the left boot heel had fallen off at one time and been nailed on a bit crookedly. The boots were familiar. The heads were not, and the buzzing bluebottle flies arose sluggishly as Matt Turlock stopped beside the two contorted and crushed bodies of Bartolomeo and his young follower Eusebio who had followed the 'Robin Hood of New Mexico' even in death.

"God," said Matt softly. He looked away from the horror of it. The protruding eyes and tongues, the blackened lips, and swollen faces. The flies crawling in the thick coagulated blood and vomit that stained their chins and the hides that snuggled so tautly about their necks.

He closed his eyes and remembered the horror and pleading in the voice of Bartolomeo Sanchez when he had asked Matt first to free him and then to kill him rather than to let him fall into the hands of Morgan Engels. *And Matt had delivered them into the hands of a soulless man like Engels!*

He remembered, too, the intense scream of terror that had come to Matt and Engels on the ridge overlooking the moonlit valley. The screaming of the boy Eusebio who had at last learned the fate which he had planned to face so bravely without knowing what it was.

He did not hear the buckboard until it was within fifty yards of him and then he looked up to see the team being reined in. A slim man dropped from the buckboard and came toward him, and suddenly he realized it was a young woman and not a man. Her hat was hanging at the back of her head, and her braided hair had been wound about her head like a crown of soft gold.

"You'd better not come any closer," he said quickly. He stepped in front of the two hide-wrapped bodies.

Her gray eyes were cold. "You don't have to hide them from me, mister," she said levelly.

There was something familiar about her. Matt narrowed his eyes. "You know about them?"

"I know Morg Engels," she said. "We heard the shooting last night. One of my boys told me that there had been rustlers on the E Bar E."

"This has happened before then?"

She nodded. "It's the Morg Engels's system of stopping rustling."

"You know him rather well then?"

"I ought to. That's my place at the end of the valley."

"That's the J Lazy S."

"Yes."

"The Sturtevant place?"

"Of course."

He tilted his head to one side. "But you said it was *your* place?"

She nodded shortly. "Can you lift them into the buckboard?"

"They look damned bad, Miss, beggin' your pardon."

She looked quickly at him. "They can't be left out here. Someone has to take care of them. Their people at least will want them."

Again, the feeling of knowing her came to him; the courage and quality of her; the fine eyes and the spirit of her. "Who are you?" he asked.

"Leslie Sturtevant," she said. "Who are you?"

Matt took off his hat. "Leslie Sturtevant! But I thought, that is, well, you see... My God! Leslie! He never told me you were a woman!"

Her eyes narrowed. "Who never told you?"

"Your brother."

It was almost as though he had struck her across the face. "Jim? You knew Jim?"

He nodded.

She studied him for a moment. "I received a letter from him before he left Fort Worth. He said he was riding with an old army comrade and not to worry. A man by the name of Matthew Turlock."

He smiled. "I am Matt Turlock," he said.

She stepped slowly backward, never taking her eyes from him. "What happened to Jim?" she said in a low voice. "What *really* happened to him?"

Her English accent was a little more pronounced now, but not as pronounced as Jim's had been, but then she must have come to America as a child. But why hadn't Jim told Matt she was a woman? And what a woman! Even at that moment, with stinking death filling his nostrils and corroding his very soul, he knew he had never seen anyone like her, and that after seeing her, it would never matter again.

"Well?" she demanded.

He glanced back at the bodies. "I don't think this is quite the place to talk." When he turned, he was startled to see a cocked pistol in her hand. She was as fast as many men he had known in his time as a gunfighter. He looked at her and smiled thinly. "Why the artillery?" he asked.

"Mister Matt Turlock," she said softly. "My brother's old army comrade, who fought with him during the Seven Days, at Antietam and Gettysburg. The man who would ride with my brother from Texas to safeguard him and his money. What *happened* to Jim and his money, Mister Turlock?"

Matt ran his tongue around his lips. He could hardly tell her the real truth. Not now in any case. "We parted company south of here," he said, and he knew instantly that she did not believe him.

"And Jim was found shot to death in one of Morg Engels's old houses near Brushy Creek. The money gone. His *guard* gone. *You,* Mister Turlock!"

There was nothing for him to say.

She looked him up and down. "Why *did* you come around here, Mister Turlock?"

He glanced back over his shoulder. The sun flashed briefly on something metallic, or perhaps the glass of a pair of binoculars, high on the ridge to the east.

"Mister Turlock?"

He turned. "I work for Morg Engels," he said quietly.

Her eyes narrowed again. "Very odd, isn't it? My brother hires you to guard him; you leave him south of here; he's found shot to death and his money gone; his guard, by a curious happenstance, starts work for Mister Morgan Engels. Or were you working for Morg Engels all the time, Mister Matt Turlock?"

The flies buzzed steadily. There was the sound of escaping gas from one of the corpses, and the foul stench crept about the two people standing there. "I'll help you with the bodies," he said, for lack of anything else to say. She was like her brother, all right.

"No," she said quietly. She stepped backward a little more. "Let them lie. I'll bring some of my men to help me. I doubt if those two poor souls lying there would want your hands on them even now."

"You're cutting things rather fine," he said. "I can't talk now but give me a chance some time."

She looked about. "Who is there to listen except them?" She jerked her head toward the two rustlers.

"You don't understand," he said,

She stood there with the pistol steady in her sum hand and her eyes as hard and level as a man's. "I understand quite enough," she said. "I'm going back to the ranch to get help, then I'll ride on into Roca Blanca, Mister Turlock. To what? To an inquest, Mister Turlock. An inquest into the death of my brother. I expect to see certain others there, Mister Turlock. Morgan Engels for one. For Morgan Engels will say that my brother was killed in self-defense, while trespassing on E Bar E land."

She knew the plot and the script well enough.

Leslie Sturtevant let down the hammer of her pistol and sheathed the weapon. "Yes, my brother was shot by Morg Engels or one of his men in self-defense. No one will know where you were, Mister Turlock, or what happened to the money Jim was bringing from Texas. Isn't that right, Mister Turlock?"

"You're telling the story," he said quietly.

She laughed bitterly. "It doesn't matter. Morg Engels always wanted the J Lazy S. With Jim gone and the money gone as well, I'll lose the ranch." She raised her head proudly. "But I'll fight to the last ditch, Mister Turlock. You can take that message back to Morgan Engels, *Judas!*" She turned on a heel and strode purposefully to her buckboard, swung up into the seat, slapped the reins on the dusty rumps of the team, and rode swiftly back toward the south end of the lovely valley.

Matt shoved back his hat, rolled a cigarette, snapped a match on a thumbnail, and lighted the cigarette, never taking his eyes from that buckboard and its lovely, and *spirited* driver. "Well, I'll be dipped in buffalo manure," he said wonderingly. He wrinkled his nose as more gas flowed about him, then turned to look toward the ridge. Once again, he saw a brief reflection of light. He walked languidly to the sorrel, keeping it between him and the watcher on the ridge.

He withdrew his Winchester from its sheath and levered a round into the chamber. Then he rounded the horse, raised and sighted the rifle, and squeezed off a fast shot. The echo rolled along the valley, and a spurt of dust rose within two feet of where the flashes had shown. There was a sudden movement in the scant brush up there, as a hat bobbed up and down and then vanished. A moment later, dust rose from behind the ridge, and the faint thudding of shod hooves on hard earth came to him. A slow grin spread across Matt Turlock's brown face.

He mounted the sorrel and rode slowly back toward the ranch. He was between the devil and the deep blue sea right now. He didn't dare tell Leslie the truth, much as he wanted to. This was no time to buck Morg Engels; not quite yet. But there was something he could do. It was chancy, downright dangerous in fact, but it was a necessary gambit in the tight and perilous game he was playing. He had no other choice.

CHAPTER FIVE

Matt Turlock was well away from the ranch before moon-rise, fleeting south over the rolling hills, riding a blocky chestnut that had a fair turn of speed and plenty of stamina. Now and then, he looked back through the darkness. Morgan Engels had been away in Roca Blanca with Cato Semmes and Monk when Matt had returned to the ranch. There had been no sign of Shorty Carnes, and Jack Vance was away for the night on the far north range of the ranch with the working vaqueros of the huge spread. As far as Matt knew, no one had seen him leave, but one could never be sure of not being watched on the E Bar E. Not Matt Turlock in any case.

He splashed across a creek and up the slope on the far side just as the first light of the moon tinged the eastern skies. Far to the east he saw a cluster of yellow lights, dim and flickering, the lights of Roca Blanca, and it was possible that Leslie Sturtevant was there if she had gone on to the inquest that day. The memory of her flooded over him, and he forced himself to drive it away, for this night he'd have to be more than just keenly alert; he'd have to have the senses of an Apache.

The moon was up high when he reached the lonely valley where Jim Sturtevant had died such a short time past. Matt dismounted and led the chestnut along below the crest of the ridge until he reached a place where he could look down upon the scattered and decaying adobes where he and Jim Sturtevant had holed up that tragic night.

There was no sign of life. The stream flowed along under the light of the moon like molten silver. The wind whispered through the scrub trees and rippled the thick grasses. The moon shone brightly on the bullet-pocked walls of the buildings.

He lay there for a time, then drew out the binoculars he had taken from Shorty Carnes's warbag. He focused them. In the light of the moon, it was almost as clear as daylight in the deserted valley. He studied the buildings foot by foot. Nothing. They looked much the same as they had the night he and Jim had dismounted there for water and had been drygulched by Morg Engels and his *corrida* of gunfighters.

Matt lowered the glasses. He wanted to wait until the moon was gone, but time was precious, and he didn't want to be missed from the ranch when Engels returned. He was walking on thin enough ice as it was, and even his ambush and capture of the rustlers wouldn't save him from the cold wrath and dark revenge of Morgan Engels.

He had to chance it. He led the chestnut farther along the ridge, then down toward the creek through a deep swale until he could get the mount no closer to the buildings without being seen. He picketed the chestnut, took his Winchester, then vanished into the scrub timber edging the creek. He worked his way through the timber until he reached a bend in the creek, where he waded across, thigh-deep in the cold rushing waters.

He padded through a bosque of cottonwoods until he could see the moonlit southern side of the main building, with its dark staring eyes of unglazed windows. Shards of broken glass reflected the moonlight from where they lay on the ground. He squatted behind a stump and studied the lay of the ground again, then he bellied through the brush, down into a shallow arroyo, along it to a pile of old building material, planking, eroded adobe bricks and rusted sheet metal, where he lay flat against the ground, took off his hat and eyed the buildings again. They seemed deserted, sure enough, yet...

Half an hour swiftly passed. He had to go in. He drew in a deep breath, then flitted like an ungainly ghost across an open area to flatten himself against the wall of an outbuilding. Ten minutes flicked past. He worked his way around the side of the outbuilding, past the tumbled ruins of a windmill structure, over a decaying litter of junk and stopped next to the sagging privy. One of the boards had split wide away from the side. He eased in and grinned to himself as he studied the main building through the half-moon on the badly warped door. Some observation post! At least it hadn't been used for quite some time.

Matt stepped outside and walked silently to the rear of the main building with his rifle cocked and ready in his hands. He stepped in through a window, and an odd feeling came over him. It was eerie in there after the bright moonlight outside, and the memory of Jim Sturtevant came swiftly back to roost. There were dark stains on the packed earthen floor of the room. The stains of Jim's blood. The shattered body would be in Roca Blanca, but somehow the spirit of the man seemed yet to be in the old adobe where he had met his death. At the thought of the way he had gone, Matt's big hands tightened almost convulsively on his rifle. Cato Semmes! There was a blood reckoning due for him.

Jim had said it was an execution. As long as he was alive, they would know they'd have a fight on their hands.

Then Jim's words came back to him, almost as though the man himself was there to utter them. *"Les needs your help. Your life is worth more to me than this money. Les can't face Engels and his* corrida *alone, but you could help if you wanted to..."*

Matt walked into the room where he had fought against the hidden riflemen that wet night. Brass crunched beneath his boots. He waited, listening, tongue touching his upper lip, waiting and listening. Nothing... It was time. He turned and walked to the filthy fireplace. He knelt and reached up inside of it to where a cavity was in the side wall and closed his hand on a thick fold of paper. He withdrew it and walked to the nearest window, riffling through it. It was all there, twenty one-hundred-dollar bills.

"All right, Turlock," the dry voice said behind him. "Drop that money, raise your hands, and turn around."

Matt whirled, hurling the wad of money straight at the face of the man who stood across the room, then dropped to the floor, at the same time drawing his Colt, cocking it, and thrusting it forward to fire. It rapped twice, the roaring of the double discharge almost splitting his eardrums. The man fell forward without a word. Matt rolled over just as a gun spat flame and smoke through a front window. "Jesus, not again," he said.

He rolled flat against the front wall. Boots grated on the gravelly *caliche* outside. "Charley?" a man called out.

Mat slowly raised his hot Colt.

"Charley? You get him, Charley?" the man called. The voice was vaguely familiar, but Matt could not place the owner of it.

Matt waited, eyes wide in the dimness. A hand came through the window and gripped the side of it. A man heaved himself into the smoky room. Then he saw Matt. He jumped back and leveled his Colt. It rapped deafeningly, and the slug plucked at Matt's hat. His Colt bucked back in his hand, and the man fell down on hands and knees, grunting in agony. "Oh God," he said thickly. He tried to raise the gun. Matt fired once. The man pitched sideways and lay still, arms outflung, staring at the dim ceiling with wide eyes that would never see again.

Matt crawled across that filthy room of death and got his rifle. He stood up and eased across the room to the north window, peered quickly outside, then stepped through to stand dose against the side of the building, in the poor shadows there.

It was as quiet as death out there after the hell and uproar in the confinement of the room, and his ears rang like a bell. His eyes smarted from the acrid burnt powder. Some of it swirled through the window on the draft and parted to flow past his head, giving him an eerie, death-dealing appearance, which was not at all deceiving, for few men could deal out death as swiftly and accurately as Matt Turlock.

He wet his lips, then softly worked his way to the back of the building. He knew now who those two men were. They were *vaqueros* of the E Bar E, lesser lights in Engels's gunfighting *corrida,* but still men who could handle six-gun and rifle along with most men, minus fighting Texans, of course. The grim thought was Matt Turlock's as he paused to eye the moonlit terrain. Had there been only two of them? He knew one thing for certain; he'd have to get them all, or head out on the owlhoot trail for Texas with hot death breathing down his dirty shirt collar.

He was just about to head for the cover of the arroyo when he held himself back. The moon was sharply etching shadows on the cold-looking, silvered earth. Nothing moved. The wind had died away. Matt tested the night with his senses, and although hot haste ran through him to get out of that silent place of death, something else held him back. Once again, he stepped out. *"No, Matt!"* the warning voice seemed to say. Cold sweat worked down his sides. The voice had been that of Jim Sturtevant, but Jim Sturtevant was surely dead!

Slowly he bent down and scooped up a handful of gravel with his right hand. He tossed it against the side of the nearest building. Instantly a gun flashed and roared not fifteen feet from him, from the far side of the house. He saw the muzzle, a thin line of black in the moonlight. He eased back around the side of the house and swiftly took off his boots and hat. He padded quickly to the front of the house and peered around the corner. Nothing but the moonlight on the naked ground. Once again, he picked up a handful of gravel, then walked across in front of the house to peer around the corner. A broad-shouldered man was crouched there. He looked toward the privy.

Matt cast the handful of gravel far out. The man jumped and turned, swinging his rifle like a duck hunter. Then he saw Matt. Both guns flashed together, but Matt had already moved around the corner, even as he fired. The other slug whined past the place where his head had been. Matt ran like a deer along the front side of the house, down the north side, along the back of the house until he turned the corner to see the man swaying and stumbling for shelter near one of the outbuildings. The man turned and saw Matt. "No, Turlock," he pleaded, then he snapped up his rifle. Matt's slug caught him in the chest even as he pressed trigger. His bullet sang thinly over Matt's head. The man fell heavily atop his smoking rifle and lay still.

Matt wiped the sweat from his taut face. He levered a fresh round into the rifle, then looked for more men. But a feeling of relief came over him. This time there was no warning voice. He walked over to the fallen man and rolled him over. The gray face of Jack Vance stared up at him, the foreman of the E Bar E, who had supposedly been working the north range of the big ranch.

Matt scouted the area. There were no more of them

to be seen. He stepped beside the sagging shed and lighted a cigarette, looking down at the sprawled body of Jack Vance, knowing full well he, Matt, had walked into a trap but that it had sprung on the three men sent to trap him. He knew well enough now that he could not go back to the ranch leaving the three of them lying there. There was only one thing to do.

He found their horses picketed half a mile from the buildings. He sweated each of the men atop a horse, then led the nervous animals toward the moonlit hills until he found a deep cleft not far from loose and shattered rock. He dumped each of the bodies into the cleft, then hauled rocks to cover them. When he was done, he erased his tracks with brush, then rode one of the horses and led the other two until he reached his picketed chestnut. He rode back to the house and spent an hour eliminating every trace he could find of that night's bloody work. The moon had vanished when he was done. He led the three horses far into the hills and picketed them loosely. When they got thirsty enough they'd break loose and either keep going, or return to the E Bar E. Let Morg Engels solve the mystery of his three missing gunmen.

Matt rode through the darkness toward the Bonito Valley, his mind weary with the load of thoughts upon it. Two thousand dollars wasn't enough to meet the due note on the J Lazy S, but it would help. Three thousand more was needed to stave off the wolf at the door. He narrowed his eyes. Morg Engels had those three thousand iron men, rightfully Leslie Sturtevant's money.

He didn't want to return to that silent ranch with the smell of sudden death hanging about it. Every nerve and fiber cried out to shy away from the place and head for the hills, to keep going plumb out of New Mexico. But that was not Matt Turlock's way.

He tethered the chestnut to the corral fence and walked quietly toward the big house. Not a light showed. Maybe Morg Engels and his sidemen were still in Roca

Blanca. He had to risk it. Without that money, Leslie Sturtevant would be helpless against the debt against the ranch.

Matt left his rifle on the back porch and then eased open the kitchen door to step quickly into the house. It was dark and quiet; almost too quiet to suit him, but there was no sight nor sound of life. A clock ticked quietly in the darkness. A mouse scurried across the floor.

Matt walked to the hallway that led to the big living room. He paused at each of the bedroom doors to listen. There was no sound from any of them. As far as he knew, Morgan Engels lived and slept alone in the big house.

He waited fifteen minutes in the darkness of the hallway, listening for sounds from the big living room, or from someone approaching the house. Then he knew he'd have to get on with his night's work. He was tired and tense, but he must do the thing for which he had come into that dark and quiet house.

He searched swiftly but efficiently throughout the room, trying to find a place where a man would keep cash. The desk revealed nothing. The table drawers held a miscellaneous collection of odds and ends. He walked to the fireplace and felt the rough field rock which formed it. Everything seemed well-mortared in place. He scratched his bristly jaws. Time was racing along. Then the thought struck him. He knelt and felt within the fireplace, in the same place he had cached the two thousand dollars in the old abandoned 'dobe to the south. His questing hand struck a ledge, felt into a cavity, and struck a tin container. He withdrew it and opened it. His fingers felt paper. Money! He withdrew the wad. Quickly he counted off three thousand dollars in one-hundred-dollar bills. "I'll be dipped in buffalo manure," he said wonderingly. He replaced the box and stuffed the money into a shirt pocket, then turned to go. Matt froze where he was. Boots had struck the wooden decking of the front porch, and he could hear the low voices of men.

Matt padded across the room and peered through a window. Morg Engels was standing at the edge of the porch talking to two men, Cato Semmes and Monk. Matt's blood seemed to turn to ice in his veins as he saw Engels turn and walk toward the door. Matt moved quickly, flattening himself against the wall as the door-knob turned. He held his breath. Engels opened the door and turned to speak. "Put the horses away, then check on Turlock," he said. He turned his head a little and looked right into the taut face of Mat Turlock. Matt's left hand pushed the door closed at the same time that his right fist connected solidly with the jaw of the rancher. He caught Engels as he sagged down toward the floor, then pressed an ear against the door to listen.

"Boss?" called Monk. "You fall or somethin'?"

Matt's throat dried up. His heart slammed erratically against his rib cage.

"Boss?" called out Monk once more.

"Come on, Monk," said Cato. "Youah been hearin' things."

"Mebbe, mebbe not!"

"Come on, dammit! It's late. I got to get some sleep!"

Matt dragged Engels to the couch and dumped him. He looked closely into the man's face. He was still out cold. There was no time to lose. Matt hurried through the house, snatched up his rifle, ran quietly toward the bunkhouse, eased open the door, then tiptoed to his bunk. Shorty Carnes was quietly snoring in the next bunk. Matt stripped off his shirt and boots, hooked his hat on a nail, shoved his rifle and hat under the bunk, then slid under the cover, drawing and cocking his Colt as he did so. He had just closed his eyes when the door swung quietly open.

Boots squeaked on the floor, and Matt could feel the presence of the two men. He lay very still, breathing slowly and steadily, knowing full well those four cold eyes were studying him.

"Restin' like a baby," said Monk.

"Yeh, the bastahd. Wheah the hell did Engels *think* he was? Chasin' some filly in Roca Blanca?"

"He ain't like you, Cato. He's a nice boy."

"Yell, like a boy copperhead. One of these days..."

They padded to their bunks.

Matt lay there with his mind as taut as a bow string. He'd have to wait until they fell asleep, but even then, it would be like treading through a den of rattlesnakes. Had Morg Engels recognized him in the split second between the time he had seen a man so close to him and the impact of a rock-hard fist? How long would the rancher be unconscious? If he cried out before those two men fell asleep... Matt's luck had been phenomenally good already that night, and maybe Jim Sturtevant's spirit *was* watching over Matt. Did spirits require rest? If Jim let him down now. Oh God, he thought, make those two ornery bastards drop right off.

Something crashed in the night. A man was yelling at the top of his voice from somewhere near the big house. Cato Semmes and Monk were racing past Matt's bunk to the door. Shorty Carnes was sitting up in bed. Cato ripped open the door and sprinted toward the house, followed by Monk. Shorty swung his thin legs over the side of his bunk. "What the hell is wrong now?" he said plaintively.

There were other men yelling and calling from the bigger bunkhouse behind the small one in which Matt and Shorty were. Matt pulled on his boots, and crammed on his hat.

"Hey, how come you're all dressed?" asked Shorty suspiciously. "How come you wasn't sleepin' in your drawers like a man should?"

"Shut up, Shorty!" Matt snatched up his rifle.

"You had yore gun belt on too and a cocked six-shooter in bed with yuh? You gone loco?"

Boots thudded on the hard ground as men ran past the bunkhouse. Then it came. "Get that bastard Turlock!" yelled Monk. "He slugged the boss. Took his money too. Get him!"

Shorty opened his mouth, but a rifle barrel was laid neatly alongside his head, and he dropped back on the bunk as nicely as a baby dropping off to sleep; a baby with a horsey face and a yellow-stained mustache.

Matt lowered his head, held his rifle out in front of him, and dived through a window to the sound of shattering glass. He rolled over and got to his feet to sprint between the two buildings, heading for the corral, and even as he ran, he turned and levered out two fast and wild shots to stop the rush of E Bar E men.

He darted alongside the corral as guns cracked and slugs searched aimlessly through the darkness for one Matt Turlock, just about to lose his position with the E Bar E. The chestnut was where he had left it. He ripped the bridle reins free and swung up into the saddle, slamming the rifle barrel against the chestnut's rump for more acceleration. They plunged down the slope with bullets snapping about them like hot and hungry hornets.

The chestnut cleared a low fence and struck out like a frightened deer, with Matt Turlock low in the saddle, and cold naked fear applying whip and spurs to both man and mount in a mad frenzy.

They slammed up the ridge, topped it, and roared down the far side toward the distant river. Two hundred yards from the river, Matt drew in the chestnut and slid from the saddle. He slapped it on the rump with the gun and watched it gallop north. Then Matt ran toward the river, and slid from the bank, gasping in the cold water as it rose to his belly, driving the breath from him.

He was laboring halfway across, chest deep in the flood

when he heard the distant rataplan of gunfire from the north. He grinned evilly, then cursed as he went in over his head. He struck out and swam until his boots hit soft bottom. Matt dragged himself out on the west bank and lay flat, his breathing harsh and erratic, his body shaking as though with ague, water draining from his clothing, and he wished to God above, with all his strength, for the first time in his short and violent life, that he had been born a girl baby.

CHAPTER SIX

is teeth were chattering so loudly that he was sure Morg Engels's boys could hear him clear from the far north end of the valley where the occasional flash of a gun pinpointed the darkness. He walked slowly up the road. The buildings of the J Lazy S were somewhere up ahead of him, but he was there before he realized it, and just as he reached to open the Texas gate, someone moved in the shadows of a small bosque. "Just you stand there, mister! Raise them hands!" the voice came from the darkness, and he could barely make out the tall man standing there.

He raised the rifle over his head with both hands.

"Throw that rifle down."

Had it been possible that one of Engels's men had cut him off? If it was one of them, he would be better off to shoot it out then and there.

"You hear me, mister?" The cocking of a gun sounded loudly in the stillness.

Matt threw down the gun.

"Raise them hands again, clasping them atop your hat!"

"The hat is wet, mister," said Matt. "I'm liable to spoil the blocking."

"I'll be damned. A comic! Well, we need one around here."

"Around where, mister?"

"Here on the J Lazy S. Where did you think you was?"

Matt grinned widely. "On the doorstep of hell," he said.

"I don't get it."

"You will. Can I see Miss Sturtevant?"

"Why?"

"I have something for her."

"Come through the gate and watch what you do with them hands, *hombre*."

Matt walked meekly through the gate. Far up the valley a gun flashed.

"What's all the shooting about?" asked the unseen man.

"Well, if you must know, *hombre,* they're chasing what they think is me."

"Who are you?"

"Name of Turlock. Matt Turlock."

"Well, I'll be dipped in a privy!"

Matt walked up the narrow winding road toward the house. Someone was standing on the porch. "Who is it, Sid?" Leslie asked.

"Turlock, Miss Sturtevant."

There was a tense pause. "I see." She opened the door. "Bring him in."

She did not light a lamp until all the shades were drawn. The man named Sid, a lantern-jawed, rawboned character with washed-out blue eyes, relieved Matt of his Colt. "He's clean, Miss Sturtevant," he said.

"Thanks, Sid. Now go back to the bosque and watch the road. If you hear anyone coming, let me know at once. Where is Manuel?"

"Up on the hill behind the barn."

"And Bennie?"

Sid grinned. "Loading his old double-barreled shotgun as far as I know."

"Don't let him do anything rash."

"No, ma'am." Sid eyed Matt. "You think you'll be safe enough with him here?"

She sat down behind a desk and placed a Colt on top of it. She looked levelly at Matt. "I think so."

Sid shifted his chew. "She's purty accurate with that handgun, Mister. Offhand, I wouldn't make no hasty moves."

Matt nodded.

When the tall man had left, she eyed Matt. "You're soaking wet," she said.

He waved a hand. "It doesn't matter."

"What happened this time?"

He grinned. "We had a little misunderstanding. A mere trifle, but I had to leave in quite a hurry."

"A habit to which you are quite accustomed," she said dryly.

"How about a truce, Miss Sturtevant?" he said wearily. He smiled a little. "I haven't done much but fight since I came into this territory."

"Isn't there something about sleeping in the bed one makes?" she said.

"One usually does," he said. "Can I take something out of my shirt pocket? It ain't a stingy gun or a spring knife, ma'am."

"Go on," she said.

He took out the soaked wad of money and tossed it onto the desk. "That is yours," he said.

She glanced at the money and then at him. "I don't understand."

"It is simply this: That five thousand dollars there is the money Jim brought from Texas."

"And you had it all the time?"

He shook his head. "It was part of the price for my life the night Jim was killed."

There was a look of scorn on her lovely face. "You *paid* your way out of it?"

"Dammit!" he snapped, shaken out of his usual calm. "Will you listen to me?"

"Go on."

He quickly told her the story of the money and how he had gotten it. She studied him. "You said there was someone watching the old adobe where Jim had been murdered. How did you get past them?"

He smiled. "They let me walk into the trap, figuring I'd show them where the *dinero* was."

"And then what happened?"

"I'm here, ain't I?" he said flatly.

"Where are *they*, Mister Turlock?"

"Back there."

"Dead?"

He nodded.

"How many of them?"

"Three, ma'am."

She leaned forward and spoke in a low, probing tone. "You mean to tell me you were trapped in that building by three of Morg Engels's men and you shot it out with them? That you killed all three of them and you're sitting there unscathed?"

"I said I was here," he answered her, and his hard eyes met her softer eyes like flicking blades of steel.

A cold feeling crept over her as she eyed this lobo of a man, this mercenary, this sure killer, this skilled professional. "And the rest of the money?" she said at last.

"I told you I took it from Engels's house."

"And how much more blood was spilled in the process?"

Matt stood up slowly and reached for his hat.

"Where do you think you're going?" she demanded.

He walked to the desk and rested his clenched hands on it, leaning forward so that he was hardly more than two feet from her. "Understand this, Miss Sturtevant," he said quietly, "you are dealing with men who will not stop at murder to gain their ends. They murdered your brother to get him out of the way. They would have murdered me if I had not lit a shuck out of that hellhole across the ridge, two jumps, and a holler just ahead of enough hot lead to fill a gallon bucket. I am a paid gunfighter, not a missionary." He placed a hand on the wad of wet money. "This is rightfully yours. Don't insult me for the methods I used to get it. It was a promise to your dying brother, Miss Sturtevant, and in my way of life that promise must be kept, no matter what I do for a living. *I kept that promise.*"

She glanced away. "Can you tell me about his last moments?"

"He knew he was done for. They had waited for us to get him, and me too. He told me how to get out of there alive. He said my life was worth more to him than the money. It was the price I paid to get out of there. I held back two thousand dollars, as I told you, and that was a damned long shot, Miss Sturtevant. Engels hired me but he was always suspicious of me. I got myself in a little more solidly with him by turning back those rustlers."

"Doesn't *that* rest on your conscience?"

"As God is my judge, I did not know what manner of man Morgan Engels really was at that time. I have no pity for rustlers, ma'am. But I thought they'd face legal justice, not the cold-blooded justice of Morgan Engels. I would never have handed those three men over to him had I known what he meant to do to them."

"I believe you," she said simply. "I have been hard on you, Mister Turlock. The loss of Jim was a great blow to me. I still cannot believe a man who loved life as Jim did, is no longer here to enjoy it. But, in his memory, and for my own satisfaction, I mean to fight this thing out until Morgan Engels is defeated!"

He smiled thinly. "Then there will be more blood spilled."

"That cannot be helped."

He nodded. "It's a way of life."

"And you? What will you do now? They'll kill you on sight. Manuel will guide you through the mountains. I can give you a good horse. You had better leave as quickly as possible."

His eyes glittered in the lamplight. "I am afraid you don't understand me, Miss Sturtevant. There was something else left to me by your brother. He said you couldn't face Engels and his *corrida* alone. He said I could help if I wanted to. Well, I am here, Miss Sturtevant."

She shook her head. "I can pay off the note now with this money." She looked up at him. "I will fight to hold this land."

"With a handful of men led by a woman?"

"That is how it will be done."

"He'll hurrah you, steal your cattle, burn your buildings, poison your waterholes, cut your fences, frighten off your men."

"I stay."

He shook his head. "This is madness!"

"I stay!"

He shrugged. "All right then but know what you are facing. Know your enemy better than you know yourself, Miss Sturtevant."

"Will you leave?"

"No," he said.

"I don't want your blood on my hands."

He grinned. "Let me worry about that."

She stood up. "Thanks for what you did for Jim, and for bringing me this money. But I can't be responsible for your death, and as sure as I am standing here, Mister Turlock, they will not stop until they *have* killed you."

Matt turned slowly. He raised his head. "It's too late," he said.

"Why?"

He jerked a thumb over his shoulder. "They're already looking for me."

She stared at him. "How do you know that? I can't hear anything."

"I can," he said simply. "Can I have my guns?"

She nodded. He walked to the table where Sid had left the weapons. Quickly he emptied the both of them of their cartridges.

"There are fresh cartridges in that drawer," she said.

He nodded. He reloaded both guns and sheathed his Colt.

"I think you are fooling me," she said at last.

He turned. "Listen," he said quietly.

The wind carried the voices of men to them, but it was the first indication she had had of their presence, and her hearing was excellent. She looked at him again and a cold eerie feeling crept over her. How had he known? *How had he known?*

"Put out the light," he said. He walked to the door and opened it a crack as the lamp was extinguished. He could not see anyone on the road, but he knew they were there.

Then the soft thudding of many hooves came to him. He closed the door. She was close behind him. "What will you do?" he asked.

"I won't run. I *can't* run," he said. He grinned.

She reached behind a chair and picked up a double-barreled shotgun.

"Don't shoot at them!" he said.

She smiled. "I didn't intend to. But you warned me that I must know my enemy better than I know myself."

"You're learning fast," he said.

"Miss Sturtevant!" called out Sid from beyond the porch. "Someone here to see you!"

She looked at Matt. He nodded. He quickly levered a round into his Winchester and stepped back to flatten himself against the wall.

She opened the door. "Who is it, Sid?"

"Mister Engels and some of his men."

"I'll be right out." She stepped just beyond the door. Already in the east, there was a faint suspicion of the false dawn.

"You rise early, Miss Sturtevant," said the dry voice of Morgan Engels.

Matt could see her composed face. "There seems to be some excitement up the valley, Mr. Engels. Hunting, perhaps?"

"Hawww," said Monk. "That's good! We *was* hunting!"

"Shut up, Monk," said Cato Semmes.

"We're looking for a man by the name of Matt Turlock," said the ranch owner.

"He's not here, if that is what you mean," she said quietly.

"Do you know him?"

She paused. "I have met him," she said.

"That's strange. I didn't know he had been around here."

"I met him yesterday," she said. "It was on your land, Mister Engels. There were two of your victims there. Rustlers, Mister Engels."

He laughed. "Victims, Miss Sturtevant? Bartolomeo Sanchez had been warned by me. He knew the penalty for stealing my cattle."

Her face worked a little. "It was utterly inhuman," she said.

"I didn't come here to discuss that. Is Matt Turlock here?"

"No."

Matt wet his lips. He could almost see them standing there like bloodhounds on the leash, waiting to be slipped.

"We found his horse at the far end of the valley. He couldn't have gotten very far."

"Why don't you look for him there then?"

"I have an idea he fooled us temporarily with that old trick, Miss Sturtevant. Quite like him. He's vicious, treacherous, and murderous."

"Coming from a peer of his, that's quite a compliment."

She was a bit of a Tartar, thought Matt. He couldn't help but grin.

"He has stolen some money from me," continued Engels.

"I am sure you'll find him...elsewhere."

Engels coughed dryly. "I hope your well-known sympathies for such people are not wasted. There is a cloud over this man, Miss Sturtevant. He came into this country with your brother, you know."

"Yes."

"But you didn't know him personally?"

"No."

"It's almost a certainty that he murdered your brother for the money he had on him."

"That's strange. You testified at the inquest that my brother opened fire on you and your men and was killed by them in self-defense."

Answer that one, Engels, thought Matt.

"That is what we think happened."

"Come now, Mister Engels! You said my brother shot at you and he was killed in return."

"It's also entirely possible, Miss Sturtevant, that it was *not* your brother who shot at us. That it was Matt Turlock. We returned the fire of this unseen man. When we entered the adobe, we found the body of your brother. There was no sign of Turlock, but he had been there. It's almost a certainty now that Turlock had murdered your brother, saw us coming, opened fire upon us, then managed somehow to escape, leaving your brother's body there, without the money of course."

Very neatly put, thought Matt.

"That story seems to suit your purpose very well."

"Miss Sturtevant, you seem inclined to favor this man. May I ask why?"

"I know little about *him*. I did not see what happened at the time my brother was murdered. I know *you* by reputation, Mister Engels."

"And?"

"I would not put the murder of my brother past you, Mister Engels."

"Strong words, Miss Sturtevant."

"You wanted a plain answer."

"Let's stop this debate and find Turlock," snapped Cato Semmes. "All this time he could be clean over them mountains!"

"May we look around, Miss Sturtevant?" asked Engels.

"Do you have a warrant, Mister Engels?"

"No."

"Then I must ask you to leave."

"I can get a warrant easily enough."

"Then go and get it."

"By that time Turlock could be across the border," said Engels.

"You will not search this place, Mister Engels!"

"You don't think you can stop me, do you?"

She stepped back a little.

"Cato, you go around the back," said Engels. "Monk, you come with me. Out of the way, ma'am."

Leslie picked up the shotgun and swept both hammers back. She held it at waist level. "There are Blue Whistlers in both barrels," she said flatly, "with split wads, Mister Engels."

There was a long pause. No man in his right mind would buck up against such a threat. The dawn light was clearly on Leslie now, and the look upon her lovely face showed that she meant exactly what she had said.

"That thing could go off, Boss," said Monk nervously.

"Best get out of heah," said Cato Semmes.

Another pause. "All right, Miss Sturtevant," said

Engels coldly. "You win this hand. But know this! You have temporarily stopped me from hunting a killer. But I will be back. I will find Matt Turlock. Further, I mean to have this ranch. I know you cannot meet the note on it. I took over that note, unknown to you. The deadline is no later than tomorrow, in Boca Blanca. If that money is not paid, I take over the J Lazy S, and nothing can stop me. *Nothing*, Miss Sturtevant."

There was nothing for her to say. Their boots thudded on the ground. A gate squeaked open and then shut. Hooves thudded on the road. Minutes ticked past. The dawn wind picked up, and the big Chicago Standard windmill ground slowly into whirring life.

She stepped inside and let down the hammers of the shotgun. She placed it in its niche in the wall behind a chair. She looked wearily at Matt. "Well, Mister Turlock?"

He smiled. "Never try to think on an empty stomach, ma'am."

"I see your point."

He nodded. "I'd be obliged for some dry clothing."

"You can take some of Jim's, if it doesn't bother you."

He shook his head. "He was my friend. During the war we often were forced to wear the clothing of the dead. A man gets used to it."

She placed a hand on his arm. "I hope you haven't opened the way to your death by staying here, Mister Turlock."

"A man can't run all his life, ma'am. I feel as though this is my last fight." He grinned. "Without pay, too. I'm slipping."

She laughed. "You are a strange man, Mister Turlock, a very strange man indeed."

"The name is Matt, ma'am."

"Matt, then."

In those two words and the manner in which she spoke them, Matt Turlock had already been paid for his last fight.

CHAPTER SEVEN

Matt Turlock had tried to cheer up the young woman during breakfast, but it was a thankless task, and in reality, there wasn't much for her to be cheerful about. True, she had the money to pay off the note against the J Lazy S, but that money had cost the life of her beloved brother. Matt Turlock had warned her what would happen if Engels started a range war with her. Her cattle could be brazenly rustled or shot down by mysterious marksmen on the open range. Strange fires would start in outbuildings and line shacks. Cattle would drop dead, swollen from poisoned water. Fences would be cut down, and the tangled wires dragged for miles across the range. Bullets would whisper in out of the dark and shatter windows. Hands would be difficult, if not impossible to get. One way or another, step by step, the slow poison of Morgan Engels would kill off the stock of the J Lazy S until there could be no income. But the land would always be there. The West Bonito Valley, well named, and well famed as the finest land of its kind in that part of the Territory of New Mexico.

"There is nothing cruder than a range war, Miss Sturtevant," said Matt. He sipped at his coffee.

A grizzled head poked into the room from the

kitchen. "Don't let that jasper scare yuh, ma'am. Old Bennie is here to fight for yuh!" He shot a withering glance at Matt. "Don't make fightin' men no more like they used to. I can still out-cook, outjump, outride, outshoot, and outkill any of the *boys* that calls themselves *men* around here, ma'am."

"You can outbull 'em too, Old Timer," said Matt

"Say!"

Leslie smiled. "Now, Bennie, Mister Turlock is our guest."

"Humph!" The grizzled head vanished.

"He means well," said Leslie.

"How many men do you have all told?"

She leaned back in her chair and drummed lightly on the checkered cloth. "Seven. Sid, he's my ramrod. Manuel, a loyal person, but a boy, really. Then there's Warner, Seb, Buck, and Gus. Then Bennie of course." She smiled.

"You damn betcha!" said Bennie from the kitchen. "Beggin' yore pardon, ma'am."

"Not very many," said Matt. "Will they fight if they have to?"

She shrugged. "They are loyal enough. I don't expect them to die for me, Matt. In addition, they are hardly gun-fighters such as you are."

"Paaah!" said Bennie. "Now in my day!"

"Bennie!" snapped Leslie. She was getting edgy.

Matt refilled their coffee cups. "It wouldn't be difficult to pay off the note, of course. Engels could hardly stop you from doing that, unless of course..." His voice trailed off.

"You mean he'd try to stop us on the road, Matt?"

"You'd never know it was him until it was too late, ma'am."

"Would he go that far?"

"Yes."

She bit her lower lip. "I don't know what to do."

He eyed her. "There is one thing you can do."

"Go on."

"Accuse Engels of the murder of your brother."

"Yes?"

"I am a witness to that, Miss Sturtevant."

"How long yuh think *you'd* last, young fella?" demanded Bennie. His head shot into view. Then he vanished as quickly as he had appeared.

"He has a strong point there, Matt," she said.

Matt nodded.

"Anything else?" she asked, almost hopelessly.

"Pay the note. Fight."

"With a handful of men?" She shook her head. "Cato Semmes, Monk, and Jack Vance alone could wipe us out."

"Not Jack Vance," said Matt quietly.

She looked quickly at him.

"He was one of the three waiting for me where your brother was killed," he said.

"He was just one of them," she said at last. Her lovely eyes studied him.

"It's fight them or be beaten by them."

"What do you suggest?"

Matt leaned forward. "Every man has his weaknesses and his price. Even men as tough as Morg Engels, Cato Semmes and Monk. Together they are a hard combination to beat. Separately it might be done."

She nodded. "It sounds easy, Matt. You know that it really isn't easy." Her eyes narrowed. "Besides, why is it your fight? You can leave. You did your job." She was startled at the change that came over his lean face.

"Blood pays off blood," he said coldly. "Jim Sturtevant was my friend. Perhaps my only real friend. We went through a lot together in the war. It was more than that, though. Sometimes a man is lucky enough to meet another man as I met your brother. Maybe up to the time they killed him, there wasn't any real purpose in my life. I am a wanderer. A wind-devil, they call men like me in some parts of the West. Come from nowhere and go no place. But before I leave this place, Miss Sturtevant, each one of those men who was at the adobe the night Jim was killed, will pay off that debt in their blood, or they'll have to kill me to welsh on the payment!"

She stood up and walked to a window to look out at the lovely West Bonito Valley, now bright and green in the morning light with fleeting clouds racing across it, chasing their madcap shadows that fled ahead of them. Cattle grazed on both sides of the rushing river. A hawk swung easily on an updraft. A horse whinnied from the corral. One of the hands was singing as he worked, and the tune seemed in time with the whirring of the windmill.

"Miss Sturtevant?" he said.

She did not answer. Her eyes were filled with the quiet loveliness of the valley.

"Ma'am?"

She bowed her head a little.

"Leslie?"

She turned, and her eyes were wet with tears. "We fight," she said brokenly. She hurried from the room.

"See what you done?" accused Bennie.

"What would you do, Old Timer?"

Bennie came into the room, filled a cup with coffee, and sipped at it for a moment. "Hell," he said at last. "I'd fight! I was a soldier once. Fit Indians too, rustlers as well. Saw my wife killed and scalped by a Comanche. Saw my brother get shot down by a rebel at Elkhorn Tavern. Since them days, I look back at all the empty years and wish sometimes I had died when I was young and full of pee and vinegar. I don't like to look ahead, bub. Old Bennie would rather die with a smokin' six-gun in his hand than to end up like an old buffalo bull pulled down at last by yellowbellied coyotes. I ain't joshin', bub! That little girl fights, Bennie Osgood fights with her."

"Thanks, Old Timer."

The washed-out eyes studied him. "I don't know whether your coming here was for good or evil, bub, but I got a feelin', as long as you *are* here, we might just beat the hell out'a that bastard Engels and his murderin' *corrida!*"

Matt stood up and walked to the window. "How about the rest of the boys?"

"Yuh want me to talk to them and sound 'em out?"

"I'd be obliged."

Bennie nodded. He limped to the door. He turned. "Was you in the army, bub?"

"Yep."

"Drummer boy, maybe?"

"No."

Bennie half closed one eye. "What outfit?"

"First Corps."

Bennie nodded. "Good fightin' men. What brigade?"

"Robertson's."

"I ain't sure I know about him."

"He was all right, Bennie. A good fighting man."

"What regiment?"

Matt was working the makings, shaping a cigarette. He placed it in his mouth and lighted it. "Fifth Texas," he said.

"Fifth Texas? That was a Johnnie outfit!"

Matt grinned. "Yeh," he said.

Bennie stomped through the kitchen. The door slammed. A moment later, it opened again, and Bennie stomped back. "Well, Matt," he said grudgingly, "there wasn't none bettern' them, even if they was Johnnies!" He turned and left the house.

Matt drew in on the cigarette. For all the brave talk, there was doubt deep within him. He had always fought under orders, a paid gunfighter from the days of his army service until he had met up with Jim again. But this was quite different. They were looking to *him* for leadership. He could always leave, for there was no profit in this business for him, other than the dark and bitter vengeance he meant to extract from Engels and his sidemen for what they had done so callously to Jim Sturtevant. But was that all? Was that the *only* reason he was staying? He closed his eyes, but he could clearly see the lovely face of Leslie Sturtevant, and he knew then full well why he was staying to throw his skill and guns into the forthcoming battle.

He walked out onto the back porch and rolled another cigarette, taking care not to step out where he might be seen by an E Bar E man peering about with field glasses. Shorty Carnes was almighty good at that sort of business, the prying little skunk.

Bennie limped across the yard and stopped at the edge of the porch. Suppressed anger was plain on his wizened face. "Well?" asked Matt.

Bennie spat, reached into Matt's shirt pocket, took out the makings, and rolled a cigarette. He took Matt's cigarette and lighted his own, then thrust the cigarette back between Matt's lips.

"Help yourself," said Matt dryly.

"Gracias!" Bennie shook his head. "We lost some of the boys already, Matt. A quartet of yellow-bellied skunks. I..."

"Four of them?"

"That's what I said! Warner, Seb, Buck, and Gus. That leaves me and Manuel, you and Sid."

Matt whistled softly. "Well, it's more than I expected at that, Bennie."

"Beats me, Matt."

"You can't blame them, Old Timer."

Bennie sat down on the edge of the porch. "I guess not." He looked about. "Hardly enough men to hold this place."

"That won't be our problem, Bennie."

"No?"

"No. If we fight, we'll have to hit them first and

harder than they can hit us and keep on hitting until we have them licked. If any of us are left, that is..."

Bennie turned. "Looks bad, don't it?"

Matt nodded. "I wish she wasn't here."

"Hell, you won't get her out'a here. She's like her brother, God rest his soul, a finer man I never knew, even if he was a furriner."

Sid came around the side of the house and nodded to Matt. "Bennie tells me the boss aims to fight," he said quietly.

"That's the idea, Sid."

The lean man shook his head. "It'll end up with all of us killed, mister."

"You can always leave," said Bennie.

"I didn't say anything about that. This is a good job, and a good place to live. Miss Sturtevant needs help. I ain't the kind of man who'd walk out on her. Besides, I hate Morg Engels's guts!"

"That's better," said Bennie. "Here comes Manuel."

A smiling young man came out of the barn and walked toward them. He bent his head in greeting to Matt. "Senor Turlock," he said softly. "I have heard of you. It is good to have you with us."

"It will be dangerous, *amigo*. Damned dangerous."

Manuel smiled. "All life is dangerous, *senor*. What is life without it? It is the wine. The smile on a flirting woman's face; the half-seen charms. The half-hidden steel of an enemy waiting for his chance to sheath his blade in you."

"My God," said Matt. "A poet!"

Manuel bowed a little. "It is my ambition."

"You're liable to die in this fight," said Matt.

"What is life but death? What is death but life?"

"A helluva good question," said Sid dryly. "What the hell does he mean, Bennie?"

"Don't ask me. I ain't no poet. He talks like that all the time."

Manuel smiled apologetically to Matt. "They are not men of discernment. Now you, Senor Turlock, *you* are a man of understanding!"

"I'm a man with a lot of work and a little time," said Matt. "How much can I depend on you boys?"

"All the way," said Bennie.

"Count me in," said Sid.

"To the hilt!" cried Manuel.

Matt tried to keep his face composed, but with a cripple, a simple cowman, a mad poet, a young woman, and himself as warriors, he had a damned good idea who was going to carry the burden of fighting for the J Lazy S.

"What do we do?" asked Sid.

"Miss Sturtevant has to pay off her note," said Matt.

"We have not the *dinero,*" said Manuel apologetically.

Matt waved a hand. "She has the money. All we have to do is make sure it gets into the right hands. It's a long road to Roca Blanca."

"When is it due?" asked Sid.

"No later than tomorrow," said Matt.

Manuel was looking up the side of the high ridge that ran behind the ranch buildings from south to north. "Look out!" he yelled.

Sid turned, and in doing so, inadvertently stepped in front of Matt. There was a flash high on the side of a tall boulder almost at the top of the ridge, followed by a puff of smoke and the crack of a high-powered rifle. Sid jerked as he was hit. He fell against a porch support, staggered sideways, and fell from the porch. Bennie rolled out of the way. Manuel dived for cover behind a watering trough. Matt dropped flat and bellied his way toward the wounded man. A second shot smashed through a window, showering Matt with shards of glass. The third shot neatly drilled a hole through the post, a foot above Matt's head. Mat gripped Sid under the arms and dragged him toward the barn. A fourth shot screamed thinly from the hard earth and tore off Matt's left boot heel, numbing his entire foot.

He reached the barn and hauled Sid inside, then he lamely sprinted toward the back of the barn and peered through a crack. There was nothing to be seen except a faint wraith of powder smoke drifting off before the light wind.

"It's begun already," said Sid faintly.

Matt limped over to him. The man had been hit high in the left shoulder. Matt stanched the flow of blood. Sid would be out of action for a long time; a long time indeed.

"Some shootin'," said Bennie. "Of course, in my prime in the old regiment, I could do better, but..."

"Shut up, Bennie," said Matt. "Go get the boss."

She came in, white-faced and tense, but she did not flinch from examining the ugly wound. It was ragged and large. Matt had seen such wounds before. She looked up at him.

"They cut a cross on the tip of the bullet," he said quietly. "Spreads it out when it hits. Dirty business, ma'am."

"Take him to the house."

"I'll be all right in the bunkhouse, ma'am," protested Sid.

"No! Boys, carry him to the house."

Matt helped them, then pulled off his boot to examine the shattered heel.

"There are some of Jim's boots left in his room," she said.

"His clothes. His boots. It just don't seem right," said Matt.

She turned slowly. "And his fight, too, Matt. Why don't you leave before they kill you? Before they kill all of us. I'm not afraid for myself, but my conscience will bother me if any of you die for me. It isn't worth it."

"That's your opinion, ma'am," said Matt.

"Keno," said Bennie.

"*Sí,*" said Manuel.

A fading picture came back to Matt Turlock at that moment. Of a column of half-starved men slogging through the mud toward Appomattox Courthouse, tattered battle-flags still carried, haversacks empty but cartridge pouches full, almost surrounded by many times their numbers of well-fed and fully equipped Yankees moving in for the final kill after four years of fighting. That had been a defeat and yet a victory. This was a cause that had everything against it, and defeat was inevitable.

"Sid is pretty bad," said Bennie. "Mebbe we ought to get a doctor."

Manuel peered through a window. "It will not be easy to get to Roca Blanca now."

"I'll go," said Leslie. "They won't stop a woman."

Matt turned slowly. "Don't fool yourself," he said. "Have you a medical kit?"

"Yes."

"A probe? Blasius pincers?"

"I think so."

Matt walked to the sink and filled a basin with hot water from the stove. He rolled up his sleeves and began to scrub his hands and lower arms. "I'll take the bullet out," he said over his shoulder.

"You?" she said.

He smiled whimsically. "You said I was quite a killer. Cannot a killer also *save a* life, Miss Leslie?"

She got the kit. It was an easy job, for the mutilated slug was quite near the surface and had not lodged in bone. He held it up with the pincers. "You can see what a cut slug would do," he said. He cleansed the wound of lead flakes, poured antiseptic into it, then bandaged it. Sid had mercifully passed out. Matt washed and dried his hands. She sat in a chair watching him. He looked at her and smiled.

"I know," he said quietly. "I am a strange man, a strange man indeed, ma'am."

She laughed quickly. "Not so strange, Matt. And, for the love of Heaven, call me Leslie!"

"Leslie, then."

She smiled again, and something seemed to pass out from each of them and blend together; something that would never separate again on earth, nor in the eternity to come.

CHAPTER EIGHT

The sun was high, flooding the West Valley of the Bonito, and nowhere in New Mexico could be seen a more peaceful and pleasant vista. Matt Turlock lay belly flat in the rippling grass, high on the ridge overlooking the ranch buildings of the J Lazy S, scanning the terrain like a scout for the Fifth Texas, which in truth he had been. A scout is like an extended eye for a commanding officer, and if he is one of the best, he can also think in the manner of his commanding officer, filing away bits of vital information and casting out that which is nonessential. Trouble with Matt Turlock this lovely day was that he was both scout and commanding officer; commanding a wounded man, a bragging cripple, a would-be poet, and a lovely young woman, with whom, to add a little more complication to the issue, Matt Turlock knew he loved as he had loved no other woman. Before meeting Leslie, none of that clinging softness had been for Matt Turlock, the man who loved the flash of gunfire, the glittering of steel, the heady wine of danger, and spilled blood. Times had changed.

Down the slope from Matt were the brassily shining clues that indicated the spot where the rifleman had fired down on the ranch. He had been a top gun, as far as Matt could figure out. Nowhere along that ridge was there a better spot for a drygulcher, and it had been a long shot, downhill to make it worse. The gods had smiled on Matt Turlock that day. If Sid had not stopped that whining slug, Matt Turlock would have been seriously wounded, or dead. He remembered well the shot Cato Semmes had made the day he had killed the escaping rustler. It had given Matt a bit of a cold feeling at the time, for he wasn't sure he could shoot that well with the long gun. Then too, there was Cato's casual appearing slaughter of the two steers who had supplied their hides for the death coats of Bartolomeo Sanchez and the boy Eusebio. Casual appearing? Matt knew well enough of the hours and hours of practice, the boxes of cartridges, and the iron will that had made Cato Semmes into the deadly gunslinger he was. *Better and faster than Matt Turlock...*

Matt focused his glasses, studying the road that skirted the west bank of the river, passing from J Lazy S land to that of E Bar E land, thence onward to Roca Blanca. Behind the valley were the tangled hills and rugged mountains. To the south was more E Bar E land. Jim Sturtevant had indeed picked a place for an ideal ranch; he had not picked a place that was easy to get into and out of, providing you were at odds ends with the owner of the E Bar E. That ridge to the east of the valley would have a man or two watching the valley and everything that moved through it during the day. There would be others further north, watching the road to Roca Blanca. When dusk came, they would move in, many of them, onto J Lazy S land, to either hurrah the place, or to wait with spiderlike patience for the J Lazy S people to make a move.

Matt grinned wryly. "J Lazy S people," he said dryly. He spat. He'd give a smart package for some of his old comrades of the Fifth Texas, Bennett Carse, Keno Bates, Mike Ord, and others. Carse had died at Gettysburg,

Bates in the Wilderness, and Mike Ord of fever in the trenches at Petersburg.

But time was ticking on, inexorably, and the note was due the next day. The money was in the ranch house. The note was in Roca Blanca. All Matt had to do was get the money there in time. There were but four of them to do the job, for Sid was already helpless.

Matt cased the glasses and walked down the hillside, keeping to the shelter of a gully. He walked to the corral, roped and saddled a clean-limbed clay bank, attached a rifle sheath to the saddle, then led the clay bank to the rear of the house.

Bennie poked his head from a window. "Where yuh think you're goin'?" he demanded suspiciously. "Pullin' out, eh? Figgered yuh would. Don't make men like they used to..."

Matt leaned against the horse. "Why don't you shut up, Bennie," he said. "You always run off at the mouth like that?"

Leslie came out of the house. "Matt, where *are* you going?"

"Roca Blanca."

"You're mad!"

"Let me have the money. Tell me where to go."

"I kin tell yuh where to go!" blustered Bennie. "Don't yuh give him that money, Miss Leslie. He'll pull foot for the border with it! If I was twenty years younger, I'd..."

"Quiet!" said Leslie. "Well, Matt?"

He shrugged. "We're being watched. I can't see how we can get past them. It would take too long through the hills and mountains. No sense in going south. East is the biggest part of the E Bar E."

"And north as well."

He nodded. "Let me take a chance."

"You'd never get past them. They'll kill you on sight, money or no money."

"You aim to sit here and let them keep us penned up?"

"If you must go, you could go after dark."

He waved a curt hand. "They'll move in so close after dark you won't be able to light a cigarette without getting a slug fired at you!"

"I can't let you go, Matt!"

"Let him go and get a bullet in his head," said Bennie sourly.

"Get the money, Leslie," said Matt.

"No!"

"Then you'll lose the ranch!"

Her eyes were troubled. "The ranch doesn't matter anymore, Matt, but you do."

"Oh my God!" said Bennie. "It's already come to that, has it?" The look from Matt's eyes sent the old man back into the shelter of his kitchen like an aged tortoise into his shell.

Leslie looked down the quiet valley. "You really think they are out there?"

"I know it."

"Can't we get help?"

"No neighbors would help. They wouldn't buck up against Morg Engels."

"There are laws and lawmen, Matt."

He nodded. "We'd still have to tell them, Leslie. Even if we did tell them, we'd have to have some proof of Engels's crimes and his intentions. We'd be laughed at. Furthermore, Morg Engels isn't going to let any of us leave this valley no matter what we want to do. He'd not be a big enough fool to let us run to the law."

"It's hopeless then, isn't it?"

"Get the money. If I can get in and pay off the note, I can also get help, somehow or another."

"It seems the only thing to do."

So it was. Matt Turlock got as far as the crossing of the river, on E Bar E land, before they struck. Rifles spat flame and smoke from a bosque overlooking the crossing. The clay bank was fleshed with a bullet. Matt suffered a bullet burn on the left bicep and lost his hat, neatly holed, fore and aft with bullet holes.

He struck the steel deep into the clay bank, turned to race back toward J Lazy S land, saw a trio of riders between him and his goal, then set the clay bank at a fence and hammered upslope toward the hills with rifles spurring him onward.

He reached temporary shelter in a tangle of shattered rock and fallen timbers. He dismounted, took his rifle and trotted back, fired half a dozen rounds to hold back his pursuers, then went back to his horse. He led it along the slopes, threading his way in and out of masses of fallen rock and tangles of timber and brush, until at last, he could look down a long, even slope toward the tempting fence line of the J Lazy S land. It looked serene enough. He rolled a cigarette and lighted it. The first puff of smoke drew a rifle bullet. "Damned fool," said Matt of himself. He lay quiet with ready rifle, but there was nothing to see, not even a telltale puff of smoke drifting off on the wind.

It was only a matter of time before Engels's men would close in on him from behind, to drive him into the sights of that hidden rifleman, or riflemen. Matt looked up at the precipitous heights behind him. It was his only chance. He crawled back, rounded a boulder, then began to scale a steep talus slope. It wasn't until he was halfway up it that he suddenly realized he was fully exposed in the open. Rifles began to crack flatly from far below, and slugs sang thinly from the rocks. His breath was coming hard and fast and his legs ached as he drove his toes in for footholds. There was nothing he could do but climb, or else turn and plunge down to the shelter below, and be trapped, perhaps killed.

Bullets flicked past both sides of his head. Another

whipped through the slack in his shirt. A fourth seemed to part his sweat-soaked hair.

"Keep running, Turlock!" yelled a derisive voice. "Where yuh aim to go?" The voice was followed by half a dozen shots. Matt fell heavily, rolled sideways and slid downhill a little, and then lay still.

"Jest like shooting fish in a barrel!" yelled the same voice. It was the cocky tone of Shorty Carnes.

The sun beat down upon the naked rocks, burning up through his Levi's and thin shirt, searing his sweaty flesh.

His head ached, and his vision was blurred. Even the metal and wood of his rifle was hot to the touch. He peered downhill. The slope shimmered, lifted, and wavered in the dancing heat waves. There was no sign of life.

Minutes ticked past. He wanted to get up and continue his climb, but he was too beat for that. The heat was already sapping what strength he had left. He felt like a nature specimen stretched on a board for dissection.

Something moved amidst the boulders. There was another movement in amongst some piled and shattered timber.

"Yuh think we got him, Monk?" called out Shorty Carnes.

"He ain't moving, is he?"

"I don't trust that sneaky bastard."

A shot snapped out. It clipped a rock close to Matt, and he had enough presence of mind left to jerk a little as though the slug had hit his body.

More time fled past, and Matt Turlock was getting sicker and weaker, as though he was stretched on a gridiron and the Devil was stoking the furnace beneath it. Salt sweat trickled into his eyes, stinging them viciously.

Boots clattered on rock. Three men came out of the tangle and stood there looking up at Matt. Monk, Shorty

Carnes, and a squat, broad-shouldered man. "We gotta go up and make sure," said Shorty.

"Listen to him," said the squat man. "The hero! From what I heard of Turlock he ain't no one to fool around with!"

"Yeh," said Monk. He spat. "He ain't breathing, I don't *think*."

"He's dead," said Shorty. "I can tell."

"Sure, sure," said the third man.

Shorty was on the prod. Like all little men, he had an immense vanity and a chip on his narrow little shoulder. "You think I won't go up there, Tom?" he asked the squat man.

"I don't see yuh moving, Windy."

"Gawd dammit! I'll show yuh!" Shorty started up the slope in his anger.

"The hero," said Monk. He laughed.

Shorty was making good time. Then he stopped and eyed Matt warily. He held his rifle ready.

"What's the matter, Shorty?" jeered Tom.

The little man wasn't so sure of himself now, but he couldn't back down now, not with *his* vanity that was all out of proportion to his size.

"Yuh want me to come and lead the way, Hero?" yelled Monk.

Shorty cursed. He forced himself up, making heavy weather of it. His breathing was harsh and irregular. It was more than he had bargained for, but he'd go on if he dropped dead to prove his point.

Matt let him get to within thirty feet. Matt fired one shot, dropping Shorty, then Matt was on his feet and eleven more rounds split the quiet, awoke the rolling echoes, wreathed the talus slope in drifting smoke, and put a pattern of singing lead about Tom and Monk. Tom went down with a slug through his left thigh. Monk vanished like the snows of yesteryear. Matt was on the way before the last echo died, churning his way up the loose, clattering rock. He dived into cover a second before the shooting started in again.

His heart pounded, sweat dripped from him, his skin burned from the sun and his sweat, and he didn't have the strength or willpower to snap a matchstick in half. "There ought'a be an easier way to go about this," he gasped out. He felt for the damp makings, rolled a cigarette, and lighted it. He still had a long way to go. He forced himself to refill the magazine of his rifle, wincing at the touch of the hot metal.

When Matt's breathing was normal, he ventured a look down the shimmering slope. Shorty Carnes still lay there, and from the looks of the man, he was dead. "Vanity, vanity, all is vanity, saith the Lord," said Matt in a low voice. He picked up his rifle and vanished into the thick tangle along the hill slopes, and no one followed him. No one follows a tiger into his natural habitat unless he is a fool.

The sun was low when he at last appeared beyond the pass and could look down upon the J Lazy S. All seemed quiet and serene, and indeed it was until the people of the J Lazy S tried to make a move.

Matt worked his way down the slopes, through the thick timber, and across some meadowland. It was dark when at last he reached a point where he could see the lights of the ranch house. He breathed in relief, slid his rifle into the crook of his left arm, and strode briskly down the slope.

He had one leg over the sagging fence when the gun broke the quiet. He hit the ground rolling, leaving part of his Levi's and part of his skin on the barbs. Lead whispered evilly through the darkness. There was no time to shoot; nothing to shoot at except those flashes, and Matt knew better than to reveal his presence. He jumped behind an outbuilding and hit the ground, rolling over until he could peer from behind a watering trough toward the house. Glass shattered at the house. The lights went out. Bullets slapped into wood, screamed thinly off metal, punctured tin, ripped through curtains, and smashed glass.

He placed his rifle in the cradle of his elbows and bellied across the hard ground to the barn. He crawled in and slid the door shut behind him. The shooting was still going on. He didn't know whether or not he had started it, but he did know that it was a major hurrahing. They had closed in after dusk, figuring that Matt Turlock was probably still wandering in the wilderness like the Children of Israel. They meant to pin down anyone at the ranch.

A horse whinnied as a bullet skinned his back. A bullet shattered a window in the dark bunkhouse. Another struck one of the rods of the windmill and screeched angrily end over end to slap into the outside of the barn, keyholing through the thin wood inches from where Matt Turlock lay.

It was a leg-weary and heartsore man who climbed into the barn loft, momentarily expecting a mutilated bullet to strike into him, and scaled the rickety ladder to a trapdoor set in the roof. He eased off the lid and crawled out on the wide roof, feeling awfully naked and unprotected up there. The moon was not showing itself as yet.

Matt lay flat, watching where the gun flashes came from, orienting each one of them, fixing them with some dim landmark. There were five positions, two on the ridge behind the buildings, one in the bosque near the gate, and two others south of the buildings in a pasture. He mentally fixed each position, then waited patiently, listening grimly as a slug ranged high and felt about through the darkness for one Matt Turlock, orphan, Confederate veteran, gunfighter, and outright idiot. The reasoning was Matt's.

The first indication of moonrise showed. The firing slacked off and died away. The last echo fled into limbo.

The wind shifted, the windmill whirred, and the smoke drifted off. Cattle bawled on the range. A dog barked somewhere up the valley.

Matt wet his lips, squinted his eyes, and raised his rifle. Two in the pasture, two on the ridge, one in the bosque. Twelve rounds. Give five to the men in the pasture, four to the men on the ridge, one to the jasper in the timber. Now! He rested the heavy .44-40 on the ridgepole and sighted in the direction of the two unseen marksmen in the pasture. Five rounds rapidly crashed out of the heavy Winchester. Matt turned, aimed uphill, and pumped out four rounds, and as he did so, a man screamed hoarsely in the darkness. Matt jumped to his feet, sighted on the bosque, and emptied the hot, smoking rifle, then jumped feet first through the open trapdoor as the first shots began to search for him on the roof of the barn.

He slid down the ladder, gathering a few splinters for his pains, heard the snap and crackling of bullets tearing through the thin warped wood of the upper floor of the barn, then dropped flat on the floor to reload. His belt loops were almost empty of cartridges. It was a cinch that the unseen riflemen had plenty of horses. Bullets swept back and forth across the ranch buildings—thudding, smashing, splintering, and always seeking blood.

Matt crawled to the front of the barn. There was no one firing from the bosque. He bellied over to the south side and peered through a crack. There was only one rifle firing in the pasture. He peered through a partly open door at the rear of the barn. There were still two men shooting up there.

The moon had begun to light the West Bonito Valley when the firing died away, leaving the acrid stench of burnt powder to drift on the night air.

Matt waited an hour, calmly smoking as he sat in a corner of the barn with his loaded rifle across his thighs. He wondered who was in the house. He wondered if they were still alive. At last, he padded to the front door and peered through a crack. It was very quiet out there, almost too quiet to suit him, but he couldn't sit in that damned echoing barn all night. There was work to be done.

He eased out, darted across the moonlit yard, and jumped on the porch. "Leslie!" he called out. "It's me, Matt!" Then he saw the sprawled body at his feet, face downward, slim and still; very, very still. For a moment, his heart almost stopped within him. He knelt and turned over the body to look into the set and peaceful face of Manuel. *"All life is dangerous,"* he had said with a quiet smile upon his dark and handsome face. *"What is life without it? It is the wine! The smile on a flirting woman's face; the half-seen charms. The half-hidden steel of an enemy waiting for his chance to sheathe his blade in you..."*

She was quite close. He stood up, and she came to his arms and pressed her tear-wet face against his chest. "He was trying to get out of the house to fight them, Matt," she said brokenly.

"Muy bravo," he said quietly. "He was a man amongst men."

"Thank God you are safe!"

"I couldn't get past them," he said.

"What difference does it make? Let's leave here, Matt! Let's run! I can't face any more of this!"

"No," he said.

"It's too much! Too much blood! We must go!"

He held by her shoulder and looked into her face. "Listen," he said in a low voice. "Your brother died for this land. Sid was wounded for it. Manuel has also died for it. I have killed men for it. The price is being paid, Leslie, and we can't run away from paying it off to the last ringing coin!"

She bowed her head. "I'm sorry," she said. "Must it be this way?"

"There *is* no other way," he said simply.

She turned and walked into the house. Matt covered the boy with a piece of canvas and walked into the house, his boots grating on glass. The interior was a shambles. Sid was lying unconscious under his bed, protected by a heavy wooden chest of drawers. Bennie held the fort in the mess of the living room. He turned to look at Matt. "Was that you on the roof, Matt?"

Matt nodded.

Bennie cackled. "Like a damned crowin' rooster. Pretty good, bub. Now me, I would'a fought 'em gun muzzle to gun muzzle on the ground, but you modern boys, you like this long-range, *safe* stuff. Oh well..."

Matt took cartridges from the desk drawer and filled his belt loops. "They'll be back," he said.

She sat down in a bullet-riddled chair. "What can we do?"

Matt rolled a cigarette and handed it to Bennie. He fashioned one for himself and lighted both smokes. "Can't leave now. The moon is like daylight outside. They could see every move we'd make."

"So?" said Bennie.

"We wait until dark again and make a break."

"Loco," said Bennie.

"You think they'll leave the job undone?" said Matt harshly. "By dawn tomorrow, this will be a charnel house, a slaughter pen. I'd rather die in the open with a gun in my hand than penned up in here waiting for the axe."

They said nothing. There was nothing to say. He had said it for them.

CHAPTER NINE

The moonlight had been almost as bright as daylight. Nothing moved about the darkened buildings of the J Lazy S. There was no sight nor sound of anyone beyond the perimeter of the ranch buildings. Matt and Bennie had loaded every gun inside the house and had placed them at strategic spots. They had barricaded the shattered windows but both of them knew well enough they could not barricade themselves against the deadliest weapon that could be used against them. Fire would be invincible. Matt hoped to God they would not fire the place at all, and certainly not before dark. To fire it in the moonlight would drive them out, and there would be no place to hide, for the surroundings of the ranch were brightly lit by the moon. After dark again, if the buildings were fired, they'd have to run a gauntlet across the illumination of the burning buildings. The darkness beyond would be hardly safe, for that too would be well-lighted by gun flashes.

There was no hope for outside help. Morg Engels would see to that. Too many of his men had died in this bloody battle, not that their lives mattered much to Morg Engels. He paid them well and fed them well. To him they were fighting machines. The only loss he felt was in losing good fighting machines, not in losing men. There was one fighting machine he meant to smash into death, by the name of Matt Turlock. It would be an obsession with him, much as his obsession for the J Lazy S range. What Morgan Engels wanted, Morgan Engels got. It was an axiom in the Bonito Valley country.

As the moon waned, faint and indistinct sounds came to the tense waiters in the house. Clinking of metal, scraping of boot leather, rustling of brush, and the indistinguishable voices of men as the ring closed in again. They had a healthy respect for Matt Turlock. He always managed to hit back much harder than he was hit. But the odds were running out on the fighting man from Texas. The sands were getting low.

The moon was gone. Bennie stirred. "What the hell?" he said hoarsely. "What's that?"

They peered over his shoulder. There was a flickering and uncertain light behind the huge, dry barn which was packed with hay. "Here it comes," said Matt. He dropped his cigarette and ground it out on the floor without thinking. They were safe enough behind the barn. No bullet could reach them. The gathering firelight began to dance back in wild reflection from the whitewashed shed to one side of it. A lazy covey of fat sparks drifted over to see what was going on at the shed. They settled down slowly like giant fireflies, and the dry wood began to smoke. A runnel of flame crept along a seam that had oozed with rosin. In a short time, the whole side of the shed was a sheet of flames. By now the whole back wall of the barn was a mass of fire, and the flames could be seen through the half-open front door and the cracks and the seams of the front wall. The hay was burning slowly in the loft.

The bunkhouse was next. The sound of shattering wood came from it as the arsonists broke up the furniture to kindle their blazes. A board smashed out the windows for a better draft. The fire took over the occupancy of the low building. A pile of seasoning timber was next, and after that, a haystack in the pasture. Drifting, burning hay dropped atop a hog shed at the far side of the pasture and the hogs grunted out of it as the roof caught and began to fill the interior with thick smoke.

Bennie coughed. He looked at Matt with reddening eyes. "Salt, pepper, and gravel in the grease," he said. "How soon before they start the house?"

Matt shrugged. Any minute now he expected to hear from Morg Engels. He had accurately called the shot.

"Turlock!" called out Engels from beyond the crackling, smoking bunkhouse. "We can still save the house and the rest of the buildings!"

"At what price?" called out Matt.

"You know what we want."

"Yuh want it in fives, tens, or twenties?" yelled Bennie. He snapped a shot into the bunkhouse.

There was a long pause. "Is *that* your answer, Turlock?" called Engels.

"Might as well be," yelled Matt. "If we give you the money we'll be shot down or barbecued anyway!"

Leslie leaned weakly against the wall. "It's hopeless," she said.

"Never say die," crowed Bennie.

Matt bit his lip. It did look like the end of the road. He knew what would happen if Engels got the money. The man's cupidity would not let him see that money go up in smoke. Matt narrowed his eyes. He looked at Bennie. "You and Miss Leslie can get near the front door," he said. "It's darker out there now that the moon has gone down. Split up the money. I'll keep Engels and his boys busy. Try for the river. You just might hide out in the brush."

Bennie looked down at his game leg and shook his head. Leslie looked toward the bedroom. "What about Sid, Matt?" she said.

"I had forgotten about him."

Bennie heaved himself to his feet. "They's a storm cellar, or whatever yuh call it under the house, built well of field stone. Trapdoor in the kitchen. We can put Sid down there. I think he'd have a good chance even if the house burned down."

It was risky, but there was nothing else they could do. If he stayed in the house and it was fired, he'd die anyway. If the house was not burned, or he survived the fire, his mouth would be stopped by a bullet. *Los muertos no hablan.*

They wet down blankets and piled them near the wounded foreman. Matt gave him a loaded pistol. "Lay low, Sid," he said. "You might be overlooked."

The foreman's face was drawn and glistening with sweat. He nodded, but there was no hope in his pain-glazed eyes.

The two men went upstairs. Bennie looked about his kitchen. "Best damned kitchen I ever had," he said ruefully.

Matt was looking at the barn. It was far enough from the house so that it was possible that sparks would not ignite the house roof, and the wind was blowing away from the house. They might just be able to hold off any would-be firebugs.

There was a sudden explosion in the loft, and the second-floor loading door was blasted outward, belching a long tongue of gas and flame that leaped the gap to the house with an insane roaring laugh to lick hungrily at the dry shakes on the back porch roof. In a matter of minutes, the whole roof was aflame, and fingers of the blaze were creeping upward.

"Devil's own luck," said Bennie. He peered through a shattered window. "Can't see a damned one of 'em, either." He glanced quickly at Matt. "How fast kin yuh run?"

"Fast enough."

"Then it's you and Miss Leslie got to head for the *rio.*"

Matt shook his head.

"Bennie came closer. "Listen, Matt. I couldn't run from here to the privy with this spavined leg of mine. Let me take 'em whilst you make a break for it."

"No!"

"Please," pleaded Bennie. "Jesus, Matt, all my life I been a damned liar. I can't outfight, outjump, outride, and outkill nobody. I can't even *outcook* nobody. 'Bout all I can do is outbull most people, like yuh once said. I never lit any Indians or rustlers. Never had a wife to be scalped by Comanches. Never saw my brother get kilt at Elkhom Tavern. I wasn't even a real soldier. I was a sutler's helper."

"You got nothing to be ashamed of, Bennie," said Matt quietly.

The man's eyes glistened. "This is my chance. I'm old, Matt, and gettin' older. Hearin' is gone, sight is gettin' bad. My guts is all shot from bad food and lousy likker. Hell, I don't want to die like a sick cow, boy!"

Matt rubbed his jaw. He looked away from the eager man.

"Matt?"

"You sure you can't run?"

"Positive!"

"Whyn't you go down with Sid?"

"I don't want to die in no hole in the ground, waitin' for my killer. Hell, I got to go anyways, boy. Might as well go first class."

"I see your point."

Bennie nodded. "When you hear me kick the back door open, Matt, you run like a striped bird, eh?"

"Keno, Bennie."

Bennic smiled. "By Jesus," he said softly. "I'll show 'em!"

Matt had his holstered Colt. He thrust another under his gun belt, a pair of derringers in his pants pockets. He told Leslie what Bennie was going to do, and when she protested, he closed her mouth with a kiss, then held her face between his hands. "Let him have his hour, Leslie," he said. "I'd want it the same way."

They stepped out onto the front porch. The ground sloped almost sharply, and there was a low hedge at the foot of the slope, and beyond that, a fieldstone fence. Fifty yards to temporary safety. The girl looked back at him with a white face. Matt heard the rear door crash open and Bennie's piercing yell. "Yippeeee! Come an' get it!" Matt pushed her toward the edge of the porch and jumped off after her. They ran full tilt down the half-dark slope, bent low, and Matt had a six-gun in each hand.

There was a great outburst of gunfire from the rear of the house. A thick pall of smoke was swirling from the building, and it concealed Leslie and Matt from those back there who were cutting Bennie down as he died to give the two fugitives a few precious seconds of grace.

Leslie pushed through the hedge and rolled over the wall, to be followed by Matt.

"What the hell," a man yelled from in front of them.

A gun flatted off from each of Matt's hands, and in the quick stabbing bursts of light, he saw the man go down. There were two others running toward him from the road. "Run, Les!" he yelled. He kicked a stone upward toward the face of the closest man, and as the man involuntarily raised a hand to protect his face, he got two soft-nosed slugs in the belly. He staggered in front of his mate and got a slug in the back from him, and in that quick moment of surprise, Matt fired over the body of the first man, and the other two went down together. Then he hurled himself down the slope, running like a deer, until he saw her climbing the wire fence on the far side of the road, looking anxiously back for him. She smiled, waved, dropped to the far side, and hid in the brush. He was with her in a moment, and they sprinted across a rocky field to the rushing river. "Can you swim?" he asked.

"Like a duck."

"Go on then!"

She pulled off her boots, hung them about her neck, and waded in. Halfway across, she began to swim, carried by the current.

Matt reloaded, waded in, holding his twin six-guns high over his head, and by a miracle, the deepest part of the river just reached his neck. He met her on the far side, and the two of them worked their way up the slope into a thick bosque, their teeth chattering wildly.

Matt looked across the valley to the flaming masses of the ranch buildings. Everything was flaming now, and great fat sparks floated across the valley to ignite the dry grass on the slopes. He could hear no shooting now. A hero had been born that night. Bennie Osgood had died as he had wished to die. *"Old Bennie would rather die with a smoking six-gun in his hand than to end up like an old buffalo bull putted down by yellowbellied coyotes,* he had said, and he had gained his ambition.

Even as he watched, he saw the entire house crumble in a flaming mass. Sid would never die now of his wound. Matt turned away. Neither one of them had really been fighting men, not professionals at least, but they had done their duty.

"I'm going to get a horse," he said to Leslie.

"Where?"

He looked up the ridge. "The only place available."

"The E Bar E?"

He nodded.

"Matt, you're mad!"

"It has to be done," he said quietly. "We can't quit now. Too many good men have died for this thing."

She pulled on her boots and stood up. "Then I'm going with you," she said.

There was no arguing with her. She was a Sturtevant. He took her by the hand and led her up the dark ridge while far behind them, the flames leaped and roared in savage glee over the ruins of the buildings. But the land was still there; *the land would always be there!*

CHAPTER TEN

The *vaquero* was whistling softly as he walked toward the corral. He never saw the thick shadow beside the low shed. A gun barrel was laid neatly just over his right ear. He was caught before he hit the ground and dragged into the shed to lie peacefully beside the first man Matt Turlock had buffaloed.

Matt crawled the corral fence to the far side, climbed it and dropped down inside. There were only two horses in the big corral, for most of the horses kept close to the ranch proper were being used that dark night along the rio in the West Bonito Valley. He talked quietly to both mounts, led them through the gate, and down the road to a small bosque where a shivering Leslie guarded two saddles. He saddled the horses, giving a bay mare to Leslie, and he took the blocky dun. He gave her a leg into the saddle. They looked back at the buildings as they rode up the lip of a swale. There was no sign of life. Far across the dark hills came the cry of a coyote.

It was an hour before dawn when they drew rein just short of the plank bridge that spanned the river south of the little town of Roca Blanca. The white-painted buildings shone ghostlike in the darkness. Matt took the horses and picketed them in the small grove of cottonwoods that edged the river. He eased his Colt in its holster and eyed the sleeping town. It had been too easy to suit him. He looked back down the road. It was dark and empty.

Leslie came close to him and kissed him. "What's wrong?" she whispered. She eyed his hard face and the granite of his eyes. "Matt?"

He looked up and down the dark, rushing river. He didn't know what was wrong himself. "Where's the marshal's office?"

"Three blocks up. Next to the Town Hall."

"Anyone be there this time of morning?"

She shrugged. "Prisoners perhaps."

"Where does the marshal live?"

"I don't know, Matt. There may be someone in the jail on guard; it's just behind the marshal's office."

"Where does the sheriff stay?"

"At the County Seat," she said. "Fifty-two miles from here."

"Great," he said dryly.

"What do we have to worry about now?"

He shrugged. *"Quién sabe?"* His eyes flicked back and forth. "I don't know. I just don't know. But I *feel* something."

She shivered and came closer to him. He looked down at her. "We've got to make the marshal's office. If any shooting starts, that's where he'd be headed."

"You don't think any of Engels's men are here?"

"I'm not taking any chances." He held her close. "We've got to play it bold, Leslie. You take the money and walk across the bridge. Stay in the shadows of the buildings."

"Where will you be?"

He smiled. "I'll be close to you."

"Can't we alert the town?"

He eyed the dark, shallow canyons of the streets. "Who knows who is waiting in those shadows? We might alert the town. We'd hardly be able to get help ahead of a hatful of hot lead."

"As you said: We can't quit now. Too many good men have died for this thing."

He nodded. "Walk softly. If you see anyone heading toward you, try to get into a building or down an alley-way. How far is that office?"

"Three blocks."

"It will feel like three miles."

He raised her face and kissed her, then pushed her gently toward the bridge. As she softly crossed it, he ran swiftly upstream to where a sagging footbridge spanned the flood. He crossed it, then padded softly toward the main street where he could see the slight figure of the girl just vanishing past the first of the buildings. He walked swiftly on a parallel course with her through a narrow alleyway, then cut up the first block, just in time to see her behind him, just about to step into the cross street. She moved toward him. Matt walked along the board sidewalk, trying to be as quiet as possible, but it wasn't easy. The store fronts were dark, and overhead was the long, block length sidewalk roof. Ahead of him it was like a dark and narrow tunnel. The street was hardly less dark.

He wet his lips and looked back. He sensed, rather than saw her. She walked like a cat.

He reached the next street, cut down it, beneath the shelter of the sidewalk roof, darted behind a wagon, then quickly across the street to the far side, where he saw a big two-story building, dark and forbidding, most likely a warehouse. He edged along it, back flat to it, Colt cocked and ready in his right hand, reaching the corner just in time to see Leslie hesitate across the street, looking nervously from right to left and then back again. She had evidently lost sight of him. "I'll be close to you," he had said. That was enough for Leslie Sturtevant. She quickly crossed the street.

Matt was far ahead now, head a little bent, probing the darkness from side to side, Colt ready to spit flame and smoke. The odds were against him. Maybe his phenomenal luck had already run dry. It was no time to think of that.

Leslie depended upon him. He was the last man left in their bitter fight to the death. They were almost two-thirds of the way to the marshal's office now. His hopes began to rise.

There was a hotel at the nearest corner and the ground level of the big building was higher than that of the building south of it, so that it had been necessary to build a wide flight of half a dozen steps on the sidewalk to raise its level to that of the hotel. The sidewalk roof followed the line of the stair flight, then continued to the open corner.

Matt softly went up the steps. There were more steps to bis right, several of them leading up to the wide double doors of the hotel's entrance. Chairs lined the walk in front of the building. He moved silently across the walk in front of the hotel, glancing back to see Leslie's head just appearing on the level of the top step. It was then that he realized he was not alone. He was almost at the corner when he saw the furtive movement in the dark street. He crouched. Two men were moving toward the steps that led up from the street, directly toward him. He sheathed his Colt.

Matt glanced back again. He hiccupped loudly and staggered in his stride, swaying as he went down the steps to the street. He hiccupped again. The two men stopped. He staggered toward them. They eyed him suspiciously. Hc heard a faint movement behind him and thudded his boots on the packed earth of the street to drown out the sound.

"Nothing but a damned drunk, Blaze," said the shorter of the two men.

Matt moved to the right, desperately trying to keep

between them and Leslie. He staggered toward them. "Got a drink?" he mumbled thickly.

"You got enough now, *hombre,*" said Blaze. He laughed.

"Get out'a the way," said the other man sharply. "What's that there, Blaze?"

"I can't see nothing but this drunk." Blaze shoved Matt. "By God!" he said. "It's someone all right."

"It's that Sturtevant filly!"

Matt swung with his left, deep into the guts of Blaze, and as the man's head involuntarily came downward, Matt swung a right from the shoulder and caught him flush on the button. Blaze went down.

"Hey, you!" the second man yelled. He clawed for his Colt. "Jesus! It's *Turlock!*"

Matt ripped his Colt free and swung it side-handed. The barrel caught the man full across the mouth, smashing lips and teeth together. The barrel chopped down in an arc as he fell atop his mate, keeping him down for the long count.

The girl was running now. Matt plunged back toward the hotel. Two men were running along the walk on the side street. They were looking toward Leslie. Matt scooped up a chair and flung it at their legs, then followed through with another as they staggered back. One of them tripped over the edge of the walk, but the second man drew and fired. The slamming explosion was doubly loud beneath the sidewalk roof. Matt had hit the deck. The slug ripped into a post behind him. He fired from the ground. The man jumped back. "Monk!" he yelled.

A boot caught Matt alongside the head, skidding along it, half stunning him. He rolled over and over until he fell down the stairs. A huge man was rushing at him, and there was no mistaking the massive frame of Monk. There was a six-gun in his hand and all he had to do was to point it and squeeze trigger and Matt Turlock's fighting days would be over. But Monk prided himself on his size and his strength, and if he could close with an opponent, so much the better for his ego and fighting lust.

Matt fired again from the ground, hardly able to see the big man. Monk grunted. Again, Matt fired. Monk staggered. Matt rolled over and up to his feet. The last three slugs rapped into Monk at a yard's range, raising the dust from his shirt and vest, but still he came on through the swirling smoke, with clawed hands and a bestial look on his flat face. Matt jumped to one side, and the big man went right past him, seeing nothing but the thick grayness, and beyond that the complete and utter darkness of death before he fell in the very center of the dusty street.

Men were yelling now. Smoke rifted. Boots thudded on the hard earth.

Matt staggered a little in his stride as he reached the far side of the street and looked back. With a sudden start, he realized he could see much better. The false dawn was on the way. He plunged along the sidewalk. There was a one-story building just ahead of him, with a small park area beside it, thick with trees, a white-painted bandstand, and a dry fountain. He could see the bars on the windows of the building. It was Leslie's goal. She was on the front steps, hammering at the door for admittance.

A man was running toward her from the other side. It was Morg Engels, pistol in hand.

"Drop, Leslie," yelled Matt.

Leslie dropped flat, and Matt fired his second Colt. Morg Engels winced. He jumped back, clawing at his face. Blood streaked it where a slug had scratched the skin. He stared at the face of death in the person of Matt Turlock, turned on a heel, and ran to disappear in the shadows. Moments later, hoofbeats drummed on the hard earth. He wasn't safe; the law has a long arm and a long rope.

Matt wiped the sweat from his face. He could hear doors slamming, windows being opened, men yelling, and women screaming. Dogs barked. He grinned. It was all over.

"Turlock!" the cold voice said.

Matt turned slowly. There was someone standing in the shadows beyond the fountain. One man standing very still. A cold feeling came over Matt.

"Quite the killah, eh, Turlock?"

Matt shifted a little. He was trying to get Cato Semmes into a better view.

"Stay wheah youah ah." Semmes's voice was more thickly accented than ever.

"You'd better run like the rest of them who left," said Matt quietly.

"I got time, Turlock."

"Your boss just hightailed it out'a town, Semmes. The war is over."

"Not for me it ain't."

They were alone in the little park. It was getting lighter now.

Matt had a chilling memory of the speed and accuracy of Cato Semmes. Semmes could beat him, all conditions being as equal as they could be, and Matt was body weary and soul tired.

There was no one near them. The townspeople were looking at the dead in the streets and trying to help the wounded.

"You've only got a little time, Semmes," bluffed Matt. His voice was not very assuring.

"Ah got time for you, killah."

"You'd never get away with it," bluffed Matt.

Semmes moved a little. He raised his head. "Seems like you and me had a little unfinished business, Mistah Turlock."

"Get goin' while you still have time!"

Semmes laughed a little, and the quality of that

laughter was cold and chilling. "Ah got time to kill you and get out of this two-bit town. Ain't nobody going to stop Cato Semmes! Nobody, youah understand?"

Matt knew now he was facing the end. He could not out-draw this man. The wind-devil would whirl no more. Yet it was hard to resign himself, now that Leslie's fight was over, now that Jim Sturtevant could rest in peace. Then Matt's eyes hardened. Jim Sturtevant! Matt remembered well the murdering shot Semmes had fired, in all likelihood into the head of the wounded and helpless rancher.

Semmes moved again and was between the fountain and the bandstand, his hands hanging loosely by his sides. "Mistah Bones," he said in a low, amused tone. "The funny man. The cahd. Seems to me youah said I had the accent and the name, Mister Bones. Yo Pappy had a cullud boy by the name of Cato, wasn't it something like thet?"

Matt nodded. He wet his dry lips.

Semmes moved forward, a slim, tall figure, walking like a lean and deadly tiger.

"Stay where you are," warned Matt.

Semmes ignored him. "I told you then thet wasn't the time or place, Mistah Turlock. But I said I'd find the time and place for youah to eat them words!"

Matt went for his Colt. Semmes drew and fired like a flash of lightning on a hot summer's night. The slug creased Matt's left leg. He staggered, and in his pain, he could not raise or fire his Colt.

"One leg at a time, Mistah Bones!" yelled Cato Semmes. "One leg at a time and then one arm at a time until youah scream for mercy!"

Semmes's Colt flashed a second time, and the soft slug struck Matt's right thigh, smashing the bone in a sickening blow. He fell as Semmes fired, and as he fell, he managed to shoot. The slug whipped through Semmes's shirt slack. The gunfighter cursed. Matt's falling had spoiled Semmes's sequence of torture and then death. As Matt hit the ground in agony, he fired again. Semmes jumped back, cursing savagely, his right arm broken at the elbow joint, but he managed to do the border shift. Even as he did so, Matt's Colt hammered out its last three rounds.

Cato Semmes whirled about, dropping his gun. He staggered back into the shadows beneath the trees, right arm hanging awkwardly, left arm clamped against his bullet-torn guts. "Ahm goin' home," said Semmes in a strange high voice. "Ahm jest goin' home to die." He fell flat on his face on the graveled path and lay still.

Matt promptly passed out on a cascading wave of burning, excruciating pain.

———

HE OPENED his eyes to see her lovely face within inches of his. She smiled. "You'll be all right," she said.

He wet his lips. "I can't get very far with a busted leg," he said. He looked wryly about the white hospital room.

She kissed him. "That's *one* way of stopping a wind-devil," she said.

He drew her close, kissed her, then closed his eyes. It was all right with Matt Turlock. A wind-devil serves no useful purpose, coming and going as it pleases, creating nothing, establishing nothing, but it is there for some unfathomable reason of God. He knew that reason now. The land in the West Bonito Valley was there; it would always be there, and God willing, so would Mr. and Mrs. Matt Turlock until their time came to pass the eternal land on to their children.

TAKE A LOOK AT JUDAS GUN AND HANGIN' PARDS:

Two Full Length Western Novels

BLOODTHIRSTY GUNSLINGERS GET THEIR REVENGE IN THIS CLASSIC WESTERN DOUBLE.

In *Judas Gun*, the prison at Yuma couldn't hold him... The blistering desert couldn't kill him... And the county's toughest guns couldn't stop him. Ken Sturgis was on the hunt for his brother Roy's killers – and not even prison could stop him.

In *Hangin' Pards*, it sure seemed that Holt Deaver had just about the worst luck of anyone in the West. At the age of twenty-five he was dead broke and on the run. He had shot one man in Chloride and had killed two others in less than a week. So when an old, whiskery, murdering no-good offered Holt ten thousand bucks to side him, it looked like a good thing. It was at least a chance for the best of everything if the gamble paid off— horses, food, liquor, and women. It also meant a partnership with a wanted outlaw and a self-conviction for Holt. But the thought of that last chance drove Holt on. Little did he reckon that even if the old rascal kept his word, it wouldn't do much good with six other bloodthirsty gunslingers on his trail.

"The joy of reading Shirreffs' work is in his mastery of pacing and his tough, gritty prose." – **James Reasoner, author of Outlaw Ranger.**

AVAILABLE NOW

ABOUT THE AUTHOR

Gordon D. Shirreffs published more than 80 western novels, 20 of them juvenile books, and John Wayne bought his book title, Rio Bravo, during the 1950s for a motion picture, which Shirreffs said constituted *"the most money I ever earned for two words."* Four of his novels were adapted to motion pictures, and he wrote a Playhouse 90 and the Boots and Saddles TV series pilot in 1957.

A former pulp magazine writer, he survived the transition to western novels without undue trauma, earning the admiration of his peers along the way. The novelist saw life a bit cynically from the edge of his funny bone and described himself as looking like a slightly parboiled owl. Despite his multifarious quips, he was dead serious about the writing profession.

Gordon D. Shirreffs was the 1995 recipient of the Owen Wister Award, given by the Western Writers of America for "a living individual who has made an outstanding contribution to the American West."

He passed in 1996.